THE MANY MASKS OF ANDY ZHOU

JACK CHENG

DIAL BOOKS FOR YOUNG READERS

CONTENT NOTE:

This story touches on topics including bullying,
racism, trichotillomania (hair-pulling compulsion),
parental death, and anorexia.

DIAL BOOKS FOR YOUNG READERS

An imprint of Penguin Random House LLC, New York

Ⓟ

First published in the United States of America by
Dial Books for Young Readers, an imprint of
Penguin Random House LLC, 2023
Text and art copyright © 2023 by Jack Cheng

Visit us online at penguinrandomhouse.com.

Library of Congress Cataloging-in-Publication Data is available.

Printed in the United States of America • ISBN 9780525553823

1 3 5 7 9 10 8 6 4 2

BVG

Design by Jason Henry • Text set in Hertz Pro

For my grandparents

SEPTEMBER

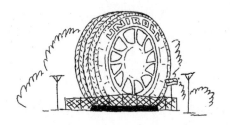

LIKE AN ANT, PROBABLY

"Andy, *did you hear me?*" Baba's eyes flick up in the rear-view mirror. He switches to English. "You always look like thinking. What you thinking about?"

"Nothing," I say, and stare out the window again. A motorcycle zooms by at full speed, weaving in and out of the freeway traffic.

Baba flips back to Shanghainese. *"I was saying, you know how difficult these past years have been for Hao Bu and Ah Dia. You have to help them, okay?"*

"Help them with what?"

"With whatever they need," says Mama from the front passenger seat. *"It's a different lifestyle here. Let's make their stay comfortable for them."*

Baba nods. "Ever since your ah dia little boy, his dream visit America. We have show he and Hao Bu best American time." Baba's eyebrows go up in the mirror.

"Xiaolei, you can make sign with they name! Have airport name sign for Hao Bu and Ah Dia see!"

"Don't people only do that for strangers?"

"Andy, *come*," my dad says in his don't-argue-with-me voice. "*Be a good grandson, okay?*"

Mama twists around and hands me her tablet. I open the drawing app, which still has my doodle from the last time Cindy and I hung out. I clear the screen.

"*Let's wait until they're settled first,*" says Baba, picking up their conversation from before.

"*You think they'll agree?*"

"*Ma might. But Ba—you know that older generation. They don't really trust doctors.*"

"*You're going to miss the exit.*"

Baba clicks on the turn signal. "*We'll take it step by step.*" I look up from the blank screen.

"Mama, Baba, I don't know Hao Bu and Ah Dia's names."

We pull into International Arrivals. Lines of cars are waiting already, parking lights red in the echoey underpass. My dad and I go through the spinning glass doors while my mom waits in the car—that way we don't get a ticket.

"*Ma, where are you!*" Baba's shouting into his phone. His voice gets deeper and louder when he's on it, like he's making up for the tiny microphone holes. "*We're just outside the baggage claim!*" he says. "*Send me a WeChat when you get this!*"

We find an open spot along the metal guard rail. I aim the tablet toward the sliding doors at the end, which have big red stickers saying DO NOT ENTER. It's mostly other Chinese families here, but there are also drivers in suits and ties, holding up their own tablets and signs. Back in the car, Mama wrote out my grandparents' names so I could draw them bigger on the screen, and Baba told me how to pronounce them. I recognize my own last name, *Zhou*, but I've already forgotten the rest.

"Andy," says Baba. "*Go ask when they're coming out.*" He points toward a guard sitting by the sliding doors. She's scrolling through something on her phone.

"They'll probably be out soon," I say.

"*Go ask.*"

"Can't you just check the app?"

"*Go. Your English is better than mine,*" says Baba. "*Quickly.*"

I hand him the tablet and duck under the rail, just as the doors at the end slide open. Out comes a business-woman with a roller bag, her suit jacket draped over the handle. Behind her is a group of maybe college students with duffels and white sneakers, and wireless head-phones around their necks. One of them has bleached blond hair—almost silver. He looks like a K-pop star.

"Andy," says Baba behind me. He points at the guard again. I go up and try to get her attention.

"Excuse me," I say, but it's so soft, she doesn't hear me. I try again, a little louder—"*Excuse me?*"—and wave my hand. The guard looks up from her phone.

"I was wondering, um . . ."

She points at the sign on the doors. "You're not allowed—"

"Okay, thanks!"

I retreat back to Baba.

"She said to wait," I tell him.

While we do, Baba goes into a story he loves, about the time he picked Mama and me up from this same airport. My dad came to Metro Detroit a few months before we did, so he could find a place for us to live, and get a car, and a job, and all his books for engineering school.

"I come with Lang Uncle pick you up," says Baba. "I waiting and waiting but you and Mama no come out. I think, what the heck! Then I go up one escalate"—he points to the escalators behind us—"and when I go up, I see you and Mama come down other escalate same time!"

I know the rest: Mama's carrying four-year-old me in her arms, and I'm reaching out for him, calling, "Baba! Baba!" As we're about to pass in opposite directions, she hands me over the railings, into *his* arms. When my dad tells the story, I can picture it all so clearly. But the only thing I actually remember is the split second I was dangling in the air between them. The feeling I was going to fall.

"Ma! Ba!" my dad suddenly shouts. He stands on his tiptoes and waves. I get a flash of worry. After all this time, am I even going to recognize my own grandparents?

But there they are, just like in our video chats—my grandma: chubby with silver curls, wearing a plain brown cardigan and pushing a cart stuffed with heavy luggage. Next to her is my much-skinnier grandpa, in a red wheelchair with a cane across his lap, being pushed by an airport worker.

Baba ducks under the rail. He rushes over so fast, I'm still frozen on the other side, holding my tablet with my grandparents' names. The ones I can't read.

Baba grabs the luggage cart from Hao Bu. He shouts over his shoulder, "Andy! *What are you doing? Come help!*"

I go under the rail.

"Wah, Xiaolei, you're getting taller," Hao Bu says when she sees me. *"Do you remember your hao bu? How come you're so skinny? What have you been feeding him?"* She says this last thing to my dad, then turns back to me. *"Hao Bu's going to cook delicious food for you, okay?"*

I'm not ready for all her questions. I just manage a polite *"Thank you, Hao Bu."*

"Where's his mother?" asks Hao Bu. *"Is it just you two?"*

"She's in the car waiting," says Baba. *"Look, old man, your grandson made you a sign!"*

I greet Ah Dia. Up close he seems tense and stiff, like he's clenching every muscle in his body. I show him the tablet and he blinks at me through his thick rectangular glasses. Chinese people don't really hug, but it feels too formal to shake his hand. So I end up just awkwardly patting him on the shoulder. Like he's a horse.

Ah Dia tips his cane down and grabs the wheelchair arm. He starts to get up.

"*Ba! Stay seated!*" my dad says, rushing over.

"*I can walk,*" says Ah Dia.

"*Old man, your son told you to stay seated!*" says Hao Bu.

"*I can do it myself!*"

Ah Dia's trying to stand, but Baba and Hao Bu want him to sit. The airport worker backs away from the wheelchair, confused about the yelling. But this same thing happens when my parents are with their Shanghainese friends. They'll all talk louder and louder until they're basically shouting. It's like a snowball rolling downhill and turning into an avalanche.

Back outside, my family avalanche-talks some more—Mama too—about how to fit my grandparents' bags in the trunk. While everyone is debating the perfect luggage arrangement, I help Ah Dia into the front passenger seat. I lock the wheelchair wheels, and reach out my hand so he has something to hold on to. He grabs it, then shifts his weight to my shoulder. His palms are meatier than I expect. His grip is surprisingly strong.

"Watch your head," I tell him. But when he doesn't react, I think for a bit and finally come up with a few words in Shanghainese: "Dang xin. Nong dou." *Careful. Your head.*

Ah Dia puts one hand on the top of the car door, ducks

in slowly, then turns and bends, and finally lands in the front seat with a plop. A couple of years ago he slipped going down the stairs at their house in Shanghai. He hurt his spine really bad. Baba wanted us all to fly back to China, but flights were expensive, and I had school. So my mom and I stayed in Michigan.

"Turn it on its side!" says Hao Bu.

"No no, stand it upright!" shouts Mama.

"Uhyo, I got it!" says Baba.

I help Ah Dia click in his seat belt. Before I shut the door again, I say, *"Careful. Your hands."*

It turns out that the luggage doesn't all fit in our trunk. Mama and I end up with a roller bag each across our laps, while Hao Bu sits on my other side, her big purse across her own lap. By the time we're on the freeway, I'm suddenly exhausted.

But at least the avalanche stopped. As we go past billboards and warehouses, and a blue steel bridge, my dad asks my grandparents—in a normal voice—about their flight and airline food, and our relatives in China. Hao Bu does most of the talking, while Ah Dia answers in short *ao*s and *mm*s. I watch him fiddle with the AC vents, then open and close the glove compartment.

Hao Bu nudges my elbow. *"Here, little buddy. For you."* She smiles and hands me a pair of silvery snack bags— airline pretzels.

I say thanks and open one. The pretzels are salty and crunchy and good. I put the other in my pocket, careful not to let it get crushed by the luggage in my lap. I know Cindy's going to like them because they're the mini kind, and she collects things that are just a little bit smaller than normal. Like, two-thirds the size. The first time we saw those eight-ounce cans of Faygo Red Pop, she pretty much lost her mind.

"Xiaolei," Hao Bu starts, then says my American name in a sing-songy voice. "Aaandy . . . *how are your studies?*"

"*His grades are okay,*" Baba answers for me. "*He always gets a few wrong on his tests. Always ninety-two, ninety-three. Never one hundred.*"

I move a little in my seat, but the luggage presses me down.

"*What year is he in now?*"

"*Going into sixth,*" says Mama. "*School starts next week.*"

Hao Bu turns to me again. There's a mischievous grin on her face. "*Xiaolei, did you know? When your ah dia was in school, he was a huge troublemaker. He hardly did his homework—most of our teachers hated him!*"

"Your ah dia, he just play ah play ah play," says Baba. "He huge playboy!" I know what Baba's getting at, but I don't think that's the right word for it.

Mama chuckles. Hao Bu smiles and shakes her head.

I watch Ah Dia again, riding quietly in the front passenger seat. I follow his eyes out the window to the trees and billboards flicking by, to the giant model car tire on the side of the freeway, the one that's so big that if you stood right under it, you'd probably feel like an ant.

SUPER SAIYAN

Cindy's standing over me when I wake up the next morning.

Or more like, when *she* wakes me up. She's shaking my shoulder, calling my name. I yawn and rub my eyes. "Why are you here so early?" I ask.

"It's already past noon, dummy."

"It is?"

She nods and looks around the living room, like she doesn't understand why I'm sleeping on our pull-out sofa bed. Our dads went to college together, and when we were in second grade, our families started renting two floors of the same house. It's called a duplex. The Shens have their own entrance upstairs from the backyard, but there's a door between their stairs and our kitchen that we leave unlocked.

I sit up. "My grandparents are sleeping in my room," I explain.

"I heard you come in yesterday," says Cindy. "Are they still . . ." She looks toward the hallway to the bedrooms.

"I think so. My mom said they have jet lag."

Her voice gets quieter. "I can't believe your parents would make you give up your room. I'd be so mad."

Should I be mad? I didn't think of it like that. Hao Bu and Ah Dia are living with us for six months, and Mama and Baba said we should give them my room so they can be more comfortable. Maybe I also stayed up too late watching TV last night.

Cindy nudges me with her knee. "Our parents went to Costco. Now's our chance." She smirks and holds up a bulging plastic grocery bag.

"What's that?"

"See for yourself."

I scoot to the edge of the sofa bed and peel off the blanket. Cindy shrieks and one-eighty spins away from me. Her ponytail almost slaps me in the face.

"*Andy*. Get *dressed* first."

I look down. Oops—I'm in my underwear!

"You might as well just put on your swim trunks," she says, her back to me still. She starts toward the bathroom. "I'll go set everything up."

"Set what up?"

It's like a miniature city: bottles and boxes, tubes and tubs. Cindy shakes the grocery bag and a flat brush with black bristles clacks onto the tile floor.

"What . . . *is* all this?" I pick up a bottle with a drawing on it of a purple fox. The pointy ears kind of make it look like the purple demon emoji. I get a weird shiver.

"Andy. We went over this," Cindy says. She grabs the bottle out of my hand and replaces it with her phone. A Korean girl is talking into the camera. The title underneath the video says BLEACHING ASIAN HAIR: THE RIGHT WAY.

Now I remember. Cindy wanted me to help bleach hers. I just didn't realize she'd be able to get everything so quickly. How does she even have the money to pay for all this?

"Thuy helped me out," she says.

Cindy always knows what I'm thinking, sometimes even before I do.

She perks up. "I forgot something. Hey, are you watching the video or what?"

I go back to the video. The girl is explaining the different steps, talking about how to mix the bleach paste. Mama started dyeing her hair last year too, after she found three gray hairs in a row and freaked out. But she dyes it dark, and the stuff she uses is only one box, not a bajillion bottles like this.

Cindy gets back as I'm finishing the video. She's changed into her purple bathing suit. Is she . . . trying to match the shampoo bottle? She hands me a pair of big rubber cleaning gloves and an empty tofu container.

"Shouldn't we at least wait till our parents are home?" I ask. "My mom can help, she—" I stop. Maybe Mama doesn't want people to know she dyes her hair.

"Andy." Cindy gives me a look that says *The whole point is to do it when they're not home.* She climbs in the bathtub and unties her ponytail, then reties everything into four sections like in the video. I breathe out. I guess we're really doing this.

"Don't worry," she says. "I trust you."

That's why Cindy's my best friend. She has enough confidence for the both of us.

I put on the gloves and find the bleach powder. I scoop it into the tofu container, then look for the other ingredients. Most of the bottles are almost empty, and I have to turn them upside down and shake to get the stuff inside to the opening. The ones I don't recognize, I just skip. It's probably better to follow the video's directions.

The last bottle is the big one that says VOLUME DEVELOPER 30. When I squeeze a glop into the tofu container, the opening makes a soft fart sound. I giggle and Cindy rolls her eyes. Then I take the brush and start mixing. It reminds me of mixing paint colors in art class, or the time Cindy and I made slime. Except this stuff is more goopy and smells like bathroom cleaner.

"Ready when you are," says Cindy, looking over her shoulder.

I take a lock of Cindy's hair in my hand. Even through the gloves, her hair feels soft and silky, not thick and wiry like mine. It's also the first time, I realize, that I've touched her hair.

"What are you waiting for?" she asks.

"Nothing." I'm glad Cindy's facing away from me, because I think my cheeks just turned red. I brush on the goop, starting with the ends, not the roots, like in the video. A little bit at a time. It's oddly satisfying, smoothing out the goop, watching her hair absorb it. I finish one section and start on the next. Meanwhile, Cindy sits super still and quiet, with her eyes closed, almost like she's praying.

"Andy, you're always so helpful," she says in a soft voice. "You really care about other people."

I feel a little dizzy when she says this, but it's probably just the bleach fumes.

I finish all four sections. There's still a little bit of goop left. We wrap Cindy's head in a plastic grocery bag like in the video, and as we do, I can already see the color changing. Cindy starts the timer on her phone and I take off the gloves. My hands are all clammy from wearing them.

"Okay, your turn," says Cindy.

"Wait. What do you mean *my* turn?"

She starts putting on the gloves. "Andy, we're going into sixth grade. We're going into *middle school*. This is our chance to make a statement."

"A statement?"

I know about middle school. Locker combinations and bells that ring every fifty minutes. Clubs and sports and school dances and health class, and a bunch of different teachers, instead of just one main one. And eighth graders. I don't know why anyone would want to make a statement in front of eighth graders.

"That's right, a statement." Cindy nods. "Besides, I think you'd look pretty cool with Super Saiyan hair."

I do think it'd be pretty cool to have hair like Goku from *Dragon Ball Z*. I could even wear my orange Turtle School shirt the first day! But then I remember: eighth graders.

"Is it me or is it kind of stuffy in here?" I reach for the door.

Cindy cuts me off. She turns on the vent fan instead. "Better?"

I look at our reflections in the mirror, Cindy with her bag-head, me with hopefully not a future bag-head. We used to be the same size, but ever since her growth spurt, she's gotten both taller and heavier than me.

"What if I, um, did something else?" I suggest. "Something not as . . . drastic? Maybe I can grow a mustache."

Cindy tilts her head. "Too . . . time-consuming," she says.

"I haven't even hit puberty," I point out.

She looks at me like, *I am not amused.* But when I start cracking up, she can't help giggling too.

Then she gets all serious again.

"Andy, *please*?" she says. "Do this with me? I mean, haven't you ever wished you could be a different person? Like, a better version of yourself? It's going to be a bigger school, with mostly kids we don't know and who don't know us. This is our one shot."

I want to say that we'd have another shot in high school. And then again when we start college. But Cindy's eyes look big and shiny, like she actually might cry. I glance at the tofu container, and at the plastic bag around Cindy's head, and then I remember the K-pop guy I saw at the airport, with the silver-blond hair. I picture him pointing at me and winking, his teeth sparkling like diamonds, saying: *You too can have cool hair like me!*

A word pops out: "Fine."

Cindy breaks into a smile so big, you wouldn't even know she was almost crying a second ago. I climb in the tub and crouch, facing the wall like she did, while Cindy mixes up more bleach goop. I notice that some of the grout between the tiles is a little pink and dirty. Baba scrubbed the whole bathroom the other day to get ready for Hao Bu and Ah Dia, even though Mama's usually the one who cleans. He must've missed a spot.

There's a fart noise. I look over my shoulder. "Is, um, everything okay?"

"It's fine, don't worry." Cindy's shaking and squeezing the Volume Developer bottle but it's only making more fart sounds. Nothing's really coming out.

"If there isn't any left, then—"

"We're okay. I'll use more of this other stuff. Turn around."

"But the video said—"

"Turn around."

I breathe out and face the wall again. I close my eyes. After a while, I feel Cindy put the first bit of goop in my hair—there's no going back now. A minute later, my scalp starts tingling. A slimy glop falls on my shoulder.

"Oops!" says Cindy. She wipes it with her glove, but that just leaves a bigger wet smear. The tingling gets more intense.

"Is it supposed to burn like this?"

"That's how you know it's working. Keep still."

I squeeze my eyes closed even tighter. I try to imagine the two of us showing up on our first day with Super Saiyan hair. I think about all the books and shows that I've read and seen, about kids with big goals like saving their family's house from getting bulldozed by the bank, or defeating the evil wizard who killed their parents, or taming the nine-tailed demon fox inside of them to become the greatest Hokage in the history of the Leaf Village. It's like Cindy said—they have to be better versions of themselves in order to get what they want.

But what if you've never thought about what you want?

I sniff a couple times, and I can't smell the bleach fumes anymore. Either the vent sucked them all up, or I got used to them, and something bugs me about both those possibilities.

We wait. Back in the living room, Cindy flops on her belly on the sofa bed and starts scrolling through dance challenges. I curl up in the side chair and doodle in one of my new school notebooks. We always hang out down here in the summer because it's cooler on the first floor. Last year, all we did was watch *Demon Slayer* and *My Roommate Is a Cat*, and eat those Asian freezer pops from 88 Mart—the ones that look like two sausage links. It was the best.

"I can't believe summer's already over," Cindy says, still looking at her phone. "It felt even shorter than last year."

"Do you think it's just going to keep feeling that way?" I ask. "The older we are, I mean."

"It's only going to get worse." Cindy nods. "The Chinese kids at that international high school . . . did you know their parents make them go take summer classes for college credit?"

"Who told you that?"

"Trevor Lang went this year." Cindy shrugs. "I heard my mom talking about it with Liu Niang Niang. You know, ChinaNet."

All the moms know everything going on with the other Chinese families through a combination of We-Chat, shouty phone calls, and showing up unannounced at each other's houses. It's like their very own Chinese gossip internet.

Cindy giggles at something on her phone. I go back to my drawing. I try to sketch Cindy's feet, but it's hard because her toes are curling back and forth. It's more of a doodle, anyway. I'm not like the really artistic kids who draw dragons or their own made-up superheroes. The stuff I draw is usually right in front of me.

Cindy pops up before I can finish. "Found one!" she says, then immediately covers her mouth. She glances toward the bedrooms. We listen for signs that we woke up my grandparents, but there's just the hum of the window AC.

I close my notebook and slide next to Cindy. She shows me the dance challenge on her phone. I watch the video loop a few times, and the people in it are moving so fast. Too fast.

"Um . . . you're gonna have to show me," I tell her. "Slowly."

"No no, it's easy!" She giggles. Then she breaks the dance down at half the speed: "See? All you do is rowboat, rowboat, windshield wipers . . . then pull-up, pull-up, airplane, spin!"

Cindy's like one of those people who has perfect pitch, who can play any song after hearing it once. Except instead of for music it's for dancing.

She stands her phone against the TV and we practice a few times until I get the hang of it. Then she hits record in the app. I mess up at the end and spin the wrong way, but Cindy doesn't seem to mind. We play it back and try not to laugh too loud. The dance looks even funnier with our plastic bag heads.

I remember something. "Hold on," I tell her. I go into

my shorts pockets from yesterday and pull out the mini pretzels. When she sees them, Cindy's eyes get wide and sparkly like an anime character. She snatches the bag right out of my hand.

"Andy, you're the best!" she says, in her happiest, most excited quiet voice. She gives me a big hug, our plastic bag heads crinkling together.

The timer goes off. I follow Cindy back to the bathroom, and watch from the hallway while she peels the bag off and checks her hair in the mirror. The goop is completely absorbed. Even the ends are a rich yellow blond. I think it worked!

Then, out of the corner of my eye, I notice the light change. I hear faint voices, car doors closing. I look toward the kitchen just in time to see Cindy's dad come in through the back, carrying two frozen ducks.

And he sees me. Wearing a plastic bag on my head.

I turn toward Cindy. She's sifting through the shampoo bottles. "I'm gonna shower upstairs," she says.

"Um . . ."

"I'll bring it back when I'm done. You have twenty more minutes for yours. Do you want my phone for the timer?"

I point at the kitchen.

"Well, do you or not?"

I keep pointing. Now Cindy's mom's standing in the doorway too. There's a confused look on both her parents' faces. It's only then that Cindy comes into the hallway to see what I'm pointing at.

And everything goes crazy.

Her parents start yelling in Shanghainese at a million words a minute. Her dad stomps into our kitchen, carrying the frozen ducks under his arms like footballs, the vein in his forehead bulging. He almost corners Cindy by the fridge, but she slips around him and darts upstairs, crying, hugging the purple fox shampoo to her chest.

Doors slam. More yelling. Hao Bu comes out of the bedroom, her eyes half-open and her hair messy from sleep. *"What's all the commotion?"* she asks. At the same time, Mama and Baba burst in through the front door with *our* groceries.

Baba looks left and right. "Andy, what happen! Everything okay?!"

Mama points. *"How come there's a plastic bag on your head?"*

I open my mouth to explain, but no words come out. My chest swells. My face goes numb. I lead them into the bathroom and wave at the mess of bottles and tubs and bleach goop. Water swooshes through the pipes upstairs, and this sets me off. I start crying too.

Baba and Mama look at each other. Then Baba goes back into the kitchen. Mama sits me down on the toilet lid, with Hao Bu watching from the doorway, and turns on the shower. She adjusts the faucet handle, making sure the water's not too hot or cold. Then she unties the plastic bag around my head.

"*Xiaolei, come,*" she says. "*Let's wash that out.*"

I rub my eyes and climb into the bathtub. It's then that I notice, reflected in the tub's faucet, my new hair—the new me.

And I'm—

Oh.

IT'S...DIFFERENT

Labor Day passes. Tuesday comes too soon.

It's different than I imagined—seeing all these kids in school, in the same place at once. It's not that I didn't know they'd be here. It's more like I forgot to picture everyone *moving*. Walking down the hallways in twos and threes, hugging friends they haven't seen all summer, clustered in groups around their new lockers, talking and laughing.

"Ohmigod you look *so* different!" Annie Zhang's telling Cindy.

"You did such a good job!" Thuy Pham adds, holding up a strand of Cindy's bleached blond hair.

From the way Cindy's glowing, you can't even tell that she and her parents yelled at each other all weekend. Or that they took away her phone.

"Andy helped," she says. "We bleached his hair too!"

I step out a little from behind Cindy. "Mine didn't come out as good," I tell them. I wore my Detroit Tigers cap this morning but made it two steps past the front entrance before the vice principal told me hats aren't allowed.

"It's not *that* bad," says Cindy.

Annie and Thuy look at my hair. My blotchy, orange-and-black hair. My definitely not-blond hair. Thuy is literally biting her tongue. I think I see Annie's eye twitch.

"It'th nyth," says Thuy.

"It's . . . different?" says Annie.

A locker slams down the hall. A kid in a gray hoodie yells, "Watch it!" and scrambles to pick his notebooks up off the floor.

Then the start bell rings, a long, crackly tone that feels too loud. Everyone hurries to class, Cindy and me included. I walk next to her and keep tight to the wall. I'm kind of glad she's a little bigger than me now. Thank god we have homeroom and first-period science together.

Hazel Heights Middle School is shaped like two big pizza boxes, overlapping at the corners.

In the middle of the overlap, there's a glassed-in courtyard with ferns and grasses and purple wildflowers, and a single skinny tree with full green leaves, just starting to turn orange-pink. There's even an old wooden bench. It all looks calm and peaceful—the exact opposite of the hallways around it.

Science is a few doors down from the courtyard.

When we walk in, the teacher, Mr. Nagy, has us stand by the tall lab counters along the edges of the room. Rows of two-person tables run up and down the middle, and posters of cells and animal kingdoms and evaporation hang on the walls. Up by the long lab counter in front, I spot a lower table with aquariums and terrariums on it. I think I see a newt.

Mr. Nagy calls us up one by one for attendance, and to give us our books and seat assignments. He's going alphabetical, so I know I'm last. When he gets to my name, his mouth starts to twist, but then he stops. "I'm not even going to attempt to pronounce this," he says.

I go up and tell him, "Call me Andy."

"Ah, that's much easier," he chuckles. "Andy it is."

I get a weird tingle across my scalp, almost like a Miles Morales spider-sense. Mr. Nagy hands me a textbook that says LIFE SCIENCES. I hurry to my seat in the back right corner, one row behind Cindy and this short red-headed kid, Kevin Walsh. When I walk by, Cindy presses her lips into a line, like she's saying *Just ignore it.*

My table partner isn't here today. At least I get some space to myself. It feels safer back here, in the corner. I dig out my notebook and the planner they gave us in homeroom. Maybe I'll get lucky and every class will have alphabetical seating.

Mr. Nagy's partway into his introduction when there's a loud knock at the door. A tall Middle Eastern kid in a gray hoodie comes in with a hall pass.

"Jameel Zebrai," says Mr. Nagy, reading his name off the pass. "Good of you to join us." He hands the kid one of the last textbooks and nods toward my table. "You're next to Andy."

"It's Zeb*ari*," Jameel tells Mr. Nagy. We briefly make eye contact. It's the same kid from the hallway this morning—the one whose stuff spilled all over the floor.

When Jameel sits down, I can almost feel the air change around me. His textbook lands on the table with a loud *slap*. I don't know if he did it on purpose, and Mr. Nagy glances our way like he's also wondering. I start drawing in my planner, mostly just to have something to do.

But as class goes on, something about Jameel makes me keep looking over. He's so tall and lanky that he barely fits into the seat. First he's staring at the terrariums at the front of the room. Then he's slouched back in his chair, twirling his pencil. I notice that, above his upper lip, he has a very faint mustache.

We make eye contact again. I look away too late.

"Quit staring," he says.

"I'm not."

"Whatchu drawing?"

I cover my planner.

Jameel points at my orange-and-black hair. "What are you, half leprechaun?"

"No."

Kevin, the redheaded kid, looks over his shoulder, then quickly turns back. Jameel snorts. It's almost impressive how he can make fun of both of us with a single word. And scary.

After a while I feel a sharp poke on my elbow. I ignore it, but for some reason, Jameel keeps at it, keeps poking me with the metal end of his pencil. The eraser is already missing. There are already chew marks on the sides. It gets so annoying that I make the mistake of saying, a little too loudly, "*Stop.*"

Cindy looks over her shoulder. Mr. Nagy clears his throat. "Mr. Zebari, is there a problem back there?"

"Why you asking me? I didn't say nothing."

"Is there a problem?" Mr. Nagy repeats.

"No problem," Jameel grumbles.

Inside me, a little alarm is going off.

I don't see Cindy again until lunch. And the only other class we have together is seventh-period honors math. So I'm with her at the start, middle, and end of school, like the buns on a Big Mac. In between, I'm on my own.

Somehow I make it through the rest of the morning. Random seventh or eighth graders laugh and say "nice hair" in the hallways, but I find out that if I use water to keep it flattened, you can't see the blotchiness as much. In language arts we have *reverse*-alphabetical seating, and kids snicker when it's my turn to say something interesting that happened over the summer. But in social studies, the attention is more on Jason Shaheen, who keeps asking Mx. Adler about

Eastern Europe, and keeps asking it in a Dracula voice.

While we wait in the lunch line, Cindy tells me about her own morning: "Sarika Shah stayed the summer with her relatives in New Jersey, and they took the train into New York City, isn't that cool? And this new girl Molly, she's doing symphony band too and—oh! I heard when Mx. Adler's in a grumpy mood they'll make the whole class write essays . . ."

I remember what Cindy said about starting middle school and making a statement. We both made statements all right, just very different ones.

"Andy, you have your iceman stare again."

"Huh? Oh—sorry." Cindy and I watched this video one time about cave-people that got frozen in ice. She said I have the same blank look in my face when I'm daydreaming.

"I talked to Thuy," she says. "She can get extra bleach stuff, but she has to wait till her parents' salon uses more bottles first. How much money do you have saved up?"

"I don't know, six dollars maybe? How much does she want?"

"More than that." Cindy sighs. "I wish we got allowances like American kids."

"We get red envelope money."

"Yeah, but that's not the same. And Lunar New Year isn't till January."

We pick up our pizza squares and apple slices. We spot Annie and Thuy and some other kids from our elementary school at one of the tables. I scan the cafeteria for Jameel, but I don't see him. I do, however, get a whiff of a bright, flowery orange smell: a group of four girls, probably eighth graders, walking our way. They're all tall and thin and wearing yoga pants and carrying fancy metal water bottles. The girl in front, a Black girl with tight curls of pastel-pink hair, is holding a stack of flyers and a roll of tape.

From the way Cindy's staring, I can tell she's noticed them too. When the tall girls pass us, the pink-haired one glances at Cindy and says, "I like your hair."

"Thanks," says Cindy, not missing a beat. "I like yours too."

"Thank you! Here, take one—" The girl hands Cindy a flyer. "Hope to see you there!"

We watch the tall girls tape a couple more flyers up on the wall, then float off into the hallways. We both look down at the paper in Cindy's hand. It says, in big bold letters at the top:

MOVEMENT

Underneath that, it says:

HHMS DANCE COMPANY
Informational meeting!
Auditorium this Friday @ Lunch!
#hhmsmove #bethere

Cindy stares at me with her mouth open a little, like she almost can't believe it. I remember a word I had to look up when reading a book once: *incredulous*. She's incredulous. Then her face changes, as if she's noticing something for the first time.

"Why's your hair wet?"

I GOT A
SPLITTING
HEADACHE

DUCK BRAINS & DEMENTORS

When I get home that afternoon, I pass out on the sofa bed and don't wake up until it's already dark, and dinner's almost over.

Baba and Hao Bu are at the table, drinking tea and talking. Baba's also picking at the to-go boxes Mama brought back from 88 Mart. It's one of our usual dinners, when Mama and Baba are too tired to cook. Except this time there's an extra foil container of roast duck.

I sit down and start filling the empty plate in front of me.

"*You're finally awake?*" Baba chuckles. "*Did you have a tiring first day? Or do you have jet lag too?*"

I shrug. I don't really feel like talking. Mama brings me a steaming bowl of rice.

"*I came out and he was fast asleep,*" says Hao Bu. She chopsticks a couple duck pieces into the dipping sauce, then puts them on my mound of white rice. I immediately move them onto the plate.

"Xiaolei, you don't want it with your rice?"

I shake my head.

"He doesn't like when the different foods mix," explains Mama.

"I always tell him that's the best part," says Baba. *"When all the flavors mix!"*

Except Baba takes it to the extreme. He'll stir everything up into one big mush, until you can't even tell the difference from one bite to the next. I like to keep each food in its own section.

Baba shakes his head and chuckles again. He nods toward the bedrooms, where I guess Ah Dia is still sleeping. *"Once Ba's over his jet lag, we can make an appointment for him,"* he tells Hao Bu. *"The doctors here are the best in the world. One of my classmates, this Indian guy, his brother's a surgeon—"*

"Uhyo, don't bother. As long as the old man moves around a bit, walks outside, it'll be enough."

"One look at his face and you can tell he's in pain—"

"You don't need to worry."

Mama chimes in: *"Ma, this is a great place to go for walks. The air's clean. Michigan's best in the fall."*

"That's right!" says Baba. *"This weekend in our backyard, we'll cook some Western food with the Shens. We use BBQ grill!"*

"BBQ grill?" asks Hao Bu.

"Hot dog, hambao!"

"*Aiya, how are you so excited now about* BBQ grill?" laughs Mama. "*You've only used that thing twice since we got it!*"

"Corn on cob!" says Baba.

"*It's probably all rusted by now!*"

"Shish kabob!"

If my mom was the kind of person who rolled her eyes, she'd roll her eyes right now.

"*Xiaoyin, make a list,*" says Baba. "*We'll go to* Costco!"

"*We can put jumbo shrimp on the* shish kabob!" says Mama, suddenly excited too. My parents will really look for any excuse to go to Costco.

"*Ma, didn't one open in Shanghai!*" asks Baba, his voice still avalanche-y.

"*That's right! I haven't been yet. It's always so busy! Is it good?*"

"*We'll take you and Ba there!* Then we have BBQ grill!"

"Free sample!" says Mama.

Hao Bu sees that I've finished my roast duck pieces, and gets me another—the head. Except I block the plate with my chopsticks.

"*Xiaolei, you don't want to eat the brains?*" asks Hao Bu.

"What's the matter, you love the brains," says Baba. "We saved the head just for you!"

"*I remember, even when you were little, you always wanted the brains,*" says Hao Bu.

I shake my head.

"*Give it to me, Ma,*" says Baba. "*I'll eat it.*"

* * *

It feels kind of nice to not talk at dinner. It feels so nice that I decide to keep doing it the next day. Cindy mentions on our walk to school how quiet I seem, even for me, but she doesn't bring it up again.

Over the next week, I realize that the best way to deal with Jameel and the others is to ignore them. When Paul Castiglione comes out of the stall in the boys' bathroom and says, "Hey Andy, who barfed on your head?" . . . *ignore*.

When Mx. Adler calls on me in social studies and Aiden Abrams fake-coughs "Carrot-top!" . . . *crossed-arms emoji*.

They're like Dementors: If you hold your breath and stay very still and quiet, they stop noticing you're there. Act like you're invisible and pretty soon you will be.

It's tougher with Jameel, though. Mainly because I have to sit next to him in science. So I try to focus instead on Mr. Nagy's lessons about plant and animal cells.

"Yo Irish!"

Chloroplasts.

"You have Lucky Charms for breakfast again?"

Mitochondria.

"Is it St. Patty's Day already?"

Nuclear membrane.

After a while, even Jameel starts getting bored. I think I'll just never say another unnecessary word for the rest of middle school.

* * *

Friday. Lunch period. Cindy made me promise to go with her to the info meeting for the dance club thing.

On our way to the auditorium, she tells me everything she's already found out about the tall girls—how the pink-haired girl's name is Viola, and she and Mai are both eighth graders, but the other girl Alexandra's in seventh, and Thuy knows Mai through—

I open my mouth to ask "How did you find all this out?" But instead I make a sound between a cough and a croak.

"Bless you," she says.

"Um, thanks?" I think the last time I talked was two days ago.

We turn the corner and walk toward the glass courtyard. Lunch bags are flopping around, lockers are closing left and right, but something about the courtyard catches my eye. The sun's really shining down today, and mixed in with the tree's peachy pink leaves are round red fruits, almost like raspberries. I spot a little bird by the trunk with one of the fruits in its beak.

Then: a loud laugh. Down the hallway, Jameel's hanging around Paul and Aiden's lockers—three Dementors in a row. And we're going to walk right past them.

I try to slow down so that Cindy blocks their view.

"Yo Irish!"

Too late.

Jameel splits off from the others and starts walking

next to us. I pretend I don't hear him, and at first Cindy doesn't realize he's talking to me. But then he steps in front of us. He holds out a pen and points to his open palm. "Draw a map of it for me," he says.

"You're in our way," Cindy tells him.

"I'm just tryna get your boy to show me where he hides it."

"What are you even talking about? Hides what?"

Jameel says the next bit extra loud, looking over at Paul and Aiden. "The pot of gold at the end of the rainbow!"

The others burst out laughing.

"Endoplasmic reticulum," I say under my breath.

"What'd you say?" asks Jameel.

I stare straight ahead. *I am not the droid you're looking for.*

"Yo, did you just Force Wave me?"

"Leave us alone," says Cindy, rolling her eyes.

"LeAvE uS AlOne," he says, in that SpongeBob meme voice.

Cindy shakes her head and pushes by Jameel. I follow, laughter cackling behind us.

By the time we get to the auditorium, everything's tingly, like my spider-sense went so haywire that it short-circuited my whole body. I picture a robot version of me in a scrapyard, my head, middle, and limbs all scattered in different places.

"Don't pay attention to those jerks," says Cindy, shaking her head. "Twenty years from now, when we're both famous dancers, they'll be delivering pizzas for a living."

I hope Cindy knows that I'm not going to be a famous dancer like she is. I also want to ask her what's wrong with delivering pizzas, because both our dads delivered food part-time when we first moved here. But I'm still too tingly to talk.

She walks into the auditorium ahead of me.

Wait—

Do I really have to wait twenty years before it gets better?

MY
PRECIOUSS S

MOVEMENT

Viola and the tall girls are on the stage goofing around when we walk in, recording each other on their phones. I watch one of them—Alexandra, I think—bend backwards, plant her hands, and kick her feet up into a perfect handstand, then gracefully lower herself down.

I turn to Cindy like, *Did you just see that?* But she's already heading for the stage.

I follow her up the side steps, past the dozen or so other kids scattered in the front rows, chatting away like they already know each other. Once I get on stage, I pretend like I'm looking around so I'm not just awkwardly standing there while Cindy talks to the tall girls.

First I check out the curtain fabric. It's very thick and velvety—definitely high quality. Then I notice a couple of big wooden panels covered in paint-splattered cloths.

I peek under one cloth: It's a row of houses that all look the same.

From backstage, I watch a few more kids trickle into the auditorium. I recognize Lucy Eugenides, who has big glasses and jean overalls and is in my honors math class, and Arj Patel, who I have language arts with. Jason Shaheen, the Dracula kid, is also here. I didn't think he was the dancing type, but then again neither am I.

Cindy and the tall girls burst out laughing about something. If Cindy has a superpower, this is it: She can meet kids who are complete strangers and two minutes later, it's like they're old friends. Meanwhile, here I am creeping in the shadows.

"Andy Zhou?"

I jump.

"I'm sorry! I didn't mean to startle you!"

I turn around. It's our elementary school art teacher Mrs. Ocampo. She's carrying a cardboard box full of tattered books.

"Andy, I thought that was you! How are you? You must be surprised to see me."

I nod. Then it clicks. The elementary school is right up the block, so it makes sense that Mrs. Ocampo would be the art teacher here too.

"How was your summer?" she asks. "Did you go anywhere exciting?"

"It was okay. We didn't go anywhere."

"I like what you did with your hair!"

"Oh. Thanks," I say. I'm pretty sure she's just being nice.

The colorful stage lights dim and brighten. While Mrs. Ocampo's head is turned, I slip away. Cindy and the tall girls slide off the stage into the front row, and I hurry down the side steps, into a seat next to Cindy.

After a while, Mrs. Ocampo comes out with another teacher, and it's someone else I know.

"Welcome to Movement. I'm Mx. Adler. My pronouns are they/them."

Under the lights, Mx. Adler's pale skin and straight silver hair are a mix of blues, golds, and purples. I remember seeing the flyer for the informational meeting taped next to the board in social studies. I glance at Cindy but she doesn't seem surprised at all. Was I the only one who didn't know Mx. Adler was in charge of Movement?

"Each February," they go on, "our dance company puts on a show for the families at Hazel Heights Middle. Last year it was *A Wrinkle in Time*. This year we will be adapting *Lord of the Flies*."

Someone raises their hand.

"Yes, in front."

"Can I be Frodo?"

"That's *Lord of the RINGS*," says someone else. "*Lord of the Flies* is the one where the boys crash-land on an island. But instead of trying to get rescued they fight each other and burn the island down."

"Spoilers! We're reading it this year!"

"You know if it was a bunch of girls they'd have figured out how to get rescued in no time," says Viola.

Cindy laughs.

"What about *Hamilton*? Maybe we can do *Hamilton*?"

"Vith Aaron Burr, ah ah ah!" says Jason in his Dracula voice.

Everyone stares.

"This year's program has been decided," Mx. Adler says firmly. "Some of you already know Mrs. Ocampo. She will be overseeing our student-run crew. That's set decoration, costumes, lighting. But make no mistake: This will be very much *your* production. I expect you to take ownership of it. And Mai, you are correct. Mrs. Hu is graciously lending us her classroom copies until then."

Mrs. Ocampo hands half a stack of papers to Viola, the other half to Alexandra, and they go around passing them out. Cindy's eyes get that sparkly anime look again. But when I see the dates and times for auditions, the rehearsals every week, the permission form at the bottom . . .

If we get picked as dancers, I'll be up on that stage, under those lights, in front of the school—the *whole* school. I imagine coming out for the first time and seeing Jameel, Paul, and Aiden in the audience pointing and laughing, which makes me mess up and trip Cindy, who knocks into the tall girls, who then topple over one by one like dominoes!

This is way different from Cindy and me doing dance challenges at home.

Mx. Adler says something and everyone's suddenly getting up to sign out copies of the books. They're breaking off into groups too—the tall girls with Mx. Adler, a handful of others with Mrs. Ocampo.

Cindy goes with the tall girls. I want to follow, but it's like someone did a *Naruto* shadow-paralysis on me. I flatten my hair to my head, and my fingers land on a single strand in the back that feels longer than the others. I barely pull and it comes right out.

It's bright orange.

HOT DOGS & HAMBAOS

That Sunday, my dad makes his whole "BBQ grill" plan with Cindy's family happen in the backyard.

It's funny, Baba's never been that into American culture, but now that Hao Bu and Ah Dia are here, all of a sudden he's Mr. Red White and Blue. He's even wearing a chef's hat and apron, except they're both from when he worked part-time at Benihana—even though he's not Japanese. I watch him scrape a small piece of burnt onion off the grill, juggle it between two metal spatulas, and flip it into the divot in his hat.

"See, Xiaoyin, the BBQ grill *works perfectly fine!"* Baba calls toward the kitchen. *"There wasn't much rust at all!"*

Next to me and Hao Bu at the patio table, Ah Dia's nodding off to sleep, then catching himself, then nodding off again. Like Jameel in science the other day.

"Ma, one of these weekends, when the weather's nice,

we'll take you and Ba to garage sale," says Baba.

"Garage?" asks Hao Bu.

"Garage sale," Cindy's dad repeats. He sits down next to us and grabs a handful of melon seeds. He cracks open a few and spits the empty shells on the cement patio. *"These Americans, let me tell you—they're always getting rid of their old stuff. They'll hold these big sales. Or sometimes they'll just put it on the curb, throw it away!"*

"You'll love it, Ma!" says Baba. *"That's how I got this* BBQ grill. *That's how we got Xiaolei's sofa bed! Guess how much it was."*

"How much?"

"Forty bucks US! That's like three-hundred RMB! They asked for one-fifty but I bargained them down."

"Wah, that cheap?"

"Aiya, Ma, don't encourage him too much," says Mama. She and Cindy's mom come out carrying trays piled with raw shish kabobs. *"He doesn't want to throw* anything *away. You haven't seen our basement yet, Ma. It's full of old stuff he got at* garage sale. *Half of it's broken!"*

"It's all perfectly good stuff! Easily fixed!"

"What have you fixed so far?"

"Who wants the first hambao!*"*

Baba serves the first burger to Ah Dia. *"Take a bite, old man,"* says Hao Bu, shaking him awake and sticking the burger in front of his face. *"It's an authentic American* hambao. *How do you like it? Does it taste like McDonald's?"*

Ah Dia opens his eyes and takes a bite, then gets to chewing. Baba gives the next burger to me. It's a little dry. I squirt more ketchup on the patty, and when Ah Dia sees me do it, he points to the bottle. So I add ketchup to his too.

Cindy's dad studies his own burger, turning the paper plate in his hands. "*I never saw what the fuss is, even back home,*" he says. He spits out the last of his seed shells and takes a bite. "*Let me tell you, I'd rather have a pork bun. Chinese food is the best food in the world. You have sweet, salty, spicy, sour . . . all kinds of flavors.*"

"*Are you eating white bread again?*" Cindy's mom scolds. "*You have to watch your diabetes—that stuff is all sugar! Wrap it in lettuce!*"

"*Try the* hot dog!" Baba tells Ah Dia. He moves the dogs onto a plate to make room on the grill for kabobs. "*You can get burgers in China, but you can't get* hot dog!"

"*Look, you can't even tell what the meat is,*" says Cindy's dad. "Hot dog like bad version of Poland sausage. Right, Andy? American pizza just bad version of Italy pizza. Even hamburger, is come from Hamburg, Germany. Real hamburger probably better!"

A tiny tomato chunk flies out of his mouth when he says this.

I nod to be polite. Cindy's dad takes another bite of his now-lettuce-wrapped burger, even though he doesn't like it, because Chinese people hate wasting food. Then he calls toward the upstairs window. "Cindy, *come down* here! Zhou Jiu Jiu made BBQ grill, *how come you're being so rude?*"

"I'll get her," I tell him.

The grown-ups' voices muffle as I go up the back stairs. The steps creak a little under the thin brown carpet. The main door at the top is open, but the door to Cindy's room is closed. Just as I'm about to knock, I stop for some reason. I find another long hair on the back of my head and pull: orange.

"Andy, is that you?"

"It's me," I answer. I guess she heard me come up the stairs.

Cindy opens the door and hurries back to something on her computer. I notice the bag of mini pretzels on the wall shelf, in between her eight-ounce Red Pop and Eliza, the taxidermy baby squirrel we found on someone's curb.

The printer on Cindy's desk clicks and clacks. It spits out two pages and she hands me one of them. The paper is still warm. It's a permission slip for . . .

"Math Olympiad? What's Math Olympiad? You want to do that too?"

"Look at the bottom—the tear-off part." She points at the signature form. There's something familiar about it. In fact, it looks just like the form for dance—

Oh.

"Our parents are never gonna let us join Movement," she says.

I spot the real permission form on Cindy's desk and compare the two. They look exactly alike. But wouldn't it be easier just to forge her parents' signatures? Also, I still have to tell her how, like, I don't really want to dance in front of the whole school.

What comes out is: "Why do I need to get *my* parents to sign the Math Olympiad one too? Can't they just sign the real one?"

"Because. If my parents find out I'm in Math Olympiad and you're not, they're gonna wonder. You know, ChinaNet."

This is getting out of control. I have to tell her. "So I was thinking, what if—"

"They ask about what we do in Math Olympiad?"

That wasn't where I was going but okay. I nod.

"Easy. We take these quizzes. Like, math riddles. It's a competition."

"People actually do that?"

"It's a real thing. Look it up."

Cindy gets a pen from the pouch on her desk. She heads for the door.

"Wait," I tell her.

"What?"

Our eyes meet. Outside it's golden hour, and the orangey-pink sun comes through the window behind

Cindy, lighting up the edges of her hair. She's literally glowing. This must be what she was talking about that day we bleached it. She's found her big thing, that better version of herself—the person she's meant to be. What kind of best friend would keep her from being that person?

"Never mind," I say.

Cindy squints at me for a second, like she suspects something. But then she shrugs and goes ahead. Our parents' avalanche voices float up from the back patio. I smell the sizzling shish kabobs on the smoky charcoal grill.

"Don't forget your form!" Cindy reminds me from the stairwell.

I pluck another hair: black.

Our dads sign our permission forms without even asking what happens at Math Olympiad. I eat some corn and a shish kabob—but only after I pull all the things off the skewer and sort each into its own pile. Ah Dia seems to really like the hot dogs. Hao Bu cuts them into little pieces to make it less messy for him to eat.

That night, after the mosquitoes drive us all back inside, I take out the fake permission form and stare at it again. Maybe it won't be so bad. Maybe I'll get some small role where I can stay in the background and not move—like a tree or a rock or something.

I pull two more hairs, both black, and doodle at the kitchen island while my parents clean up. Baba's shaking the trash from his tall chef's hat into the garbage bin, and Mama's trying to fit the buns and uncooked hot dogs into the freezer.

"*Aiya, there's no more room,*" she says. "*We need a second fridge.*"

Baba shrugs. "*Maybe we can find one at a garage sale.*"

CANADIAN QUARTERS

It's the second week of school—only thirty-seven to go, according to my planner. And it's weird, but . . . I think I've memorized Jameel's schedule.

Third period, he comes out of the boys' locker room after gym, down the hall from my social studies classroom. So I take the long way around. At lunch, he'll clown around with Paul and Aiden, but sometimes he's at a different table with a bunch of Chaldean kids, including Dracula Jason. Other times I won't see him at all—probably because he got detention.

I guess that's the thing with Dementors: You have to learn their every move before they learn yours.

And even then you have to stay on guard.

Like Tuesday after school, when I'm supposed to meet Cindy to walk her to symphony band, I almost run into Jameel by the drinking fountain. He's trying to talk to this popular girl, Lily Danielopoulos, who's trying not to get talked to. I duck around the corner and wait. He shouldn't be there much longer because he usually gets a ride home.

"Andy Zhou!"

I jump.

"Sorry! I keep doing that!" It's Mrs. Ocampo again, standing in the doorway to the art studio.

"That's okay," I tell her.

"I meant to talk to you more at the info meeting," she says. Her tote bag's overflowing with colorful scraps of fabric. "Are you planning to audition this week? I didn't realize you were a dancer too!"

I nod. Then shake my head. There's an awkward silence, like she's waiting for me to say more. I remember the permission slip. I dig inside my backpack until I find it.

When Mrs. Ocampo sees the form, she makes a funny face. Uh-oh, she knows it's fake! The jig is up! But then she flips the sheet over—to my doodles from the barbecue.

"Ignore those," I tell her.

"Are these shrimp tails?" she asks.

I nod.

"I really like your line work," she says. "It has a lot of character."

"Thanks." She's probably just being nice again, because that's what teachers are supposed to do.

"Would you like to keep this?" Mrs. Ocampo asks. "I can photocopy it."

"You can have it," I tell her.

"Are you sure? Are you taking art with me this year?"

"I am. Next semester." I glance around the corner: Jameel's gone. When I turn back again, I see Mrs. Ocampo looking back and forth between me and the hallway.

"Um, I have to meet my friend and stuff," I tell her. I hurry out of there.

As I walk away, I hear her call after me: "See you at auditions, Andy!"

"Where were you?" Cindy asks. "I waited."

I catch her just as she's heading into symphony band. "Sorry. I was turning in my permission slip," I tell her. "For Movement." Not that I really planned that.

"Oh, great!" She beams. "Let's practice after school tomorrow." She waves at me, then takes her violin case into the music room. I stand at the doorway for a second and watch her say hi to some of her band friends. Cindy has so many friends—Dance Friends and Band Friends, Lunch Friends and Class Friends. But I guess it's nice to be her *best* friend. Her Everywhere Friend.

By the time I step outside, the buses have already left, and the school feels emptier. Calmer. I put on my Tigers cap and pull it down toward my eyes. Some kids walk ahead of me, while others get into vans and SUVs. The cross-country team is in the middle of the soccer field, stretching in their shorts and T-shirts. And even from this far away, I can hear the clatter of Cindy and everyone in symphony band, warming up their instruments.

It's my first time walking home alone this year. Cindy's a fast walker, so by myself I can take my time. Along the streets are trees with leaves as big as my face, and dangling seeds that look like long green beans. The sky's super clear, but there's a cool wind. It's not quite fall yet, but summer's definitely over.

Around the next block, I pass our old elementary school. The beige brick building already seems smaller than I remember. A kid in Mrs. Antonioni's room looks out the window at me and the other walkers, maybe wondering what middle school's like. Last year Cindy and I were sitting on their side of the glass.

And now I know what it's like.

The kids ahead of me turn onto side streets and go into their houses. By the time I'm a couple blocks from home, I'm the only one left—no one in front and no one behind.

A memory bubbles up. In fourth grade, I saw this repair guy fixing the vending machine in our cafeteria. While the machine's cover was open, he told me how it worked—how coins went down the rails and got read by magnets and tiny lights and sorted into their right places—the quarters with the quarters, the dimes with the dimes. How it could tell if you put in something that was the wrong size or weight, even if by a little.

Then he dug a Canadian quarter out of his pocket. He dropped it into the machine, and I watched it roll down the rails, past all the different coin holes without so much as a hiccup, and clack into the return slot, rejected.

The house feels different as soon as I walk in. My bed's folded back up into a sofa, and the window's open, the curtains billowing a little in the breeze. I hear the clatter of bowls and dishes—Hao Bu must be up and about. Then I remember what Baba said about jet lag, how it's worse flying west to east, how having jet lag is like having the flu: "You feel tired and tired and tired, and then one day you suddenly not tired anymore!"

In the kitchen, all the cabinet doors are open. Hao Bu's standing on a chair, rummaging through a cupboard.

She looks over her shoulder. *"Eh? Xiaolei, you're back? Do you have any homework?"*

"I'm back." I nod. *"I have a little bit of math."* I actually have social studies too, and also science. For science we have to color in drawings of plant and animal cells and label all the parts. But I don't know how to say that in Chinese.

Hao Bu digs through the cabinets again. I take off my backpack and collapse onto the sofa. My eyes fall on the copy of *Lord of the Flies* Cindy checked out for me, waiting to be finished. But for some reason, I don't feel like finishing. I pull a hair: black.

"Where's the dried seaweed?" I hear Hao Bu mumbling to herself. *"And there's no oyster sauce? How could they be out of oyster sauce?"*

"Hao Bu, do you need something?" I ask.

"*Xiaolei, tell me, where's the grocery store? Hao Bu has to buy some things.*"

If Baba were here, he'd probably say, "Let's go to Costco!" But Hao Bu's looking for Chinese groceries, and we get those from 88 Mart, where Mama works. That's on the other side of the freeway, though, and I don't want my grandma to get lost or hit by a truck.

"*I'll go with you,*" I tell her. "*We can walk there.*"

"*Can you go with me? That'd be best.*"

The toilet flushes. Ah Dia's awake too. Hao Bu steps down from the chair and goes into the bathroom to help him.

"*Old man, we're going to get groceries!*" I hear her say. "*You want to come with us? Your grandson says we can walk there.*"

"*You go,*" says Ah Dia.

She turns off the light behind them as they come out. "*Old man, you have to get some exercise. You can't use your jet lag as an excuse anymore. We're going for a walk later, okay?*"

"*Okay, okay.*"

"*Hao Bu will get some money,*" she tells me, and disappears into the bedroom.

Something about having all the cabinet doors open makes me nervous, so I go and shut them one by one. In the living room, Ah Dia makes like he's going to sit down on the sofa. I go over to help but he waves me away. I turn on the TV, so he doesn't get bored while we're gone, and I hand him the remote for the Xiaomi box. Mama and Baba use that to stream their Chinese shows.

Ah Dia looks over the top of his glasses at the buttons. Then he points the remote at the TV and starts clicking around. From the way he's going through the menus, it looks like he already knows how to work it.

"Xiaolei, how much money should we bring?" Hao Bu's back. She's holding a tattered envelope bulging with hundred-dollar bills. There must be at least two thousand bucks in there—I didn't realize my grandparents were rich! Then I remember how Baba sends them money every few months, so maybe it's from that.

On our way out, I notice Ah Dia sitting very still in front of the TV. I get a weird vision of his body as a stone statue, with moss all over. But then it goes away, and I just see the scene from a Chinese drama, reflected in his glasses.

HI-CHEWS & CENTURY EGGS

To get to 88 Mart, Hao Bu and I have to cross the freeway into Hazel Heights, where there's a bunch of Asian and ethnic stuff, and car mechanics and old appliance stores, and fewer trees. My school, Hazel Heights Middle, is on our side, the Oakdale side. It's not in Hazel Heights at all. Mx. Adler told us in social studies it has something to do with moving district lines, and then they got grumpy and made us write a surprise essay about Spanish Conquistadors.

Today, the sun's throwing a harsh glare off the windows of the tall brown apartment building in the distance. Under the pedestrian bridge, half the lanes on the freeway are blocked off for construction, and traffic is barely moving. The bridge also has a metal fence that curves up and over like a tunnel. Cindy told me once that it reminded her of a secret passageway, the kind in Narnia or *Bridge to Terabithia*. Except the only places it takes us are shopping plazas and home, and none of those seem like magical kingdoms to me.

Inside 88 Mart, Hao Bu grabs a cart and we go right past the section with all the hair and beauty products. I forgot this was even here! Maybe in all those bottles and boxes is something that'll make my blotchy hair more like Cindy's.

We're already in the produce area, though, so I'll have to go back. Hao Bu rips a couple plastic bags from the roll by the squash and fills them with bundles of cilantro and chives. She squeezes the big white radishes and winter melons, grabs bags of bok choy and foam trays of shiitake mushrooms wrapped in plastic, and extra-tall tubs of tofu.

"Your hao bu's gonna make douwu jiang for you, okay?" I nod. I think that's soy milk? I didn't know you could make it at home.

When we get near the seafood counter, I see Mama in her face mask and gloves, slime and guts on her thick rubber apron, descaling a fish. In China she used to be a nurse, but she couldn't do that here without an American nursing degree. So now instead of sewing people up, she cuts fish open.

Mama bags the fish and hands it to a customer, then spots us and waves.

"Eh, Ma, you didn't have to come! I would've brought groceries back for us!"

"Uhyo, it's no problem!" says Hao Bu. *"The walk was good for me. Such a nice day too! And you know what my grandson here said when I asked him where the store was?"*

"What'd he say?"

"He said, Hao Bu, I'll go with you!"

While Hao Bu and Mama talk about what's good to buy in the store, I sneak away to the beauty products. There are multiple shelves of the stuff—facial masks and shampoos, whitening creams, and pearly boxes in Chinese or Japanese or Korean with I'm-not-really-sure-what inside. I've never paid too much attention to this section before. But then again, I've never had a reason to.

I grab a box off the shelf. It has a picture of an Asian lady with big round eyes, light skin, and silky blond hair. When I flip it over to read the back, I hear a voice.

"Yo Irish, you getting some facial cream?"

The voice is weirdly familiar. It sounds like—

Jameel.

Jameel.

He's smirking at me from a display of Japanese candy. What's *he* doing here? I don't know whether to run or hide, but I do know one thing: It's not a good look standing next to the feminine beauty products.

I quickly put the box back and walk toward the candy. "I wasn't getting facial cream. I was coming here."

"Sure you were."

I already forgot my rule about not talking to Dementors. I should've kept the hair dye and walked away.

I wait for Jameel to say something else mean, but he just goes back to the racks of Hi-Chews and Puchaos, the boxes of Pocky and choco-koalas, trying to decide what he wants. It's almost like he doesn't mind that I'm here, like he's not trying to suck my soul out of my body.

"What flavor you like?" he asks. "Bet it's grape, isn't it?"

"Ew, no. Grape's the worst," I blurt out.

"It really is."

Did we just . . . agree on something? I scan Jameel's face. Is this a trick?

"So then which one?" he asks.

He really wants to know. I look over the racks. Then I reach for the mango Hi-Chew and hand it to him.

"Not bad, not bad." Jameel nods. "But yo, check this out." He puts the mango back and picks out one with a kiwi on the wrapper.

"This the real stuff," he says. Except instead of *stuff* he uses a different s-word.

He hands me the kiwi and grabs another for himself. He looks left and right, and for a split second I wonder if he's going to steal it. But then he calls out: "Ma! Can I get a Hi-Chew?"

His mom comes over pushing a cart with mostly vegetables in it. Her hair's wavy brown and streaked with blond highlights, and she's dressed like she just came from a business meeting. Light glints off her necklace—a thin gold chain with a cross on the end.

"Jameel, you're already getting ramen," she says. "You have to put one back. You can't have both."

"Ma, they're completely different! Ramen's food, this is dessert."

"You still have to pick."

"Fine," he grumbles. He looks back and forth between the candy and a foam ramen bowl in the cart, like it's the hardest choice he's ever had to make. He puts the candy back on the shelf.

Jameel points at me with his thumb. "Ma, this is Andy. We're lab partners in science."

I think it's the first time he's called me by my actual name. But it's not like he's going to make fun of me right in front of his mom.

"Well, Andy, it's good to meet you," she says, smiling. She turns back to Jameel. "See, didn't I tell you if you really tried, you'd make some nice friends?"

"What's that supposed to mean? Just 'cause he's Asian he's automatically a good kid?"

"I'm just saying that Andy seems like a nice—"

"What, you think he gets straight A's too? Maybe he's good at math and knows kung fu—"

"Jameel." His mom glares at him like, *Not here.* Jameel grumbles and folds his arms across his chest. Was he just . . . defending me? And does he realize his mom called us "friends"?

Just then I see Hao Bu coming toward us. Her cart's

overflowing with meat and veggies, and a dozen bottles of different sauces and cooking wines. She's also loaded a fifty-pound bag of rice onto the bottom rack.

"This is my grandma," I say. Hao Bu smiles politely at Jameel's mom, who nods at the full shopping cart. "Wow, look at that. Are you throwing a party?"

Hao Bu just nods and keeps smiling her polite smile, looking back and forth between Jameel, his mom, and me.

"She only understands a little English," I explain. "She just came from China last week." I translate for Hao Bu: "*Hao Bu, this is* Jameel. *We . . . go to the same school.*"

"Hello, yes," she says in English, still smiling.

Jameel chews his fingernails. He looks around, distracted by something. "Ma, let's go, I gotta feed him."

What? Who? Is there a third grader he keeps in his closet and tortures?

"Well, it was nice meeting you, Andy," his mom says. "Maybe we can have you over sometime. You too, Ms. . . . ?" She looks back and forth between me and Hao Bu, waiting for an answer. I know Hao Bu doesn't have my same last name since Chinese women usually keep their last names when they get married. But I don't remember what hers is. Meanwhile Hao Bu's still just smiling blankly.

"Ma!"

"Okay, okay, it was nice meeting you," says Jameel's mom.

Hao Bu points at the kiwi Hi-Chew in my hand. *"You want to buy this candy? Get it. Hao Bu will pay for it."*

I look over at Jameel. He and his mom are getting in line to check out. I almost can't believe this is the same Dementor who calls me "Irish" at school. Who called me that even a minute ago. Around his mom at least, he seems like any other kid.

Hao Bu grabs a couple more things and we get into a different checkout line. When the cashier scans the Hi-Chew, she puts it on the ledge next to the card machine for me instead of bagging it. I peel open the shiny outside wrapper, then the paper one around the individual piece. I pop the soft candy in my mouth. It's a burst of kiwi flavor, with that mellow vanilla aftertaste that all the candies have. Jameel's right—it's delicious. Maybe even better than mango.

I catch Jameel staring at me as he walks out of the store with his mom. He frowns a little, like he regrets picking ramen. I stop chewing, and the rest of the candy melts slowly in my mouth.

At dinner that night, Hao Bu tells Baba every detail of our trip to 88 Mart, how when we came out, we realized that we couldn't carry all the groceries.

"And I asked Andy, how are we going to get all this home!" She laughs. *"But your son, he said, Let's go get Mama. Let's go get Mama. Luckily, Xiaoyin was able to borrow a cart for us."*

I listen to Hao Bu tell the story, and scoop another spoonful of braised pork and chestnuts onto my plate. When we got home, she made it seem like she was just going to whip something up, but while I did my homework she cooked an entire feast: chilled cucumber and stir-fried bok choy, chives with bright golden chunks of scrambled eggs, tilapia steamed with ginger and green onion, *douwu yi*—rolled tofu-skin crepe things in a sweet brown sauce. And cabbage and rice cakes. And a pork shank soup with bamboo and winter melon! It's so much food. And it's all so good.

Even Mr. Red White and Blue thinks so. "I vwery mwiss yourmw hwao bwu cwooking," says Baba, his cheeks puffed like a puffer fish.

"Aiya, Ma, you shouldn't have gone to all the trouble," says Mama.

"It's no problem! No problem at all!" Hao Bu ladles more soup into my bowl, making sure I get extra chunks of pork and bamboo. Then she goes back to spoon-feeding Ah Dia. *"Come on, old man, another bite."*

Ah Dia shakes his head. *"I don't want any more."*

"How can you not want more! You barely ate anything!"

"I ate enough!"

"Andy, *did you know? Your ah dia used to cook delicious food too,"* says Baba. There's a grain of rice stuck to the corner of his mouth. *"Your hao bu's chive and egg is great, but your ah dia's was even better!* The egg so shiny and yellow. Like golden."

"*What's Ah Dia's favorite food?*" I ask.

"*Your ah dia loves zhuo,*" says Hao Bu. We call it that in Shanghainese but I've only seen it labeled rice porridge or congee at Chinese restaurants. "*Zhuo with fermented tofu and century egg.*"

"*Xiaolei also loves century eggs,*" Mama adds.

I nod. Cindy says it's gross because it's basically a pickled egg, but she's the only Chinese kid I know who thinks so. I don't care how it's made—it's the best.

After dinner, I go upstairs and give Cindy a Hi-Chew. I wait for her to comment on the flavor, but she eats it without saying anything. She's too focused on looking up songs and dances for our auditions, trying to find the perfect ones. I can't even think about being up on that stage, even if it's just in front of Mx. Adler and Mrs. Ocampo. Like, I physically can't think about it. It's like staring at the sun.

I pop another Hi-Chew and pick up Cindy's copy of *Lord of the Flies*. I find the spot where I left off in my own book, but my mind keeps wandering to how Jameel acted at 88 Mart, the look on his face as he and his mom were leaving. I pluck another hair. It's black.

"Andy."

I drop the hair. I look up.

Cindy's ponytail is undone, and she's smoothing her silky blond hair between her fingers, almost in a shy way. "Who are the best characters to audition for?

Ralph or Piggy, right? Aren't those the main ones?"

"Well, there's Jack too." I stop. "Wait, you haven't read it?" If she'd even read the first chapter, she'd know that Jack's another main character.

"I don't think Mx. Adler's expecting us to *finish* the book yet," Cindy says. "I can just watch the movie or something."

"But—"

"You haven't answered my question though. If you *had* to pick someone, who would it be? Who's your favorite?"

Definitely not Jack. But I don't know about Ralph or Piggy either. Piggy has good ideas, but nobody pays attention to him. And Ralph is supposed to be his best friend on the island but he doesn't stand up for Piggy when the others bully him. Then someone else comes to mind.

"Simon."

"Who's he?"

"He kind of keeps to himself. I mean, he talks to the other kids, but there's something about him that's, I don't know, different. He's on the island with everyone, but he's also apart from them. He sees things."

Cindy's face scrunches up. "He sees things?"

"It's like, if Ralph and Jack are Gryffindor and Slytherin, and Piggy's a Hufflepuff, then Simon's the Ravenclaw."

"Jeez, you're more into all that than Ms. Daly is." Cindy frowns. "You know those books have all kinds of problems, right?" Ms. Daly is our honors math teacher. She was the same exact age as the characters when the books came out, and her room's decorated with all Hogwarts-themed stuff.

"I know. I mean, I've only read a couple of them," I tell her. "Anyway, Simon has a scene in the middle where he's talking to the Lord of the Flies."

"There's an *actual* Lord of the Flies?"

"Well, it's really just the dead boar head that the hunters—"

"Wait, so Simon has a *solo*?"

"I guess."

"Interesting . . ." I can see the wheels turning in Cindy's head. I eat another Hi-Chew and peel back the extra bits of the outside wrapper. There's only one candy left. I think about offering it to Cindy, but then a funny idea pops into my head. I put the candy back in my pocket.

"Okay, I know what to do," says Cindy.

That was quick.

"Do you still have your Halloween costume from last year?"

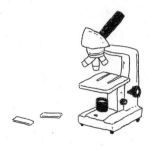

ACCIDENTAL GENIUS

"So you remember your steps, right?" Cindy says the next morning in science. "First you sky-poke, sky-poke, dribble left . . ."

I check the clock on the school's TV system. I glance at the open door.

"Andy."

I look back at her. "I remember the steps."

Cindy squints at me. She knows I'm up to something. But the bell rings, so she spins back around in her seat. Just as Mr. Nagy's about to shut the door, Jameel shambles in and sits down next to me, all limbs and noise. I wait for him to settle.

Then I take out my last kiwi Hi-Chew.

I put it a few inches to the left of my notebook, far enough that it's on his side of our table. I don't look over, because I almost don't want to see his reaction. Maybe

I saved him a candy because I felt bad about not giving him one at 88 Mart. Or maybe it's to get him to stop calling me names. A peace offering.

I hear him undo the wrapper and chew loudly. I can almost feel him smirking next to me. Mr. Nagy's at the front of the room, talking about our lab day with microscopes, demonstrating how to twist the lens heads and turn the focus knob. But then he stops.

"Mr. Zebari, no gum in my class."

"It's not gum," says Jameel. "It's candy." He winks at me.

"No candy either."

I tense up. It's over. Jameel's going to say I gave him the candy, and then I'll get detention for giving it to him, and it'll go on my record and I'll flunk sixth grade and I'll never get into that international high school!

Except Jameel doesn't tell on me. Instead he makes a show of swallowing the rest of the Hi-Chew. He turns to me and rolls his eyes, like he's saying about Mr. Nagy, *Can you believe this guy?*

"First warning," says Mr. Nagy. "One more and you're going to the office."

"Whatever happened to three strikes?" asks Jameel.

"I mean it."

A hush falls over the class. Jameel crumples the candy wrapper into a little ball. Then, while Mr. Nagy's looking away, he flicks it off the table, hitting Kevin Walsh square on the back of the neck.

Kevin's ears twitch. He freezes, like his own spider-sense just activated and he knows not to turn around. I watch Jameel chew the corner of one of his nails, even though his other finger already has a Band-Aid around the top.

Maybe I made a mistake being nice to him. Dementors don't care how nice you are.

Mr. Nagy finishes the demonstration. He hands out some worksheets and tells us it's our turn. There are microscope stations at the counters along the walls, and boxes of glass slides next to the lab sinks. We're supposed to wet two slides and put a strand of hair between them, then write down what we see.

It's four kids per microscope. Jameel and I get paired with Cindy and Kevin, which makes me a little tingly. All of a sudden everyone's plucking hairs from their heads, so I don't feel so weird doing it too. I find a longer one and pull: It's bright orange, with a little black at the root.

Cindy and Jameel are jostling for position by the sink with a bunch of other kids, trying to get slides from the box. Kevin looks at me, then sticks his hands in his pockets.

"Take turns, please," says Mr. Nagy, like he's talking specifically about Cindy and Jameel. "No pushing. Let everyone have their turn."

Cindy comes back first. She puts one of her shiny bleached hairs in between two glass slides, then climbs on the lab stool and sets them under the microscope lens. She turns the focus knob like Mr. Nagy showed us—and perks up.

"Andy, look at this!"

I sit and look into the eyepiece: Her hair's like a thick rope or flaky tree branch, glowing gold at the edges. Wow!

I move over so Kevin can have a turn. Meanwhile Jameel's back with his own glass slides. I watch him try to pluck at his hair, but it's so short, he can't get a good grip.

"Yo Irish, let me get one of yours," he says. He starts reaching for my head but I duck just in time.

"Come on, help a brother out!"

"Maybe let's just look at Cindy's hair?" I suggest. "It's already in the microscope."

"I want the full experience," Jameel says. He chews at his finger again.

"Then use that."

"Use what?"

I pretend like I'm biting my nails. Jameel's eyes widen.

"Irish, you're a genius."

He takes off the Band-Aid, then squeezes his finger over one of the wet slides. I was talking about his fingernail—not *that*. Jameel dabs the tiniest drop of blood on the slide and covers it with a second slide. The red dot flattens into a wider, see-through pink circle.

Jameel smirks. He whips around to the microscope.

Kevin sees him and immediately jumps off the stool. Jameel replaces Cindy's slides with his, then frantically twists the heads to change the zoom. He looks up.

"Yo Andy, check this out!"

I glance at Cindy, who looks like she's about to shoot fire out of her eyes at Jameel. But part of me also wants to see what it looks like under the microscope. So I go.

When I put my eye over the viewfinder, I notice little gray clouds. I turn the knob to try to make the image clearer. The clouds are still a little blurry, but they're *definitely* moving.

"Are those . . . blood cells?"

Jameel nods triumphantly.

"Wait, what? Lemme see," says Carter King from the next group over. He climbs onto the stool. "Whoa!"

"Cindy, do you want to—" I start. But when I turn around, her arms are folded across her chest. Kevin's behind her, staring down at his feet.

Carter pulls his cousin Caleb over. Other kids hear and start swarming our microscope.

"Now, now, no pushing," Jameel says, imitating Mr. Nagy. "Let everyone get a turn."

There's enough of a commotion that Mr. Nagy comes over too. When he sees what's on the slide, his whole face turns red. His bushy gray eyebrows look almost like they're made of smoke.

"Who's responsible for this?" he asks.

Everyone falls quiet. I think about what my parents

would say if I got in trouble and hesitate. Cindy's the one who points at Jameel. "It was him. He did it."

"Zebari. Outside."

Jameel holds up his hands. He looks to me for backup. "You never said we couldn't—"

"Let's go. *Now*."

Jameel clicks his tongue and heads for the door. Mr. Nagy grabs the microscope by the neck and follows him out. Even when they're in the hallway, we can still hear them.

"*I will not have you disrupting my class, you understand?*"

Mr. Nagy lowers his voice, and after a second he comes back in and sets the microscope on the front counter. He tells us to continue with our worksheets.

When he leaves again, I know it's to walk Jameel to the office.

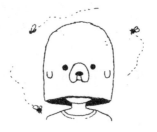

A WEIRD SIXTY SECONDS

Jameel doesn't come out of the boys' locker room third period. He's not in the hallways before lunch. I wonder if he got suspended. Did they call his mom at work? It seemed like he got in way more trouble than he deserved to, all for looking at blood cells.

And it was my idea to do it in the first place, sort of.

I try to shake the thought away. Cindy's getting ready for our audition, brushing her hair in the mirror stuck inside her locker door. I pull another strand of mine but I forget to check the color.

I don't realize I'm thinking out loud until I say, "Do you think Jameel got suspended?"

"I hope so," says Cindy.

"But why?"

Cindy rolls her eyes. "You were there. He was disrupting the class."

"Yeah, but that was earlier. With the Hi-Chew. I mean, the candy. He was just being curious. Isn't that what science is all—"

"Andy, it's *blood*. He could've given everyone hepatitis."

"I don't think Jameel has—"

"It's just not *sanitary*, is what I mean." She turns to face me. "Mr. Nagy would've done the same thing if it was you or me."

Would he have? Or would he have just explained nicely why we shouldn't be messing around with blood, without sending us to the office?

Cindy turns back to the mirror. "You should be glad anyway. Do you *like* it when he makes fun of you?"

"I don't," I say.

Of course I don't. Except when Jameel called me "Irish" earlier—it was different than before. Like he didn't mean it the same way. But does that make it okay?

Cindy sighs. "Andy, just—don't make a big deal out of it." She shuts her locker and nods toward my backpack. "You brought it, right?"

"I brought it," I say, still wondering about Jameel.

One of the tall girls—the seventh grader, Alexandra—is in the middle of her audition when we walk into the auditorium. Viola, Mai, and a couple other kids are sitting in the front rows, while Mx. Adler takes notes and Mrs. Ocampo records video on her phone.

I feel my stomach drop. I didn't realize we'd be on camera—and with other kids watching!

Cindy and I slip quietly into the second row. Alexandra twirls and hops on stage. From the way she's dancing, I'm guessing she's had ballet lessons.

I look over at Cindy. Her eyes are locked on Alexandra. She's even shifting a little in her seat to Alexandra's routine. I try to remember the moves we practiced—was it sky-poke, basketball dribble . . . or basketball dribble, *then* sky-poke?

Everyone claps. Alexandra's done. Mx. Adler asks who wants to go next and Cindy pops up. She taps me on the shoulder. I look at her like, *Do I have to?*

Now she's giving me a death stare. I guess I do have to.

I take a deep breath and pull the mask out of my backpack. I tent open the bottom. It's Jake from *Adventure Time*. I made it for Cindy and my Halloween costume last year.

"Andy and I are auditioning together, if that's okay," she tells the teachers. "I'm going to be Simon. Andy's the boar."

I slide the mask over my head. It still smells a little like paint. I get it lined up just in time to see Mx. Adler gesturing toward the stage, like they're saying, *I'll allow it.*

Cindy leads me up the side steps because it's hard for me to see through the tiny eye holes. She walks me to the spot where she wants me to stand, and gives my hand an extra-hard squeeze. Maybe she's warning me not to mess up. Then she lets go and starts the song she picked out on her phone.

The poppy music builds, the beat pulses through my head, Cindy's sneakers squeak and slap the stage floor. I hear my cue and . . .

I can't move. My body is completely frozen.

The dance is only sixty seconds long, but it feels longer while it's happening. I close my eyes, because I don't want to see how mad or disappointed at me Cindy must be. I don't want to see the tall girls probably snickering in the front row. For some reason, I imagine the dead boar head in the book, flies swarming out of its blank eyes and mouth, except instead of on an island, it's in the principal's office, telling Jameel in an echoey demon voice, *YOU'RE SUSPENDED.*

It's a weird sixty seconds.

Once the music stops, the rest happens so fast: kids clapping, Cindy leading me off the stage, the two of us back in our seats. I feel a little dizzy, like, *What just happened?*

Mx. Adler writes something on their clipboard. Someone else gets up to audition. When I take off my mask, Cindy's looking straight ahead, but not really watching the other dancer set up—iceman stare. She's probably so mad at me for messing up my part, she can't even face me.

I pull a hair: orange.

"Cindy," I whisper. *"I'm sorry I—"*

"It's okay."

"I don't know what hap—"

"It's okay, really." She gets up.

"Where are you—"

"Let's go to lunch," she says.

I follow her up.

"Andy." Mrs. Ocampo waves at me. "I love that mask you made. It's paper mache, right?"

I look at the lopsided mask in my hand. I nod.

She smiles. "You did a great job with it."

I glance at Cindy to see her reaction. There's a flash of something in her face. But then it's gone.

GARAGE SALES IN THE HOT SUN

Jameel's in school the next day. He didn't get suspended after all. I guess I'm . . . relieved?

In science, Mr. Nagy has him sit at the front of the room, at the table with the terrariums. It's normally for kids to make up tests and quizzes they missed, but I think Mr. Nagy just wants to keep an eye on him. Jameel stares into the glass cages the whole time, and hurries out as soon as the bell rings. He doesn't so much as look at me. Does he hate me because I basically made him get in trouble?

I avoid him in the hallways, just in case.

Jameel's not the only one acting weird. I notice Cindy doing the iceman stare again at lunch, not really touching her food.

Then I catch her looking toward the auditorium when we pass it in the halls.

After school, she says she has a ton of homework and

goes straight up to her room, even though she has the whole weekend to finish.

"Ba, Andy, let's go," says Baba.

It's Saturday—hot and sunny. One of those days that says maybe summer isn't over after all. Ah Dia's eyes are glued to another of his Chinese dramas. He either doesn't hear Baba over the TV or he's *acting* like he doesn't hear. Upstairs, Cindy's practicing her violin, and messing up more than usual.

"We could all stay here and watch shows with Ah Dia," I suggest. "Plus I have some homework?"

"Finish it later," says Baba. He turns off the TV.

"I was watching that!" says Ah Dia.

Cindy's violin squeaks. Mama shuts off the window AC, and Hao Bu brings Ah Dia's sneakers over. She starts putting them on for him but he tries to kick them off. Hao Bu slaps at the air. *"Quit messing around. Your son wants to take you to garage!"*

An avalanche-talk later, we're all in the car.

I feel better once we start driving. We used to go garage sale hunting all the time back when Cindy and I still went to Chinese school on Saturdays. Our parents would pick us up from the Chinese Community Center, we'd all get KFC for lunch, and then we'd cruise up and down the main roads near big subdivisions, looking for garage sale signs at street corners.

Cindy and I were as excited as our parents. They'd

let us buy toys and board games and sports stuff they'd never let us get at stores, because no Chinese person can pass up a good deal.

Ah Dia included. Once we find the first garage sale, he gets out to look with everyone else. I watch him test an old sewing machine, turn its wheel and press the foot pedal. He picks up a duck carved out of wood, then puts it back down. At the other end of the driveway, Hao Bu's flipping over plates and dishes, looking at the handwritten price stickers on the bottom.

"Wah, these are only twenty-five cents?" she asks my mom.

"And you can bargain them down!" says Mama. *"Twenty-five cents for two."*

"Twenty-five cents for THREE," says Baba.

Later we come across a subdivision sale, which makes my parents especially excited. Baba parks under a shade tree and we all get out and walk. At one house I find some hair clippers. We already have a set at home, actually. I could use them to shave my head!

But then I think about Cindy. If I shaved my head now, would she think I was giving up on her? On this plan to reinvent ourselves? I should've asked her to come along this morning, I realize too late.

I pluck a hair: orange.

A couple houses down, Mama finds some poofy winter coats for my grandparents, and my dad finds a pair of barbells.

"What are you planning to do with those?" asks Mama.

Baba curls his biceps. *"I'm going to get super buff. You just watch!"* But when the owner rejects his offer of 80 percent off, he leaves them behind.

We keep driving. Mama makes us all put on more sunscreen and hands us bottles of water. The next time we stop, Ah Dia's tired and wants to stay in the car. It turns into another avalanche:

"What's the matter, old man?" asks Hao Bu. *"You still have jet lag?"*

"Here, drink some more water," says Mama.

"I'm fine," says Ah Dia.

"Ba, I'm telling you, we should really get a doctor to—"

"I'll stay in the car with him!"

"Ma, I'll do it! You go—"

"I'm fine!"

Mama ends up staying with Ah Dia so that Baba and Hao Bu can shop some more. I go with my dad and grandma. Even in the scorching sun, it feels kind of nice to be outside. At one house, I find a box with some old paperback kids' books that remind me of *Lord of the Flies,* which I still haven't finished. The story keeps getting darker and darker. I just have a feeling that something terrible is going to happen.

When I put the books back, I notice a leather journal lying flat at the bottom. It's one of those fancy sketchbooks, the kind with the elastic band and a pocket in the back. I open it and the creamy pages inside are completely blank. The sticker on it says only three dollars!

Like I said, no Chinese person can pass up a good deal.

I show the sketchbook to Baba, who flips it over, sees the price, then hands it back to me and tells me to bargain for *one* dollar. He gives me four quarters out of his pocket. While he's not looking, Hao Bu sneaks me an extra two bucks.

I take it to the owner, a lady sitting in a lawn chair in the shaded garage, and I hand her all three dollars.

Baba and Hao Bu keep browsing, but I hurry back to the car before the seller lady can change her mind. This might be the first good thing that's happened to me all year. As I walk up, I see Mama in the driver's seat, windows rolled down. I hear her talking to Ah Dia in a soft voice.

"...*just worried,*" she's saying. "*We're all worried. Humor him and go for a check-up. It'll reassure us.*"

"*Ao.*" Ah Dia nods. I'm not sure if he's saying he understands or if he's saying he'll go. I open the back door and get in.

Mama looks over her shoulder. She puts on a more cheerful voice. "*Xiaolei, what did you find?*" she asks.

I show her and Ah Dia the sketchbook. "*It's for drawing,*" I tell them.

"*You're still drawing?*" says Ah Dia. Still?

He goes on. "*When you were younger. You were al-*"

ways drawing." He winces a little, but not because of the memory. Ever since Baba mentioned that Ah Dia's in pain, I've noticed it more. His face will scrunch up sometimes, as if he's just eaten a sour plum.

"*You'd draw all the time,*" he repeats. "*Drawing on the walls. Drawing on the table. Drawing everywhere.*" I'm expecting him to say more, but he stops. It's the longest conversation we've had since he got here.

I run my hand across the leather sketchbook cover, then open it to the first page. The spine crackles a little.

"*Ah Dia, when you were little, did you draw too?*" I ask.

"*I sang choir,*" says Ah Dia. "*Played music. Die zi*—flute. *Because of . . .*" Then he says something I don't understand.

"Cultural Revolution," Mama translates. She hands me a pen from her purse. "Start in 1966. Government say people only allow make traditional art, traditional music. Forbid Western-style art. Your grandparent all were kid. Government make they go work on farm."

Ah Dia looks out the window, and I get the feeling that he's done talking for now. Mama pulls out her phone and asks, "Andy, when is Math Olympia start? Is this Monday?"

"The Monday after," I answer. I pluck another hair, and when I do, I notice a small, smooth spot on the back of my head.

Mama types something into her phone while Ah Dia keeps staring out the window, watching automatic sprinklers chuck water over someone's lawn. Baba said that Ah Dia's always wanted to visit America. Is it at all like what he expected? Garage sales in the hot sun? Automatic sprinklers over wide green lawns?

I write my name inside the sketchbook cover. On the first blank page, I try to draw Ah Dia's hand, his bony knuckles resting across his walking cane, almost like knobs on a tree trunk. I start thinking about Jameel again, the way he looked at me on microscope day, and the way Cindy *didn't* look at me after I messed up our audition . . .

And then I get an idea.

I finish my drawing. It's not my best, but it's not terrible either. I show it to Mama and Ah Dia, and I watch him stare at it for a few long seconds. There's a smear of sunscreen near his left eyebrow.

"Very good," he says in English. "I very like." He hands back the sketchbook and looks out the window again.

It's still hard to imagine Ah Dia as a bad kid growing up. But I'm starting to notice how he doesn't like being told what to do. I wonder if he ever got detention. Do they even have detention in China? Mama and Baba said in the old days, teachers there would rap your knuckles with a wooden ruler if you were misbehaving. Does that still happen today?

And what was it like, being made to go work on a farm as a kid? Did they have fun raising the chickens? Or did they spend all their days toiling away in the fields. Did all those kids in one place turn into warring tribes, like in *Lord of the Flies*?

I can't find the words to ask. I don't really get time to, either, because my dad and grandma come back to the car, talking and laughing. Hao Bu's cradling a set of mixing bowls, and when Baba pops into view, he's carrying four fishing rods, three tackle boxes, and wearing a floppy bucket hat with a bunch of colorful fuzzy lures on it. His mouth is open in a smile almost as wide as the hat.

"Old man, look! We're going fishing, American-style!*"*

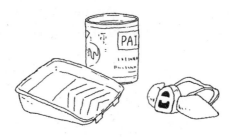

NEW TO CREW

It rains the next day. Like, an absolute downpour. Fishing has to wait.

The storms carry into Monday, and at school, water pelts the courtyard tree and bench like glass pebbles. It's only just starting to let up in the afternoon, when Cindy and I go by the auditorium to see if the cast list has been posted. It hasn't.

"What's taking so long?" Cindy wonders out loud. But I'm secretly relieved. It means I still have time.

"We can drop you off on the way," says Cindy. Her mom's picking her up for a dentist appointment.

"I have to go talk to a teacher," I say, hoping she doesn't ask which one. "I'll meet you at home."

Cindy shrugs. I wave goodbye, then hurry off to the art studio.

When I get there, the door's wide open. A girl in an

oversize blue T-shirt is setting up drop cloths along a pair of huge wooden panels. I recognize the panels—they're the ones I saw backstage in the auditorium. The set from last year's *A Wrinkle in Time* show.

The girl looks over. I recognize her from the informational meeting too. She has straight black hair and pale-brown skin, and I wonder if she's Filipina like Mrs. Ocampo—or maybe Latina. She waves hi and tells me her name is Eva Jiménez.

"Yeets Ahndy, ah!"

I turn around. It's Jason Shaheen. He walks in with Lucy Eugenides, who's wearing her trademark glasses and jean overalls. "Hey Andy!" she says.

"Andy!" Mrs. Ocampo comes out of the back closet carrying an easel and a blank canvas. "We're getting a jump start on this year's production. You came just in time!"

I did?

Mrs. Ocampo sets up the easel at the front of the room and tells everyone to gather around. The others put down their backpacks and rain jackets and pull up chairs. I sit too. Wait—what did I come here to do again?

"All right, let's dive in," says Mrs. Ocampo. "Feel free to shout out ideas. Props, costumes, whatever jumps to mind when you think *Lord of the Flies*!"

"Piggy's glasses!" says Lucy, adjusting her own. Mrs.

Ocampo writes *glasses* on a note and sticks it on the canvas.

"The cahnch!" says Jason. Mrs. Ocampo stares for a second, then writes *conch* and sticks it up.

"Fire. We need fire," say Eva in a slightly creepy way.

"They're from an English boarding school," says Lucy. "So they probably have uniforms."

"Yeah, charred by fire," Eva adds.

"Vith some blahd!" says Jason.

"Oh! And the parachute!" says Lucy.

I remember why I'm here. To talk to Mrs. Ocampo about the audition.

"Anything else?" she asks, looking to me. "No bad ideas. Just whatever pops up in your mind's eye."

I remember that vision I had of Jameel and the boar's head. In the principal's office. I raise my hand.

"Andy?"

"The boar?"

"Ooo yeah," says Lucy.

Mrs. Ocampo smiles. She writes *boar* and sticks it up.

"And the hunters need spears. Sharp ones," says Eva.

"Vooden stakes?" Jason frowns.

Mrs. Ocampo puts up a few more stickies, then looks over the canvas.

"This is a terrific start," she says. She pulls off the *conch* and *glasses* stickies and moves them to the bottom corner. "I can get us these. If you all think of more ideas, feel free to add them!" She caps her Sharpie and puts it with the stickies pad on the easel ledge. The others go up, chatting about who wants to work on what.

Now's my chance.

"Mrs. Ocampo?" I ask. "Can I talk to you about my and Cindy Shen's audition?"

"Of course!" she says. She turns to Eva. "Eva, you want to get everyone else set up to paint? Andy, come, step into my office."

Mrs. Ocampo's office turns out to be the supply closet in the back of the art studio. It fits her desk and a couple of chairs, and that's about it. I stay in the doorway and glance back at the others. Eva's handing aprons to Jason and Lucy. She also puts on a rubber face mask with two big air filter thingies. It kind of makes her look like Nausicaä of the Valley of the Wind.

"So Andy, what can I do ya for?"

I try to focus. I tell Mrs. Ocampo what I rehearsed over the weekend . . . sort of: "So, I know we kinda messed up our audition the other day. I mean *we* didn't— Cindy didn't—because I was supposed to basketball-dribble and then sky-poke but the mask and lights and it was hard to see? And anyway it's not Cindy's fault because she did everything she was supposed to and did it really well, probably, so I don't think you should count it against her. And stuff."

Mrs. Ocampo nods. "I'll be sure to let Mx. Adler know," she says, then looks me in the eyes. "Cindy's very lucky to have you as a friend."

I feel my cheeks get hot. "Thanks," I tell her.

"You know, I'm glad you're here. I was thinking that it would be wonderful to make our boar costume for the show out of paper mache. Or the head, at least. What do you think about that? And I'll say it once more—I just loved that mask you brought to your audition."

I look away so I don't blush again. Eva pries open a paint bucket with a screwdriver and starts pouring white paint into a metal tray. Now Jason and Lucy have their own Nausicaä masks on. They're holding long rods with paint rollers at the end. Are they going to—?

"Andy, I was wondering," says Mrs. Ocampo, sitting back. "Would you like to join our production crew? And be our paper mache man?"

I snap back to the conversation. Me? Join crew?

"What do you say?" Mrs. Ocampo asks. "Sound fun?"

I turn the idea around in my head, like an unsolved Rubik's Cube. If I join crew, I can be in dance club with Cindy—but without having to dance. It's even better than being a tree or rock, because I won't have to be on stage at all!

I nod. Maybe a few too many times.

"That's wonderful! And I already have your permission

form, so you're all set. That is, unless you want to stay and help today too. I could call one of your adults and ask, if you'd like."

I shake my head. "I can't today," I say, without telling her the real reason: My parents aren't expecting Math Olympiad to start until *next* week.

"Next Monday then!"

"Okay!"

On my way out, I see Eva roll, onto the old backdrops, the first ribbon of white paint.

HUH.

SPIKY LIZARDS & ONE-PUNCH MAN

I leave the art studio with a pep to my step—I'm almost skipping.

Going by the courtyard, I can tell the rain's a lot lighter. Water's beaded up on the glass walls, and more drips from the tree's peach-colored leaves. A pair of cardinals, one red, one purply brown, land on the skinny branches. They tweet and flick their tails, then both fly off.

In all the weeks since school started, I haven't seen a single person—not even the custodian—go inside. Or is it *outside*? Maybe neither.

Rattling metal. Someone clicks their tongue. It's Jameel, down the hallway. I watch him struggle and struggle and finally get his locker open. He grabs his backpack, throws a book and a mess of papers in, then slams the door and gives the knob a twist.

I flip my rain hood over my head. I hurry toward the

front entrance. Even though Jameel hasn't talked much to me lately, I'm not taking any chances.

"Yo Irish! Wait up!"

Something about how he says it makes me stop and look. He comes up alongside, his backpack hanging lazily off one shoulder.

"You walking home?" he asks. "Or you got a ride?"

"Yeah," I say.

"So which is it?"

"Walk. Walking. I'm walking home."

"Cool. Me too."

We walk side by side through the mostly empty halls. Jameel doesn't really say more to me, and I'm not going to rock the boat by talking to him. A couple cross-country runners come out of the boys' locker room, their shoes squeaking on the floor. Molly Sienkiewicz slings her French horn case across her back and mumbles, "I'm so freaking late!" The whole time, my rain jacket makes little zwishing sounds. *Zwish zwish.*

Outside, we round the pickup circle and head down the wet gray sidewalk, away from school. I'm expecting him to turn onto a side street at any moment, but he sticks by me, looking off into the distance like he's thinking about something—or someone—far away. I know that look. It's my iceman stare. I also notice how different this is from walking with Cindy, how whenever there's any quiet, she'll fill it. How even if Cindy's not talking, she'll hum songs and make little sound effects.

Zwish zwish.

I turn toward my street. Jameel does too.

He asks before I can: "You following me?"

"I'm not."

"You sure?" He squints at me. I squeeze my backpack straps. I feel a joke coming, or a new nickname. Instead he points past my house toward the freeway. "I'm that way."

I've never seen him go this way before, but then I remember how he normally gets a ride home.

As if he knows what I'm thinking, he says, "My uncle picks me up usually. But his car's in the shop. My ma don't like me walking."

"Me too," I say. "I mean, not mom. In the shop—our car isn't." Why am I talking like Yoda? I take a breath. "My mom doesn't like me walking either. And stuff."

"Huh," Jameel says.

My head floods with questions. I want to ask him about Mr. Nagy and detention. Is that why he stayed late today? Did he get into trouble with his mom? How did his dad react? What if your parents can't pick you up after school, and you don't live close enough to walk? Do you just have to stay there until they leave work?

I hold out my hand. The rain's stopped. I pull back my hood.

Jameel points. "Yo, isn't that your grandma?"

I get the spider-sense tingle again. I remember kids asking me stuff like that before at my old school, when they saw an elderly Chinese lady. As if we all looked alike. But then I see who Jameel's pointing at. It *is* my grandma. And Ah Dia's with her. She's waving at us.

We walk over. *"Your ah dia wanted to see your school!"* says Hao Bu. She laughs and shakes her head. *"I tell you—this old man, you try to get him to walk and he wants to stay inside. Then suddenly when it rains, he wants to go for a walk!"*

"My school's that way." I point the direction we came. *"Hao Bu, you remember* Jameel? *My classmate."*

"Ao, Jamee? Hello, yes. Jamee!"

"Hi, Granny," says Jameel, extra polite. He and Ah Dia stare at each other for a second and neither of them says a word. It's kind of awkward. Hao Bu's carrying a folded-up umbrella, big enough for both her and Ah Dia.

"Do you want me to show you my school?" I ask them.

"I'm tired," says Ah Dia, still staring at Jameel.

"Next time then," says Hao Bu.

As the four of us walk the rest of the way, Jameel starts fidgeting with the zippers of his backpack. He pulls out a set of keys from the front pocket. There's a little plastic figurine dangling from the ring, and I immediately recognize the bald head, yellow suit, and red gloves. The white cape. It's One-Punch Man!

"*You* watch anime?" Now I'm the one who's incredulous.

"Everyone watches anime." Jameel shrugs. "Hey, wait—you seen *Demon Slayer?*"

"That's one of my favorites!"

"What about *Kaiji: Ultimate Survivor*?"

"I haven't. What's that?"

"Bruh, you gotta! It's a classic!"

Jameel launches into a description of what the show's about. Before I know it, we're standing in front of my house. Hao Bu helps Ah Dia up the porch steps, then points at Jameel but says to me, *"Is* Jamee *coming over to play?"*

I look at Jameel, who's waiting for a translation. He's spinning his keys around the key ring, catching One-Punch Man, letting him go. Catching him. Letting him go. I think about Cindy and Movement, Hi-Chews and garage sales and duck brains, and it's like something in me short-circuits. I lose any ability to talk.

Jameel spins his keys around and catches them one more time.

Then he says, "Yo, you wanna come over?"

I promise Hao Bu I'll be back before dinner. It turns out Jameel lives in the tall apartment building across the freeway overpass, with balconies facing out toward the traffic. I always thought it was a weird thing to have a view of, but I don't say that out loud. As we walk toward the building, with its wet brown brick, it almost looks like a fortress.

Jameel lives on the ninth floor. Inside, his apartment unit has beige carpet instead of old wood floors like our duplex. We take our shoes off at the door, and when he closes it behind us, there's a small wooden crucifix under the peephole.

The wind outside howls and whistles, and rattles the glass balcony doors. It's either picked up from before, or it's just stronger up high. Poppy music's coming from the other room, and in the narrow kitchen near the door, there's a framed painting of Jesus Christ—one of those ones where you can see his glowing red heart.

Jameel goes into the fridge and gets a juice and string cheese for me, and another set for himself. When he hands me the snacks, he seems younger for some reason.

"Hey Andy, wanna see something cool?"

He called me by my actual name again. And this time his mom isn't even around.

I follow Jameel down the hallway, toward his room at the end. I get a quick look at some of the family photos on the wall. There's the usual school and wedding pictures, and others with relatives at parks and big dinners. There's also a portrait of someone in a marines uniform who looks like an older version of Jameel.

We pass by a bedroom with two teenage girls inside doing homework. *AP Chemistry,* according to the books in their laps. The music's coming from here.

"'Sup Katie," Jameel says to one of the girls, and leans against the door frame. If his face were an emoji, it'd be the kissy-face one. The girl who's *not* Katie gives

Jameel the side-eye, then gets up and shuts the door. I'm guessing that's his older sister.

Jameel laughs it off. "Come on," he says.

The vertical blinds in his room are drawn. It's darker than in the living room. When we walk in, Jameel's whole body changes, like he's touched an electrical wire. He rushes over to the low dresser. Tries to turn on two lamps above a big glass case.

"Samira!" he barks at the wall between his room and his sister's. Maybe it's the low light, but his eyes look almost wet. "Why'd you turn off my lamps!"

"It wasn't me!"

Jameel fiddles with a power strip behind the glass case, then checks the lamps again. His body's blocking my view, so I can't see what he's so worried about.

"They're supposed to be on!" he says. "He needs his rays!"

"I didn't touch your stinking lamps!"

Jameel goes to the window and opens the blinds. Light floods the room. That's when I see who "he" is. *What* he is—a lizard. A pale green lizard with spikes all over his face and throat, and smudges of yellow around his eyes and mouth. He's basking on a gnarled and twisted log.

Jameel comes back over and fusses with a timer on the power strip. The lights finally go on, along with a third fluorescent tube inside the terrarium. He opens the top and scoops up the lizard, and puts him over his shoulder.

"His name is Vegeta," says Jameel, his voice softer. "He's a beardie—a bearded dragon."

Jameel covers Vegeta's body with his hand, I think to check for temperature. It almost looks like he's burping a baby. He moves closer so I can pet Vegeta, and I run my finger against the lizard's chin and cheeks. The spiky head does kind of remind me of the Dragon Ball Z character.

Vegeta raises a tiny hand. Is he waving at me? I look back at the empty terrarium. Around the twisted log are pieces of chewed-up lettuce, and strips of bumpy shed skin. I see little droppings too, black with white tips. Then I notice, next to the glass cage, a smaller plastic one with half an egg carton inside, crawling with insects. With crickets!

Are they . . . Vegeta's food?

"You wanna hold him?" asks Jameel. When I turn around, Vegeta's right in my face. I back into the dresser. I almost knock over the crickets.

Jameel laughs. "Don't kiss him, Irish—you could get salmonella!"

I laugh a nervous laugh.

"Here," he says, and reaches out with Vegeta again, more slowly this time, like he's asking for my permission.

I offer my shoulder. Jameel sets Vegeta on top, and Vegeta sits there for a while, letting me pet his pebbly skin. Then he starts crawling! His tiny claws poke through my shirt as he climbs up the side of my neck, over my ear, all the way to the top of my head. Vegeta stops, then just sits there. On my head. There's a bearded dragon on my head!

Jameel laughs again. "He likes you!"

What if I move and he bites me or something? Or gives me salmonella. "What if he poops on my head!" I say.

"It's pee too." Jameel grins. "It's a combination pee-poop!" But then he takes Vegeta off and puts him on his own head. Vegeta looks left and right, admiring the view—as if he's at the helm of a ship. I burst out laughing.

Jameel puts Vegeta back on his log and grabs a pair of long silver tweezers by the cricket cage. "You wanna feed him?"

I look back and forth between the two cages. "You do it."

Jameel smirks. He pops the top off the cricket cage and waves the tweezers around. "I choose . . . *you*."

The tiny cricket wriggles between the tweezer arms. Jameel lowers it onto Vegeta's log. Vegeta opens his mouth and then, in the blink of an eye, the cricket's inside his mouth. He chomps up and down, insect limbs flying everywhere. I get a weird shiver.

Jameel puts the top back on the cricket cage, then strokes Vegeta's scales with his knuckles. He goes to the window and adjusts the blinds, pulling the string up and down, trying to get the light perfect.

His sister stops in the doorway and plops a big draw-string sack on the floor. "Jameel, it's your turn. Laundry."

"Do it yourself, bruh! I ain't touching your dirty underwear!"

"You're so annoying!" says Samira, storming away. "*And stop talking like you're Black! You're not Black!*"

"This is just how I talk, bruh!" Jameel shouts, then looks back at me. "You got any sisters?"

I shake my head.

"Lucky." He closes his eyes and tilts his head back, making his Adam's apple stick all the way out. I've seen him do this when he gets called on in class. It means: *Do I have to?*

I want to ask him if he also has a brother—if that's his brother in the portrait with the marines uniform.

But I don't ask.

Jameel pops up, like he's suddenly changed his mind about laundry. "BRB," he says, then gathers his own clothes off the floor. He throws them into the basket in his closet, puts his sister's bag on top, and hurries out the door.

"*Samira, where are the quarters!*"

"*Where they always are! You're such a doofus!*"

Jameel swears—I think. Maybe in Aramaic, which I know a lot of Chaldeans speak. I hear the main apartment door close, and then I'm by myself in the room. In *Jameel's* room. Well, not totally by myself—I'm here with a bearded dragon!

I look at the terrarium again. Vegeta's basking on his log, eyes closed, soaking in heat and light from the one overhead lamp. I open the string cheese and juice and get a closer look at the crickets, hanging out on their egg carton. A tiny pale brown one raises its antennas and lets out a soft chirp.

Then I notice something. Quiet. Samira's music has stopped, and outside, the wind's not howling anymore. The sun comes in and out of the clouds, turning the light in the room from warm to cold, back to warm again. It feels like before Hao Bu and Ah Dia got here, when I'd come home from school and my parents were still at work, and I had the house all to myself. I was alone, but not lonely.

Sounds from the other room. Jameel and his sister at it again. This time about who gets to use the TV.

"You're not even watching!"

"We weren't before but we are now!"

Jameel storms back into his room. From the looks of it, he lost the argument. He grabs his laptop off the desk. It's an old gaming one with worn red and silver paint. He's either had it for a long time, or he got it as a hand-me-down.

I follow Jameel into the living room, where his sister and her friend are watching a Korean drama I've seen Mama watch at home. Jameel slides open the glass door, and we go out onto the balcony.

"Don't hog the bandwidth," says Samira. Jameel sticks out his tongue at her. He slides the door shut. I sit in one of the two metal patio chairs, while he wipes the rainwater off the glass table with the bottom of his shirt. Then he puts his laptop along the far edge and angles it so we can both see. He loads the show he was talking about before: *Kaiji: Ultimate Survivor*.

Jameel seems to calm down as we watch. I can't keep track of his moods. Which Jameel's going to come out next, the Dementor Jameel or the one who takes really good care of a bearded dragon? Halfway into the episode, right after the main character gets thrown onto the gambling ship and has to win a card version of rock, paper, scissors to save his own life, Jameel asks me a question.

"Hey Andy," he says. "Do you think the world's fair?"

"Fair?"

"Yeah, you know, fair. Do you think it's a fair place. Like, if you're a good person, if you stick to what you know's right, even though no one else agrees, you get rewarded in the end. And if bad stuff happens, it means you deserved it."

He says it without looking away from the screen, like he doesn't care about the answer. But somehow I know he cares a lot. Is the world a fair place? I want to tell him yes. Of course it is. But then I remember how he got in trouble just for being curious about blood cells, and I'm not so sure anymore. I reach back and pull another hair. It's orange.

"Never mind," Jameel says.

The laptop freezes. The screen goes dark. Jameel hits the power button a couple times, but nothing happens. He clicks his tongue, then runs inside to get the charger.

My eyes drift away from the laptop, out toward the balcony view. I go up to the railing for a better look. As far as I can tell, we're the only ones in this apartment building sitting outside. I can see the freeway below, traffic flowing smoothly in spite of the construction, a river of cars curving far into the distance. I can even make out some of the tall buildings in downtown Detroit.

It's a pretty nice view.

That afternoon, when I walk home, I'm almost floating. For once, the freeway overpass actually does feel like a bridge between two worlds—the normal one, and one where Jameel and I are friends.

At school the next day, the cast list for the winter dance show finally gets posted. Viola's Jack, Mai's Ralph, and Alexandra, the ballet dancer girl, is playing both Piggy and the boar. For the role of Simon, it says . . . *Cindy*.

And I'm listed under "Crew."

OCTOBER

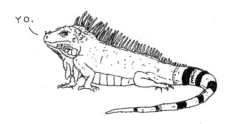

CREW KID

October comes quick and sudden, like someone got bored with the rest of September and skipped ahead.

The flowers in the glass courtyard fade, and the tree turns a reddish purple. Its leaves start to wither and drop. My hair's changed too—my black roots have grown in, making the orange blotches less noticeable. Mama wanted to cut it for me, but then you'd see the little bald spot where I've been pulling my hair. So I made her trim just the edges.

Cindy did get a real haircut. Her hair's shorter now—down to her chin—which somehow makes her seem more mature. When we found out she got cast as Simon, she didn't jump up and down like I thought she would, even though it was the exact role she wanted. "See? Nothing to worry about," she said. But it felt like she was talking more to herself.

No one bothered to take the cast list down. Now it's wearing graffiti in colored pens and markers: hearts and stars next to some names, drawings in the margins, joke names added and crossed off. Someone wrote *Van Helsing* under "Hunters." I think I know who.

A poke at my arm. Monday. Science. Jameel twirls his latest destroyed writing utensil—the tube of a ballpoint pen. At the front of the room, Mr. Nagy's grading our quizzes on photosynthesis and cell energy.

Jameel pokes my arm again. "What's this, Irish? You painting me a picture?"

I raise my elbow to get a better look. There's a streak of dried paint on the flat side of my forearm, from helping with the backdrops *last week*. How is that still there? I try rubbing the gunk away.

"I'm molting," I whisper. "Like Vegeta."

Jameel snorts. His jokes haven't exactly stopped, but I've learned to joke back.

"Hey, come over after school today," he says.

"Can't." I glance at Cindy. Her knees are bouncing in rhythm under her table.

"Then let's go over to yours. We always hang out at my place. It's only fair."

"Jameel, I can't. You know I have—"

"Math Olympiad. Yeah, yeah, you told me. Whatchu do there anyway?"

"We take these tests. They're like math riddles. It's a

competition." I know I felt weird lying to my parents, but now I'm glad for the excuse. I'd never hear the end of it if Jameel found out I was in a dance club.

"Whatchu win?" he asks.

"Huh?"

"What do you win, if you do good on the tests."

"A certificate."

"Sounds like fun." He puts the pen tube to his lips and blows air at the back of Kevin's head. Kevin swats at it, as if there's a fly. Jameel cracks up.

I nudge him with my elbow. I point at our textbooks, which we're supposed to be reading quietly to ourselves. He nudges me back: "Come on bruh, you can skip Math Olympiad one time."

I'm saved by Mr. Nagy, who comes around with our graded quizzes. I get my usual 9/10. Mr. Nagy puts Jameel's quiz facedown on the table, and when Jameel flips it over, he grumbles something and shoves the paper into his folder. I check my arm again: The paint's gone, but the skin where it used to be is red and raw.

"Here," Jameel says. He flops an orange envelope over my textbook. It says *Andy* on the front, and the corners are clean and crisp. Unlike the usual homework or notebook that's gone through a tumble in his bag.

"What is it?"

"Open it."

I slide my finger under the flap and take out the card inside. There's a lizard with a speech bubble coming out of its mouth: *IGUANA HAVE SOME FUN?*

I flip open the card. It's an invitation to Jameel's birthday party.

"It's a small party," he says, weirdly shy. Something inside me softens. "Mostly just my fam. But look—" He taps the inside of the card. "We're going to Reptomania!"

"Reptomania?"

"That huge reptile zoo? I never told you about it?" Jameel nods toward Cindy. "You can invite your girlfriend if you want."

"She's not my girlfriend."

"In that case, put in a good word for me." Jameel winks.

I have no clue how to respond to that so I laugh and kick his foot under the table.

"Ow!"

Mr. Nagy shushes us, tells us to read *quietly*. Cindy looks over her shoulder and I cover the card with my hand. She glares at Jameel, then at me. And when she turns back around, I slide it into my sketchbook.

Maybe I'm imagining it, but at lunch later Cindy talks more to Annie and Thuy, almost as if she's ignoring me. She keeps her head down in honors math too, and then, after school, she's not waiting at her locker to walk to Movement together. I stick around for a couple minutes just in case, but when she doesn't show, I head for the auditorium.

Inside, Cindy's already on stage stretching with Alexandra. Viola and Mai are next to them, hand in hand, laughing and chatting about something. Sometimes from class I'll see the tall girls floating through the hallways, as if they have permanent hall passes. They've started carrying around their *Lord of the Flies* books too, like it's part of their uniform—along with the yoga pants and water bottles.

Cindy spots me. Waves me over. She's also been carrying her copy of the book, though I'm still not sure if she's read it. I hurry up the side steps and follow her stage left, which is actually on the right if you're sitting in the audience. Mx. Adler had to put up signs saying LEFT and RIGHT because everyone kept getting confused.

We go over by a stack of chairs. Cindy looks me in the eyes, her pupils big and black. I can't pull a hair with her watching, so I touch my bald spot instead. And when my hand drops back down, she grabs it.

"Andy, I feel like we haven't hung out in forever," she says. "Just the two of us." She's not ignoring me—I *was* imagining it.

And she's right. Between homework and symphony band and PSAT prep, which both her parents and mine got us workbooks for so we can take it early *next* fall, I guess I've been spending more time with Jameel than with her. She has to know that we're friends by now. Or at least After-School Friends. And Science Friends. At lunch and in the hallways, Jameel still hangs out more with Paul and Aiden, who I have absolutely no interest in—

"Andy."

I'm iceman staring.

"Let's hang out this Saturday," she says.

"My dad wants to go fishing then." I frown.

Her hand loosens a little. I try to hold on. "But you could come with us," I say. "Or maybe we can hang out Sunday?" I glance over her shoulder at the thick velvet curtains. I remember something: "We still have to figure out our Halloween costumes! I mean, they have to be *really* good if we're going to get more candy than last year."

"Oh. Yeah . . ."

"We should skip that celery guy's house, though. You know, the one who—"

She lets go. "Don't you think we're a little old for trick-or-treating?"

"But it's our favorite—"

"Circle up, everyone!" Mx. Adler is clapping and calling all of us to center stage. Rehearsal's starting. Cindy grabs both my hands this time, and gives them a little squeeze.

"Sunday's fine," she says.

But before she lets go, she adds, "Andy, you're my best friend."

And there's a weird sadness in her voice.

Mx. Adler doesn't have many rules for Movement aside from Be Respectful and Always Stretch. The other main one is that we all do the warm-up together, even crew.

Normally I don't mind the exercises. Some of them are actually kind of fun. But today, as Mx. Adler has us all spread out and sit on the stage floor, I wish I could go straight to the art studio.

"Today's exercise is called Egg," says Mx. Adler. They tell us to hug our knees to our chest. Lower our heads. We're trying to make ourselves as small as possible. I squeeze until I can't get any smaller, and then I squeeze some more. This, I know how to do.

"Now, give yourself the freedom to move," says Mx. Adler. "Slowly. Whichever way you choose. Keep your eyes closed if possible. But be attentive to those around you."

I peek. The other kids are unfolding themselves, reaching arms up, sticking legs out. Cindy starts crawling like a baby. I stay in the same pose as before.

"Follow your body where it wants to go."

My arms are locked. I don't want to go anywhere. I'm allowed to stay like this, right? Because what if I move the wrong way? What if I knock into someone and injure them? Mx. Adler said our rehearsal space is supposed to be safe, free from judgment. We're all doing weird things with our bodies here. But the safest I feel is like this—head down, hands around my knees. Small. Unhatched. Egg.

"That's enough," says Mx. Adler, after I don't know how much time passes.

I stand up too fast and get a little dizzy. We step back into a loose circle, link arms, and bow—the same way we end every warm-up. I stay for a second and watch Cindy and the tall girls line up to practice their first dance number. Then I hurry off to the art studio.

As soon as I walk in: relief. Like I can hit pause on Cindy and Jameel and focus on something else for a while. Without much talking, we grab our stuff from the tall cabinets along the walls, and pick up from the week before.

Today, Eva's working on the fire that the boys in the story try to keep going to signal for help. Since Mrs. Ocampo said we can't have real fire, Eva had the idea to cut up old T-shirts, dye the strips red, yellow, and orange, then tie them to a fan to make fake flames. During Egg, Eva stretched her arms and legs all the way up and down and just planked the whole time. I'm pretty sure she's some kind of wizard.

Meanwhile, Lucy's cutting a mountain shape out of an extra backdrop panel. She helped her mom and dad fix up their house and she's super good with power tools, which I think makes Mrs. Ocampo nervous. So she's having Lucy use a hand saw instead.

Jason Shaheen is surprisingly good with a sewing machine—or at least he's a fast learner. The first thing he sewed after Mrs. Ocampo showed him how to use it was a black-and-red vampire cape. Now he's working on the parachute, which, unlike the cape, is actually in the story.

Then there's me, paper mache guy. Mrs. Ocampo thought the boar mask should be big enough to seem *menacing*—that was the word she used. So instead of inflating a balloon and papering it over like I did for my Jake mask, I'm using bendy craft wire to build a frame first.

While we're all doing our parts, Mrs. Ocampo works on her own art—these collages she makes from different kinds of fabric. She also plays "chill" music off her Bluetooth speaker. I wouldn't have guessed she listens to that stuff, but it blends nicely with the toothy scraping of Lucy's saw, the *rat-tat-tat* of Jason's sewing machine, the sloshing of Eva's buckets of water and dye. The ceilings in the art studio are taller than in the other classrooms, and you can see all the metal air ducts like in the gym. With the windows open too, it's like there are more places for my thoughts to go—they can float up or out into the trees.

One thought: I really like working with wire. It's easier than drawing, in a way, because the lines are already there. All I have to do is put them in the right place.

Another thought: It's weird that you can dress up to go trick-or-treating one year and everything's fun, then the next year you're suddenly too old for it. Cindy's kind of right, though—I don't remember seeing many middle schoolers, unless they were taking their little brothers and sisters around. But still—did we stop liking candy?

My thoughts keep floating up, up, and out. I'm above the trees now, over the school, over the freeway past my house. Right at this moment, Jameel's probably home feeding Vegeta. Or arguing with his sister. I wonder again what present I should get him, maybe a book about lizards? (I haven't ever seen him read for fun.) Or a Blu-ray of some anime? (He can stream everything, though.)

Maybe I can draw something—maybe I can draw Vegeta! He's asked me a bunch of times to see my sketch-book, but I've only shown him a page or two because my designs for the boar mask are in there. The other day Cindy and I actually filled out an old Math Olympiad quiz she found online to show our parents. Wouldn't it have been easier just to tell them—and Jameel—the truth, from the start?

I feel a sharp prick of wire. I shrink back into the room. There's the tiniest, pin-sized dot of red on my index finger. I stare at it for a second, then stick my finger in my mouth. I look around, at everyone else quietly working, everyone in their own little worlds . . .

If we told the truth from the start, maybe I wouldn't be here.

And I like being here.

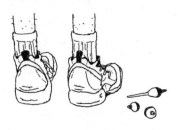

ASIAN CARP

On Saturday, after checking the weather for the millionth time, after Baba went as far as lighting incense in Hao Bu's incense holder and praying for clear skies (and Baba isn't religious *at all*), it's finally a nice enough day to go fishing. Or as he calls it, "Fishing, American-style!"

We drive out to one of the Metroparks, where we've gone a bunch of times in summer before, especially when we first moved from China and didn't have a backyard like we do now. I still remember being on a lake beach for the first time and hating the wet sand, how it stuck to my arms and feet. But then, after the sun had dried the sand enough, I could wiggle my toes and it would fall right through the cracks between them, leaving my skin smooth and silky. From then on, I didn't mind the stickiness anymore. It was worth the feeling afterwards.

Of course, we're not here for the beach this time. Once we're inside the park, we don't stop to walk the trails or admire all the yellow, orange, and red leaves. We head straight for what's either a big pond or a small lake to go *Fishing, American-style!*

We claim a picnic table near the shore and bring the rods and tackle boxes to a long wide pier sticking out into the water. There's a red warning sign—ASIAN CARP: INVASIVE SPECIES! REPORT ANY SIGHTINGS!—that makes me a little tingly when I see it. The banks are lined with tall reeds and cattails, looking like hot dogs roasting over a green fire.

Speaking of hot dogs, we're still working through the 96-pack from Baba's BBQ grill day. They've been the subject of more than a couple avalanche arguments, including one when we were loading the car:

Baba: *"Xiaoyin, there's no need to bring those. We're going to catch a bunch of fish to cook!"*

Mama: *"What if we don't catch anything? We have to use these up!"*

Baba: *"I'm going to catch a big one! You'll see!"*

Mama: *"But they're going to go bad!"*

Baba: *"Hot dogs can't go bad!"*

Nobody suggests throwing them away. Like I said, Chinese people hate wasting food.

"Your ah dia use go fishing when he boy!" says Baba, his bucket hat flopping as he talks. He rummages through his tackle of hooks and bobbers and plastic worms while Ah Dia stands by and watches. "But he fishing very different from fishing American-style. Just use stick and string!"

Baba gets the biggest bobber he can find and ties it to the end of his line. Then he adds a plastic fish lure with two enormous triple-hooks coming out of it. I look around and other people fishing are using live worms with *much* smaller bobbers—and much smaller hooks. A couple little boys at the end of the pier are throwing rocks at lily pads.

"What do you want, old man?" asks Baba. Ah Dia looks over the tackle boxes and points to some metal sinkers. Baba laughs. *"Don't use those, Ba. You won't catch any big ones that way."*

"I want those."

"Are you sure?"

Ah Dia nods.

"Andy, *come help your ah dia!"*

I find instructions in one of the tackle boxes that show how to tie the knots. So I tie the sinker and a hook onto Ah Dia's line. *"What do you want to let the fish eat?"* I ask him, because I don't know the Chinese word for *bait*.

Ah Dia squints toward the pond, at the reeds and patches of rippling water, almost as if he's imagining where he'd be hanging out if he was a big fish, and what he might like to eat.

"Andy," says Mama. *"You two use this."* She sneaks us

a hot dog. I look at Ah Dia. He nods. I break off a nub and stick it on the hook.

"Oop!" shouts Baba behind us. His bucket hat's suddenly in the pond. He reels it back in, then wrings out the water.

"Ba, Andy, make sure your hook's not stuck in anything before you cast," he says over his shoulder. He stares at the wet bucket hat for a second, then plucks one of the fuzzy lures off and adds it to his line. Ah Dia and I move farther down the pier, away from Baba.

I turn the crank on the reel so there's not too much extra line, then hand the rod to Ah Dia. When I do, the end of it starts jiggling wildly. I notice that Ah Dia's hand is trembling. I reach over and help steady the rod while he figures out how to work the reel. He has that sour-plum look on his face.

Before I can ask if he's okay, Ah Dia covers the shaky hand with his other one. He brings the rod back, then flicks it forward. The hot dog nub sails in a small arc into the lake.

"Good one, Ba!" my dad calls from down the pier.

"You two want to sit?" asks Hao Bu. She brings over a metal folding chair for Ah Dia and a cloth one for me.

Ah Dia shakes his head. He cranks the reel until the line tightens.

"Uhyo, don't be so stubborn, old man," says Hao Bu. *"You'll get tired standing too long. Come, sit."*

"I want to stand," says Ah Dia.

"*Suit yourself.*" She shrugs. But then she sets up the chair for him anyway.

Mama hands me my own fishing rod. She's already put a hook and hot dog nub on for me. I try to follow Ah Dia's example, but I don't cast mine as far. Still, I crank the reel until the line's tight like his, and sit down in my folding chair. After a while, I feel Ah Dia press his hand down on my shoulder. He uses it as a brace, and lowers himself into his chair too.

We wait. Mama brings hats for me and Ah Dia. Rubs sunscreen over our faces and necks. She gets me my sketchbook too, and I open it to a fresh page and look for something to draw. It's such a clear day that I can see farther than usual. The sun's shimmering off the water's surface, and people are kayaking in the distance. The two little kids run out of rocks and race back to the shore, hunting for more ammo.

I watch Ah Dia's hands again. They're steady now, gripping the fishing rod. But his whole body's tilting a little to the side. He's wearing a pair of new white walking shoes that Mama got for him from Costco, so I try to sketch those.

Baba yells. We all look over. He starts frantically cranking his reel, getting more and more excited.

"*Did you catch something?*" asks Mama.

"*Definitely!*" says Baba. "*Wah, this one's a fighter! Xiao-yin—quick, get the net! It probably huge bass!*" Mama and

Hao Bu hurry over with the net. I lean forward to get a better look. But when Baba's line comes out of the water, the only thing he's caught is a pile of weeds.

"I think it got away," he says.

"All worked up for nothing!" says Mama. Hao Bu shakes her head and laughs. Then Ah Dia's reel makes a sharp whirring sound. The end of his rod bends and unbends. I think it's an actual fish!

"Andy, *go help!"* shouts Baba. Ah Dia tries to stand up. I drop my sketchbook and help. Ah Dia cranks and pulls, then cranks some more. The rippling V where the line meets the water darts left, darts right, comes closer and closer until . . . a fish flops into Mama's waiting net. A tiny fish. The size of my hand.

"Lucky catch, old man!" says Baba. *"Hurry, let's take a picture!* Andy, *you too—get in with Ah Dia!"*

I lean in and smile. Baba snaps a photo. Mama fills a plastic bucket halfway with pond water so we can keep the fish alive before we cook it. While everyone else is busy with that, I see my own fishing rod bend too! I pick it up off the pier and start reeling it in. But all I get is an empty hook—the hot dog's gone.

The two little kids race down the pier again. One of them stops in front of me, pulls the corners of his eyes into slits, and runs away laughing.

Spider-sense tingle. Like there's an itch deep inside me that I can't reach. I look around: Mama's helping Ah Dia with more bait, Baba's reeling in more seaweed, and

Hao Bu's looking for something in the cooler. No one else saw what happened.

I pull a couple hairs. I run the fishing rod over to Mama.

"What's the matter? You need more hot dog*?"*

I shake my head.

"You're done already?"

I nod.

"Watch, old man. I'm definitely going to get one this time," Baba says, casting again. *"Xiaoyin, get the knife ready!"*

"Uhyo, get it on your own!" says Mama. *"I butcher fish day in and day out. I'm not doing unpaid work."*

"Fine, I'll do it myself!"

Ah Dia casts again too, using more hot dog bait. Right away, he gets a second bite. It's another small fish, about the size of the first. Despite Mama saying she's not doing any more work, she still helps Ah Dia pull the hook out.

When I look over again, I see Baba breaking off a piece of hot dog to use as bait. And those two little kids are gone.

WHAT ELSE WOULD YOU CALL THEM?

After lunch the next day, I tell Cindy upstairs about how we caught a dozen little fish the same size as the first two, and people were coming up to ask what kind of bait we used. Mama was happy to give away the hot dogs.

"They said the fish were crappies," I tell her. We talked our parents into letting us do our PSAT practice tests together in her room. "Other kinds of fish you have to throw back if they're too small but the crappies you don't have to. And my dad's so into fishing now, he went again by himself this morning. He's hooked."

Cindy glances up from her workbook, but only for a second. She doesn't laugh at my joke. It's not like her to be so quiet—I can even hear her stomach gurgle.

I sit up a little. "Also there was this sign. It said to look out for Asian carp because they're an invasive species and stuff."

She doesn't react to this either. I almost pluck a hair but stop just in time. I rub the little bald spot instead.

"The sign was like, right by the pier," I go on. "It was really in your face."

"It's like what Mr. Nagy talked about in class," she finally says. "Ecosystems have a natural balance. Invasive species throw off that balance. Biodiversity and all that."

"It's just—why do they have to call it *Asian* carp? Does that seem weird to you?"

Cindy shrugs. "They're native to Asia. What else would you call them?"

I go back to my practice test. I'm on a math problem about the cost of manufacturing an electric truck. I read it a second time, but I start to feel all itchy inside again, and I pull another hair. I know I should stop, because the bald spot is getting bigger. But sometimes I don't even realize I'm doing it until it's too late.

Cindy finishes her test. She flips to the back of the workbook to check her answers in the answer key.

I tell her about the kids who did the slit-eyes thing.

Cindy looks up. "How old were they?"

"I don't know, maybe five or six?"

"They're just dumb little kids," she says. "They probably didn't even know what they were doing."

"I'm pretty sure they knew it meant—"

"Andy, I'm sorry that happened, but sometimes it just does. They've probably, like, never even seen an Asian person before."

Cindy goes back to the workbook. But I still have that weird itchy feeling. Maybe she's right. Maybe it's no big deal, and I'm being too sensitive. I pluck another hair.

"I missed two," Cindy says, without sounding either proud or disappointed. She tosses the workbook aside and sinks into her bed, starts scrolling through her phone.

I read the math problem a third time, but it's like it's written in an alien language. Cindy's stomach gurgles again. I close the workbook. "You wanna watch anime? I'll finish this later."

"Sure." She shrugs.

I grab her laptop from her desk. But even after we start *Dennou Coil,* which Jameel and I watched and I thought Cindy might love because it has cats in it, the whole time she barely looks up from her phone.

This wasn't what I thought it'd be like hanging out with Cindy again. If we're just gonna lie around and half watch TV, I'd almost rather be downstairs working on Jameel's birthday present.

But isn't this basically what we did all summer? So how come it's not fun anymore?

The next week, I feel tired and grumpy, like I got jet lag without getting on a jet.

The weather on Monday doesn't help: bloated gray clouds, dark as dusk, so dark that the leaves on the courtyard tree look almost black. Thunder rumbles in the background, and it feels like it could pour rain at any second. But it never does. There's only the threat of rain, which is somehow worse.

Everyone's in a bad mood, not just me. Jameel's quiet in science and missing from lunch—detention again, I think. In social studies, after we read out loud from the textbook about European art and literature, Mx. Adler has the whole class write a surprise essay about the Crusades.

Then in Movement, while us crew kids watch the dancers practice the boar hunt number to get inspiration for the costumes and lighting, Alexandra slips and starts sobbing uncontrollably.

In the art studio afterwards, Mrs. Ocampo changes her "chill" music to something more upbeat. "To compensate for the weather," she says. But it just sounds wrong.

And then there's Jameel's present.

I try and try but no matter what, I still can't get the drawing right. First, Vegeta's arms come out too big. Then they come out too small. Or his eye's lopsided. Or his head's twisted in a weird way. I don't even work on it for most of the week because I know whatever I draw is just going to suck.

"Andy, *draw later*," says Mama. *"Eat your breakfast."*

I look up from my sketchbook. It's Saturday already. The day before Jameel's party. I'm running out of time.

At the table, spoons and bowls and chopsticks click and clack as my family passes around the toppings for *zhuo*. There are jars of pickled cucumbers and carrots, fermented tofu in little dishes, a big plastic tub of cottony pork *song*, and the century eggs that Cindy hates, cut into little wedges and drenched with sesame oil and soy sauce. I also get whiffs of the red-braised fish that Hao Bu made this morning, from a couple perch that Baba caught last night—and proudly descaled and gutted by himself. We were all surprised.

Mama's still staring at me. I eat a spoonful of *zhuo* and watch Baba swirl everything in his own bowl into a pukey brown mush. I cringe a little.

"Ma, while I was waiting to catch these big fish," Baba says, adding in a couple fish chunks, *"I thought, hey, I have some time. Let me call my friend's brother—that one who's a surgeon."*

Hao Bu pulls a few scales off a piece of fish, then spoon-feeds it to Ah Dia.

"He said they had some patients cancel recently," my dad goes on. *"It's really lucky. We'll first take Ba in for an evaluation. If everything looks promising, they'll schedule him for surgery."*

"How much will it cost?" Hao Bu asks. *"Isn't surgery here really expensive?"*

"Let me and Xiaoyin worry about that."

"Uhyo, save your money." Hao Bu loads another spoonful of fish. *"Come on, old man, one more bite."*

"*Ma. We talked about this,*" Baba says. "*I already booked a—*"

"*No doctors! No surgery!*" Ah Dia shouts suddenly. Fish sauce dribbles down the front of his sweater. Hao Bu wipes it with a napkin, and Mama goes and wets a towel for the stain.

Baba looks down at his pukey *zhuo* bowl, like he's mad but also doesn't want to start an argument. I know he cares about Ah Dia, but it's weird that he and Hao Bu keep talking about Ah Dia without talking *to* him, even though he's sitting right here. Why don't they ask what *he* wants?

I look over my drawing. I accidentally gave Vegeta a third arm. I rip the page out—a little too loudly. Loud enough that everyone stares.

I let out a breath. "Mama, Baba, can you take me to get a birthday present for my friend?"

"Why you want buy present?" asks Baba. "You don't give drawing?"

I shake my head. "I need something else."

"Which friend is again?" asks Mama. "Is Chris?"

I had a friend named Chris in second grade who invited me to his birthday party, but my parents always forget that he moved away. Do they think I only hang out with Cindy and a kid who doesn't live here anymore? That I can't make any new friends on my own?

"His name's Jameel," I tell them. "You don't know him. We're lab partners in science."

"*What kind of person is he?*" asks Baba.

I want to say that Jameel's tall and lanky, that he loves anime and lizards and jokes around a lot. That he started the year as a Dementor, but now he's a friend. Except I don't, because when Baba asks what kind of person he is, what he's really asking is, *Is he Chinese?*

"He's not Chinese. He's Chaldean. Hao Bu and Ah Dia met him."

"*Ma, Ba, you know Andy's friend?*"

"*Who?*"

"Jameel," I remind her. "*Hao Bu, you met him at 88 Mart that time. And then by my school.*"

"Jamee . . . ao, Jamee! Yes, Jamee. Nice boy, yes."

"Chaldea?" asks Mama.

"Is Iraqi," says Baba. "Like neighbor Mr. Khan except Mr. Khan Muslim. Chaldea is believe in God, Jesus Christ."

"Muslims believe in God too," I point out. We're getting off topic. "Can you take me to get him a present?"

"What kind present?" asks Baba. "How much?"

That part I still haven't figured out yet. "I don't know, maybe we can go to a pet shop? Jameel has a lizard—"

"Oh! We go to mall!" says Mama.

"*That's right! Ma, we haven't taken you and Ba to the big mall yet!*" shouts Baba.

The avalanche begins.

"*Aiya, I told you to take them last week!*" says Mama.

"*Where is there a mall!*" says Hao Bu.

"*I'm staying here!*" says Ah Dia.

"*Ba, you can walk around! It's good exercise!*" says Baba.

Mama grabs our jackets from the closet. I guess we're going to the mall.

SALAD BOWL

The mall we go to is the big fancy one near the automotive parks where Baba works. The entrance has two sets of heavy glass doors, and pushing through them, I imagine going through an airlock: On the other side, a whole planet of activity.

My dad suggests that we split up. He and Ah Dia will meet us later at the food court. I don't know if he'll try convincing Ah Dia to see the doctor again, but I do know for sure they're going to look at gadgets. Every time we come, Baba just goes and looks at all the new phones and gadgets, but he never buys any of them.

There's no pet or reptile store in the mall, so Mama suggests we check out the toy store on the second level. Maybe I'll find something there. Walking toward the glass elevators, we pass Indian grandmas in flowery saris and Muslim girls wearing colorful hijabs. I spot teenage Chaldean boys with really nice hair, and Chinese tourists with arms full of shopping bags, and little Black kids in superhero capes, spinning the giant marble spheres by the fountain.

In fifth grade, we learned how America is a salad bowl of different cultures, and Metro Detroit especially because all kinds of people started coming in the early 1900s to work at the car factories—Black people from the South, immigrants from Poland, Ireland, and Italy, and from parts of Asia and the Middle East too. Other than at school, I think the place I get the salad bowl feeling most is here, at the mall.

I guess because we all need to buy stuff.

"Ma, what do you think?" Mama asks Hao Bu as we get on the elevator. *"How's it compare to the malls in China?"*

Hao Bu looks left and right through the glass, and kneads her hands like she's worried about something. But then she offers a few words of English: "Same, yes. But different."

Inside the toy store, I'm instantly overwhelmed. There are too many colors, too many things spinning and whirring and buzzing and clacking. I have to start in a corner of the store and go one aisle at a time. I see a bunch of stuff Jameel would like, but they're all not right for one reason or another:

A drone that we could fly off his balcony! (Too expensive. Baba would never let me get this.)

A rubber band shooter! (His mom would take it away.)

A remote-control fart machine! (His sister would hate me, and right now she thinks I'm nice.)

What if by the time I walk down the last aisle I still haven't found anything? What if I all I can give him for a present is a lopsided drawing of a bearded dragon?

But then I see it: One of those big-head vinyl figurines of Vegeta—the character from *Dragon Ball Z*!

It's perfect, and it's on sale for ten dollars, which is cheap enough for Baba to grumble but not say no. Hao Bu offers to pay, and Mama refuses to let her. They mini-avalanche over it. But while Mama goes to the register, Hao Bu slips me a ten-dollar bill anyway.

Afterwards, my mom shows my grandma the soap shop where they give out free samples of soap and hand lotion. We go to the store that sells kitchen stuff and try free cappuccinos from their thousand-dollar coffee machines. In one of the big department stores, Mama finds sweaters on clearance for me and Ah Dia, then she and Hao Bu test out different perfumes and lipsticks, and get their other makeup done for free from the ladies wearing all black behind the counters.

I don't even mind, because Hao Bu looks like she's having fun, and I'm glad I found Jameel a present. By the time we go up to the third-level food court, Baba and Ah Dia have been waiting for half an hour.

"*Ma! Xiaoyin! What were you guys doing!*" says Baba. "*I sent you like ten WeChats! I called both of you and no one picked up!*"

"*Our phones were on silent!*" Mama and Hao Bu laugh, their faces rosy with makeup.

Baba shakes his head, then he laughs too, in a better mood than this morning. When we split up again to get our lunches, I wonder if he finally convinced Ah Dia to see the doctor.

"*Old man, you go with your grandson,*" Hao Bu tells Ah Dia, and slips me some more money. Ah Dia doesn't resist like usual. Instead, he shuffles toward me. I take his hand and scan the stalls, trying to figure out what he might want.

Mama goes to the panini place, and I see Baba take Hao Bu to try the fried chicken sandwich place—because KFC opened in China when he was a kid and he's obsessed with fried chicken sandwiches. For some reason, my eyes land on the fast-food Chinese place.

We never get it because Baba says it's not *real* Chinese food. It's Americanized. I remember what Cindy's dad said when we were grilling in the backyard, about pizza and hot dogs being American versions of other foods too, and then Jameel's voice pops into my head. If he were here, he'd probably say: *Don't matter if it's authentic—delicious is delicious, bruh!*

"*Ah Dia, do you want to try American Chinese food?*"

"*Whatever you like,*" he says. He squints at the steaming bins under the glass case, and looks over the line snaking around from the register. "*A lot of people waiting,*" he says. "*Must be good.*"

While we wait, I scan the menu, trying to decide what I want Ah Dia to try. I settle on General Tso's chicken (I can already hear Baba groaning). In fact, I see Baba and Hao Bu pointing at us from the fried chicken sandwich line, Baba laughing and shaking his head like he can't believe I'm taking Ah Dia here.

Then I notice, out of the corner of my eye, a fluff of pink curls. A group of girls leaving the juice place, smoothie cups in hand. I recognize them—it's Viola and the tall girls! But as I watch them take the escalator down to the second level, I count one more of them than usual.

The extra one is Cindy.

I raise my hand to wave, call out her name. But I stop. I glance at Mama and Baba, both still in their food lines. Maybe it's that they'd hear me, and they'd tell Cindy's parents, and I promised to keep Movement a secret. Or maybe I stop for a different reason.

I look again. When did Cindy get as tall as them? She's thinner than before too. She's carrying a smoothie cup like the others, but she also has a small red-and-black shopping bag from the place that sells yoga pants. I imagine the four of them in the store, the tall girls helping Cindy find the perfect pair, a pair exactly like their own, and Cindy trying on the pants, and then Viola anointing her, telling her, *Now you're one of us.*

I watch them step off the escalator, walk along the glass railing, and turn into the Halloween store.

My stomach drops. I feel Ah Dia's hand on my shoulder. At first I think it's to comfort me, but then I feel him squeeze, *hard*. Suddenly all his weight presses on me. My shoulder gives and I spin around. Before I know it, we're both on the floor. The rest of my family's rushing over.

"Ba! Ba!"

"Old man, get up!"

"No no, don't move!"

"Andy what happen!"

Mama helps me up. There's a small crowd around us now. A couple strangers are yelling for help, while everyone else in the food court gives us horrified looks, their eyes wide and their hands over their mouths. Someone else hurries over calling, "I'm a nurse!"

Mall security shows up out of nowhere. They're telling Ah Dia to lie still. He's moaning, his voice is faint. Where are his glasses? Baba's explaining that Ah Dia has a bad back. Hao Bu's in tears, scolding him, telling him to be more careful. A wheelchair shows up. Someone puts a brace around his neck. Then they sit him up and carry him into the wheelchair. I see his glasses on the ground and scoop them up. The metal frame's all bent out of shape.

The next thing I know, mall security is clearing a path for us out of the food court. My shoulder throbs. I remember Cindy, and I look for her.

But she's nowhere in the crowd.

IGUANA HAVE SOME FUN?

Mama sits down on the edge of the sofa bed and runs her hand through my hair. It's almost noon the next day.

"Andy," she says, "is time for your friend party."

Hao Bu's in the kitchen with a somber face, quietly frying up red bean sesame balls. I hear Baba's loud phone voice outside, talking to his friend Lang Uncle.

"Yes. He seem is better now," Baba says. "We take to emergency room. They do X-ray, say is look okay. Ah? Visitor insurance?"

Mama's hand grazes my bald spot. I pull the blanket over my head.

"I don't have to go," I tell her. "I can stay here. Help Ah Dia."

"Mama and Baba here," she says, peeling the blanket off again. "Hao Bu here. You go. Have fun." She puts my new sweater next to the pillow. She's already cut the tags off.

"But I don't have a present," I say. In all that happened yesterday, I dropped Jameel's gift in the food court. I didn't realize until we were already home.

Mama leans toward the side table. She picks up one of the bad Vegeta drawings I ripped out of my sketchbook and holds it up for me to see.

"*Mama will wrap this for you, all right?* Is good drawing. *Quickly, get dressed.* "

"I wanna wear my hoodie."

"Okay. I just wash," Mama says, going into the closet for wrapping paper. "Is in Hao Bu and Ah Dia room."

When I walk in, Ah Dia's sitting up in the bed, with pillows behind his lower back. He's watching his Chinese dramas. My parents moved the smaller TV from their room into his and Hao Bu's.

"*Ah Dia, how are you feeling?*" I ask. He's still wearing the foam neck brace they gave him at the mall. He has a black eye too, and the bruises on his arms are purple and green.

"Okay," he says in English.

"*I'm getting my clothes,*" I explain.

The laundry basket's next to the dresser. I get a whiff of incense from the sticks in the holder on top. The line of smoke flutters a little, then steadies again. Some of my old stuff is still on the dresser—the I HEART NY snow globe, the picture from the Millennium Falcon when we went to Disney World. But now it's mixed in with Hao Bu and Ah Dia's stuff. There's their black-and-white wedding photo, Hao Bu wearing a lacy white gown. And a newer studio one of them in costumes from old Chinese dynasty times. Ah Dia's glasses in the photo don't have lenses in them.

I take off the shirt I slept in. Leave my sweatpants on. I fish my orange Turtle School shirt out of the laundry basket. I have a bruise too, on my shoulder from where Ah Dia tried to brace himself while he was falling. I look at it in the wall mirror and touch the edges. It's still a little sore.

"*Xiaolei,*" says Ah Dia. He pauses his show. I finish putting on my shirt. He points toward me, his finger more curled than straight. "*You're going to* Jamee *birthday party?*"

I nod. Our eyes meet for a second, and even though he doesn't say it out loud, I somehow know that he's telling me he's sorry. What I want to say back is: *It's no big deal. It's just a little bruise. But I'm worried about you. I don't want you to get hurt.*

What comes out is: "*Ah Dia, be careful.*"

"Ao." He nods.

I find my hoodie and throw it on over the shirt. Our eyes meet again, and then I go.

Back in the living room, Mama's putting the final piece of tape on the wrapping paper. It looks like she found a frame for the drawing too. She hands me a card envelope with an open flap and a pen for me to sign with. I take out the card—it has a sloth eating a melting ice cream cone. When did she even get this?

"Andy, you want Mama drive?" she asks.

I shake my head. "I can walk." I sign the card.

Before I go, Hao Bu gives me a fried sesame ball to try. It's warm and sticky and good. She puts a batch into a plastic food container for me to bring to Jameel's. Mama gets me a bag for everything, then zips up the front of my hoodie.

"Have fun," she says.

"I will." Then I add, "Thanks, Mama. Thanks, Hao Bu."

Outside in the driveway, Baba's done with his call. He's crouched on the gravel next to the garbage and recycling bins, quietly cleaning his fishing gear with the garden hose. He sees me and waves.

"Don't stay out too late," he says in a soft voice.

"I won't."

I glance up at Cindy's window. The curtain's closed, but a light's on inside.

On the way to Jameel's, my brain is in a weird fog—like the face-in-the-clouds emoji.

When I get to the overpass, the freeway below isn't clogged like usual. Cars are zooming by, maybe faster than the speed limit. I stop for a second in the middle of the bridge and press my face against the metal fence.

There was a room yesterday, next to the mall security

office—in a back part of the building I didn't even know was there. I remember the nurse asking Ah Dia if he could feel his hands and legs. Mall employees escorting us to the parking structure. Baba cradling Ah Dia in his arms, laying him into the reclined front seat of our car. On the way to the hospital, I sat in Mama's lap, which I haven't done in years.

Someone throws a drink cup out their window. Another car runs it over. Maybe if I was better at drawing, we wouldn't have needed to go to the mall in the first place. Maybe if I was paying attention, I would've caught Ah Dia before he fell. I pull two hairs, one black, one orange.

No—something distracted me. Cindy and the tall girls.

Why didn't she tell me she'd be at the mall with them? Has she hung out with them outside of school before? I guess I don't tell her every time I hang out with Jameel, but still—why would she go to the Halloween store with them after saying we're too old for trick-or-treating?

I glance at Jameel's apartment, and I notice a bunch of people standing on his balcony. He said it'd be mostly relatives, but did he invite Paul and Aiden too? It's not too late to go home. I can message him and say we had a family emergency, which we kind of did. Just a little white lie, like being in Math Olympiad.

A gust of cold wind fluffs my hair. I look down and my

arms are folded across my chest, like I'm holding myself in Egg.

I squeeze myself extra tight.

Then I walk the rest of the way across.

Jameel's mom is the one who opens their apartment door. She's wearing gold earrings and a frilly black-and-white blouse. Even from the hallway I can hear all the people talking inside.

"Andy!" she says. "It's so good to see you again. Come in!"

I hand her the container of sesame balls.

"What's this?" she asks.

"A Chinese dessert," I answer, because it's weird to have the first thing I say to his mom be "sesame balls."

"You're so thoughtful!" she says. "Do I need to refrigerate these? Come, come—"

She leads me into their kitchen and puts Hao Bu's dessert on the counter, next to heaping plates and big foil containers of delicious-smelling Iraqi food. It reminds me of a Chinese party, but I notice that there's other stuff on the counters too, like two-liter bottles of Vernors and Faygo Rock & Rye, and jumbo bags of barbecue-flavor Better Made chips—things my own parents wouldn't really set out at a Chinese party.

Jameel's mom sweeps me up in a wave of introductions. It turns out that Jameel has *a lot* of relatives, and I think maybe every single one of them is crammed into his apartment. Everyone's dressed like they just came from church, and I count at least nine aunts and uncles—even more kids. Jameel's sister, Samira, says hi, and so does Sarah Sitto, who's in our grade and who I actually didn't know was one of Jameel's cousins. Other than Sarah, though, I'm the only one from school. Paul and Aiden aren't here . . . yet.

"Jameel's talking to his brother," his mom says, nodding toward the bedrooms. "Why don't you go give him his present yourself?"

The door to Jameel's room is closed halfway. I knock lightly and push it open, expecting to see him with his older brother—the one in the marines uniform. Except inside, it's just Jameel by himself at his desk. It's a video chat.

He looks over his shoulder, nods at me, then moves some stuff off the bed next to him, like he wants me to sit. He goes back to the chat. In the video, Jameel's brother is on the bottom bunk of a bunk bed. From the lamplight behind him, it looks like he's somewhere in the world where it's already dark. I sit with Jameel's present in my lap and try not to listen in. But I can't help hearing.

"You know it's hard on her," his brother's saying. "It's *been* hard. You're a smart kid. Mom's just looking out for what's best."

"Don't I get a say, though? I mean, Dad got him for—"

"And I'm telling you, focus on school. It's like Uncle Leo always says: We're des—"

"Descended from kings, yeah yeah."

"Look, if you get your grades up, it won't be an issue anyway. You'll have more options. That's not a bad thing."

As I listen in, I start to pick up clues about Jameel's family. His dad's not in his life anymore, and I want to ask why. But how do I even bring up something like that? Last night, after Mama and Baba helped Ah Dia settle into bed, everyone just went off into their own rooms. We never even sat down together to go over what happened—probably because we'd have to all relive it.

But then . . . is there ever a right moment to talk about this kind of stuff?

Maybe Jameel letting me be here, letting me listen in, is his way of talking. Or at least making room for it. I imagine a narrow dark hallway between us, with two doors on either side. His door's cracked open a sliver, just enough to let in the light.

"Gotta hit the hay," his brother's saying. "Oh-five-hundred start tomorrow."

"You coming back for Christmas?"

"Jameel, you know how these deployments work. I don't get leave unless it's for a special reason."

"Yeah . . ."

"But I'll put in a request. For you. You have my word. Soon as I know, you'll know."

Jameel sits up a little. "Okay."

"All right, I'm—"

"Wait." Jameel turns the laptop toward me. "Yousif, this is my friend Andy. Andy, this is my brother, Yousif."

We wave at each other. Jameel turns the laptop back.

"Happy birthday, brother," says Yousif. "Think about what I said."

The call ends and the video window closes. Jameel stares at the desktop wallpaper for a second, then shuts the computer lid. He forces a smile. I can feel that hallway between us darkening again, the chance to ask him fading.

He tilts his chin at the present. "That for me?"

I nod. I hand him the card and gift, and he sets the card aside on his desk. I'm expecting him to rip the wrapping paper off the package, but he unwraps it more carefully, gently sliding his finger under the pieces of tape.

"I don't know if I got him exactly right," I say.

Jameel's eyes get wide when he sees what's in the frame. "Are you kidding me? This is amazing!" He looks over the drawing and then starts undoing the little metal holders for the cardboard backing.

"Hold up, you gotta sign this for me," he says. "This gon' be worth money someday."

I feel my insides glow. "Okay."

I sign the corner of the paper, and Jameel replaces the backing and stands the frame next to Vegeta's cage, angling it just right. I look back and forth between my drawing and the real thing—maybe I didn't do such a bad job after all.

Jameel's eyes meet mine. He's all smiles. I think he's going to come in for a hug like Cindy would. But as soon as I open my arms the tiniest bit, he takes a half step back. Stuffs his hands in his pockets.

I look away. My face burns, my eyes land on the crickets. There are so many of them, in that tiny plastic cage. Do they feel cramped at all? Or have they gotten used to it? How comfortable can it be, living on half an egg carton?

One of Jameel's uncles pops in the doorway. "Come on, boys, time to eat!" he says. "Then it's off to Reptomania!"

Jameel crumples up the torn wrapping paper and throws it in the wastebasket under his desk. Then he draws the blinds closed—all without making eye contact again—and we join the rest of the party.

WONTONS

On Monday, Jameel's *still* raving about Reptomania. He raves about it all through Mr. Nagy's lesson on Gregor Mendel, and he even plops his lunch bag down at my and Cindy's table in the cafeteria, talking about water monitors and cow-spotted pythons and the blue rhino iguana we saw. It's official—we're Lunch Friends now too.

Cindy interrupts him. "What are you even talking about?" she says.

"Irish here came to my birthday party," says Jameel.

"Oh really." Cindy gives me a look. I can't tell if she's annoyed at Jameel or disappointed in me, or both. But her attitude annoys me back.

"Yeah," I say. "Really."

"Yo, remember the alligators?" Jameel says.

"Yeah! It was so weird they didn't even move or blink. I thought they were fake at first!"

"That's exactly what I thought!" We fist-bump.

"That's nice," Cindy says, then turns to talk to Annie and Thuy.

"Oh yeah, my ma was mad hype about those sesame balls. She wants your grandma's recipe."

"I'll ask."

"I got something for you," says Jameel, unzipping his lunch bag with a smirk. He pulls out two foil-wrapped cylinders and hands one to me. When I open it, the smell of the spices instantly takes me back. Maybe even more amazing than Reptomania was all the food at Jameel's house. The cauliflower stew and buttery biryani, the fried potato things stuffed with beef, flatbreads called *lughma* that I ate too many of. And the boiled sheep head dish Jameel's uncle brought and was really excited that I liked—there's leftover meat from it in this wrap!

"Mmm, braaaiinnsss," I say, taking a big bite.

"Braaaaainnnsss." Jameel laughs. There were a lot of zombie jokes yesterday.

"That food was so good," I tell him. "My mouth wanted more—"

"But my stomach was full!"

We fist-bump again.

Cindy gets up with a tall-girl flourish and goes to sit at the other end of the table. I feel guilty at first, like maybe I was rubbing it in too much—the fact that I went to Jameel's party. But then a switch flips inside me. Jameel's my friend, and Cindy's not even trying. And meanwhile *she* was out with the tall girls buying yoga pants and looking at Halloween costumes!

Jameel starts talking about Reptomania again, but I interrupt him. "Hey, you wanna come over after school?"

"Don't you got Math Olympiad?"

"I'm skipping it."

"Hao Bu, Ah Dia, I'm home," I call out. "Jameel's *here too!"*

Hao Bu shuts off the kitchen faucet and dries her hands on a towel. Mixing bowls and cutting boards with different ingredients are set out on the counters. She's probably making another one of her feasts.

"Hi. Yes. Jamee. Welcome." She smiles.

"Hi Granny," says Jameel, extra polite.

"Your baba took Ah Dia to see the doctor," Hao Bu reports. *"But that was a few hours ago. Do you think they should be back already?"*

"They probably went fishing," I say.

Hao Bu laughs. For some reason, just being around Jameel puts me in a jokey mood.

"What'd she say?" Jameel asks.

"My grandpa fell the other day," I tell him.

"Bruh . . . is he all right?"

"He has some bruises but no broken bones or anything. My dad took him to the doctor's to get some more tests."

Jameel goes quiet. "I'm sure everything's fine," I tell him, even though I don't know if it is. As the words leave my mouth, they sound exactly like what Cindy would say.

I power on the living room TV and get a couple cans of root beer from the fridge. When I turn back around, Jameel's staring at the screen, which is paused in the middle of an episode of *Three Kingdoms*—the last thing Ah Dia was watching. I also notice that some of my early Vegeta sketches are still on the table by the sofa. I quickly shove them underneath.

"Bruh, what show is this?" asks Jameel, still looking at the screen. "I think I seen this before."

"It's *Three Kingdoms*," I tell him. I hand him a root beer and unpause the TV. "There's that one video game series about it."

"Oh yeah!"

"The games are mostly about fighting, though," I say. "But there's more to it than that. There's strategy too. And even magic. This is a newer reboot, but I think the story's hundreds of years old. It's like a Chinese *Game of Thrones*."

"Hundreds? Sounds more like *Game of Thrones* is an American *Three Kingdoms*."

He has a point.

Jameel cracks the can open and takes a sip, and we spend a couple minutes watching the show and talking about what kind of root beer is the best. We both agree that glass bottles are better than either cans or plastic ones. Jameel opens his mouth and lets out a loud burp. He looks toward Hao Bu in the kitchen. "Oops. Sorry!"

Hao Bu laughs. I laugh and burp too. It turns into a whole burp-talking thing, as I tell Jameel about how Baba's been trying to show my grandparents American stuff, and now he's obsessed with fishing.

"He went like three times last *guoweeeeeek.*"

"Did he catch anything *goouwuwuwuood?*"

"The other day he got some *pergghghgch.*"

We laugh until our sides hurt. Then there's a nice calm, after we're done laughing, when all I hear are the voices on TV and the sound of Hao Bu chopping vegetables. I feel that dark hallway between us light up again. I flash to the awkward moment at Jameel's party when I thought we were going to hug.

I tell him anyway—about the kids at the park who did the slit-eyes thing.

Jameel listens, taking a slow sip. Then he asks, "So what'd you do?"

"I ignored them." I shrug. "They're just dumb kids. I can't let it get to me." Why do I keep echoing Cindy?

Jameel clicks his tongue. "Bruh, that's messed up. You're as American as they are. You should get to go to the park and not have to deal with BS like that." He takes another sip. "Wanna know what I'da done?"

"What?"

"Pushed 'em in the water. How they gon' learn otherwise?"

But what if those kids couldn't swim and drowned? What if their parents saw? I get what he's saying—I should stand up for myself. But wouldn't pushing them have just made things worse?

I almost pull a hair. I rub my bald spot instead. Jameel tips his can up and chugs the rest, then lets out another loud burp.

"Yo, you should take your grandparents to a cider mill," he says. "Cider donuts, bruh!"

"Oh yeah!" I'm glad for the subject change. "Hot cider! Apple picking!"

"Corn mazes—no, *haunted* corn mazes!"

I try to laugh. I'm totally not scared of haunted corn mazes.

"There's that place that does zombie paintball hayrides too."

"Whaaaaaat? We should go!"

Hao Bu brings a big mixing bowl over to the dining table, and Jameel gets up to see what she's doing. I follow him. There's a mound of pink-and-white ground pork inside the bowl, with flecks of green onion and tiny shrimps. She sprinkles a big handful of salt over the mixture, stirs it up with chopsticks, then adds even more salt.

"Yo, what's your grandma making?" asks Jameel.

"Wontons." I think she might be making them for the Chinese party at the Langs' place this weekend. According to the ChinaNet, they just bought a new house.

Hao Bu looks at me. *"Do you and* Jamee *want to help me fold a few wontons?"*

I look between the giant bowl of filling and the multiple stacks of square wonton skins. I wonder what Hao Bu's definition of "a few" is.

"Can I try?" asks Jameel, without me having to translate. We sit down at the table. This isn't exactly what I expected us to do the first time he came over.

"Look me," says Hao Bu, gesturing toward Jameel. She peels a wonton skin off the stack and chopsticks a nugget of filling into the middle. Next, she folds the top edge down, leaving a small gap between that and the bottom. With a flick of her wrists, she turns it into a perfectly shaped wonton—like a magic trick. Finally, she dabs a finger into a shallow water dish and pinches the corners together, locking the shape in place.

"Hold up, I need to see that again," says Jameel. Hao Bu and I both giggle.

Hao Bu takes the finished wonton and puts it in an empty metal baking pan. Then she shows us again, much slower this time. Fill. Fold. Twist. Dab. Pinch. If Cindy were here, I bet she could turn it into some kind of dance. No—she'd probably just take over the whole operation and end up bossing Jameel and me around.

Hao Bu fills a couple wrappers for us. I've helped Mama make wontons before, so I know what to do, even if they don't look as perfect as Hao Bu's. Jameel's first try comes out messy and deformed.

"Half the filling is on the outside!" he says, laughing. Hao Bu laughs too, then gives us each a stack of wonton skins.

Our second tries come out better. Jameel manages to keep most of the filling inside. By the fourth and fifth ones, he's gotten the hang of it.

"It's kinda like tying your shoes," he says. "When I was little, I couldn't get it, no matter what. My dad showed me a million times, Yousif showed me, Samira kept making fun of me. I was prolly six or seven. I wouldn't wear shoes with laces in them for forever. Then one day I was all, lemme give it another shot, and I got it! It's like I didn't practice in all that time, but I learned anyway."

Jameel opens and closes his hands as he talks, the tips of his long bony fingers dusted with flour. I've never noticed before how much he uses his hands to talk—like he's wearing a puppet on each one. Hao Bu looks between me and Jameel, as if she understands what he's saying, even if she might not know all the words.

"Yo, let's race!" says Jameel.

"You sure you wanna?" I smile.

"Sure I'm sure. Ready set go!"

It feels good to do something I've done before. There's always a next step. Put the filling in the middle. Fold it over, twist and flip. Water, pinch, tray. Start another. I watch Jameel rock back and forth a little, and I bob my head, like there's some invisible beat that we both hear. It takes me back to the art studio, working with the other crew kids while Mrs. Ocampo plays her "chill" music.

A thought creeps up: Today's not just the first time

I've skipped Movement. It's the first time I've skipped *anything*.

I think back to what Jameel asked that time on his balcony—is the world fair? Do bad things happen because you deserve it? I search Hao Bu's face. Did Ah Dia fall the other day because I was *bad*? Or years ago, when he first fell at their house in China . . . was it some kind of punishment for being a bad person?

No. It was a random accident. It didn't *mean* anything. But my grandparents had to live with it anyway.

Somehow that seems even more sad.

Jameel's still rocking back and forth a little. Fill. Fold. Twist. Dab. Pinch. Completely in the zone. He mentioned his dad earlier—in that story about shoelaces. I take a breath.

"Jameel, your dad. Is he . . ."

I think of all the different ways I can put it. *What's the deal with your dad? Why wasn't he at your party? How come I've never met him?* All the ways I can dance around the d-word. I remember when I told Mama and Baba my favorite number was four, they said I should find a new favorite number because four in Chinese is unlucky. *Sì* is a homonym of *sĭ—death.*

I ask: "Is your dad still around?"

Jameel stops wrapping. Our eyes meet. I don't look away this time.

"He died two years ago," Jameel says. "He kept getting these bad headaches. He didn't like going to the doc's normally. Would just pop a coupla aspirin and call it a day. But they got bad enough that he finally had 'em checked out. Turned out he had a tumor."

Jameel looks down at the mixing bowl. "Even with treatment and everything, he just got, I dunno, more and more out of it. Like, less himself. He'd forget things, forget who we were. It got to be that we couldn't even visit him in the hospital 'cause he'd yell all this nasty stuff about us."

Jameel takes a breath.

"I'm sorry," I tell him.

"But that wasn't even the worst part," he says. "The worst was, for the longest time, none of us knew about it. Us kids, I mean. Him and my ma tried to hide it from us. They didn't want to worry us, they said after. We only found out 'cause Ma broke down and told Yousif."

Jameel balls his hands into fists, then unclenches them. He looks at me again, his eyes wet. He snuffles.

I snuffle too.

"Your dad's the one who gave you Vegeta?" I ask.

Jameel nods. "Last birthday present he ever got me," he says. "It's funny, him and Ma *never* let us have any pets. Chaldean parents are, like, anti-pet. But then one day Uncle Leo just showed up with a beardie. Said it was Ba's idea—he wouldn't take no for an answer. Now my ma's saying she'll take Vegeta away if . . ."

"If you don't do better at school." That's what Yousif

156

was talking about in their video chat. I shake my head. Take Vegeta away? But also . . . I've seen how Jameel is at school. "She probably just wants to help—"

He clicks his tongue. "I'm sick of people saying that. What about what I want, huh? She never even asked me what I want. I'm not no little kid no more."

I stay quiet. A car drives past outside with an electric hum. I picture lights and cables in a hospital, a room with a big round machine.

Jameel lets out a sharp breath. "Sorry. Didn't mean to—" He starts wiping his hands with a kitchen towel. "It's just, every year around this time—I dunno, I don't do so good."

"Sorry," I say again. But it doesn't feel like enough.

Jameel rubs his eyes. Hao Bu puts her hand over my wrist. *"That's enough wrapping,"* she says. *"I'll finish the rest. Why don't you and* Jamee *go watch TV."*

We do, but Jameel does the iceman stare the whole time. He doesn't stay long afterwards. He doesn't even want to taste the wontons we folded, so Hao Bu sends him home with a freezer bag full of them instead.

When he's absent from school the next day, I wonder if it's because of me, like I made him stick his hand into a kind of fire. The rest of the week, even when he's his usual jokey self, what he told me about his dad is always there, in the background.

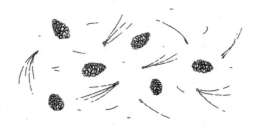

WHO YOU CAN AND CAN'T
BE FRIENDS WITH

Every few months, our group of Shanghainese families take turns hosting a party, where we each bring a different dish to share and eat it buffet-style. Cindy once told me this is called a *potluck*, but we've always just called it a Chinese party.

This time, it's at the Langs' new house. We drive north on the freeway, all the way to 25 Mile Road, and turn into a subdivision surrounded by tall pine trees. Baba first met Lang Uncle at the community center where Cindy and I used to go for Chinese school. Lang Uncle's Taiwanese, and Xu Auntie is Shanghainese, and they've both been in Michigan for a lot longer than we have. We even call them Uncle and Auntie instead of the Chinese words.

As we pull up, I see the cars first, a line of mostly SUVs

parked along the street and up the half-circle driveway. The house itself has gray wood paneling with big clean windows. It almost looks like a cabin. Inside, there's a tall entry area with a dangling chandelier, and I can hear chatter from the other rooms, conversations in mid-avalanche.

I politely say hello to Lang Uncle and Xu Auntie, then stand by holding the tray with Hao Bu's spring rolls while the grown-ups talk.

"How are you doing?" Lang Uncle asks Ah Dia. *"Are you feeling better?"*

"I took him to get an MRI *scan this week,"* answers Baba. *"But we're still waiting on the results. Kingston, thank you so much for help us figure out."*

"The healthcare system in this country—what a mess." Lang Uncle shakes his head. "Let me know if there's anything else I can do."

Baba smiles and quickly changes the subject, like it's all no big deal. I wonder if that's not a Cindy thing but a Chinese thing. He and Mama start peppering the Langs with questions about the house:

"How many rooms are there?"

"How many square feet is it?"

"How much is the heating bill?"

Lang Uncle says he'll give them a tour. Xu Auntie takes the spring rolls from me and tells me all the kids are in the basement. My grandparents and I follow her into the kitchen, Hao Bu holding Ah Dia's arm. Even though he's not wearing his neck brace anymore, he still hesitates when he moves, almost like he doesn't trust his own body.

I say a quick hello to the other moms, who are all standing around the big kitchen island. They ask me how school's going, and comment on how skinny I am, how I should be eating more, asking if I feel cold wearing shorts underneath a hoodie. I politely answer, then escape downstairs.

The Langs' basement is finished, unlike ours back home. The stairs don't creak going down, and they're covered in nice carpet—the thick kind that's the color of Oreo ice cream, and loops over instead of having ends that stick up. Downstairs, the Feng twins are playing a smash fighting game with Lydia Tong on one of Trevor Lang's retro consoles, while a couple of the younger kids are sprawled out on the floor watching cartoons on their tablets. Someone's grandma is sitting on the sofa, bouncing a toddler on her knees, and Trevor's in the middle of a battle royale round, talking into his gaming headset at the desk along the wall.

The only one who isn't here yet is Cindy. When we left this afternoon, her parents' car was still parked by the side of the house. At school this week, she stopped sitting at our usual table at lunch. I wondered if it's because Jameel started sitting with me, or if she went to go sit with the tall girls instead, wherever *they* sit—I think in the auditorium.

I pull up a chair and watch Trevor for a while, then join the console game in front of the TV. After a few rounds, I notice a faint, flowery orange smell. I turn around and there's Cindy in the big recliner, staring at her phone, probably texting with the tall girls, looking like a queen on a royal throne.

Are we having a fight? Is it even possible to have a silent fight with your best friend?

It must be.

But it doesn't seem like you can end a silent fight with more silence, more ignoring each other.

Xu Auntie comes down the stairs. "Okay, everyone, time to eat!" she says, waving us up. "Let's go. Kids first, get your food and then the adults will have theirs. Trevor, set a good example."

Cindy's the first to leave, followed by the twins. Then Trevor quits his match and the rest of us go, me at the very end.

Upstairs, the Chinese party is in full avalanche. The moms are clustered around the dining table, gossiping about ChinaNet rumors and bragging about deals they scored. *It was already on clearance, and then I had my extra twenty-five percent off! It came out to three eighty-seven!*

Hao Bu and Ah Dia are sitting in the den with a couple other grandparents, chatting by the stone fireplace. Meanwhile, I can hear the dads in the living room, cracking melon seeds and talking about money.

"*Take your salary and multiply it by twenty-five! If you can have that much saved, you can live off the interest!*"

Everyone's drinking wine.

Just as Cindy grabs a plate from the counter, she gets pulled aside by one of the moms:

"Cindy? *Wah, I hardly recognized you. You've lost some weight!*"

I slide in and grab my own plate. I load it with Hao Bu's spring rolls, Liu Niang Niang's beef strips and celery, and Jia Ahyi's candied lotus. Zhang Jiuma's salt-and-pepper shrimp and Xu Auntie's smoked fish. To be polite, I get a little bit of everything, even though I'm not hungry, and when I come back around for napkins and chopsticks, Cindy moves past me without a word.

It reminds me of this one warm-up we did in Movement, where we had to all keep walking around without stopping, covering every part of the stage, not letting any space stay open for too long.

Except sometimes you and another person would try to go to the same spot. You'd almost crash into each other, and leave new openings where you both were before. Mx. Adler didn't explain afterwards what we were supposed to learn from it—they never do that for any of the warm-ups—but I think it was about being aware of not only where you're going, but where everyone else is going too.

Right now, where Cindy's going is to a sofa in the den. Where I'm going is a different sofa in the den, next to Hao Bu and Ah Dia.

Cindy and I are sitting apart, but somehow it still feels like we're crashing.

Hao Bu pats Ah Dia's knee and gets up. *"Old man, what do you want to eat?"*

"Whatever," says Ah Dia.

Lang Uncle comes over and checks the fireplace. He turns a little knob and the fire gets bigger—I didn't realize the logs in there were fake. I focus on my food, taking a small bite of each item on my plate. I tried hard to keep it all separate, but I piled too much on. Everything's spilling into everything else.

Cindy gets up suddenly, like she can't handle even being near me. She slides open the glass door to the deck, takes her plate of food outside, and shuts the door behind her. She stops in front of the wood railing for a second, her back toward me, then walks out of view.

I flash to a random memory: Lucas de la Cruz, on the playground in fourth grade, sitting by himself on the seesaw because his best friend Diana had just moved away. I left the game of kick-and-catch, pretending I had a stomachache, and crouched on the sidelines close to where Lucas was. The ground was covered in wood chips. I'd pick up a handful and release it, pick up and release, and every once in a while I'd look over my shoulder at Lucas. I wanted to talk to him, to tell him I was sorry that his best friend left, and be the other end of his seesaw. But I couldn't move.

And now I remember how that ended. With Cindy

leading Annie and Thuy over. I still don't know how she did it, really. Maybe she just walked up to Lucas and said, "I'm sorry about Diana. Do you want to go swing on the swings with us?" Because when I looked again, the seesaw was empty, and they were all on their way to the swings.

Could it have been that easy? Just to go up and say out loud what you were thinking?

Hao Bu comes back with plates of food for her and Ah Dia, and leaves again to get napkins and water. Ah Dia nudges my knee, then points a curled finger toward the sliding door. He doesn't say a word, but I think I know what he's getting at.

I set down my plate and go.

Outside, Cindy's leaning against the railing at the other end of the deck. Her sweatshirt sleeves are pulled over her hands, and her plate is on the patio table behind her. She's barely touched her food.

"Aren't you cold out here?" It's the only thing I can think to say. Cindy looks at me, then stares back out at the woods. The deck's littered with baby pinecones. They cover the top part of the railing too. To our left and right are other decks, belonging to other houses, all of them looking out toward the tall straight trees.

It should be peaceful, being out here. So why does every cell inside me feel like it's going to split in two?

A sharp crack in the distance, almost like thunder.

But the sky's clear. Then I see the bushy gray tail—it's a squirrel, breaking off branches as it leaps from one tree to another.

"Be careful around him," says Cindy. "He's bad news."

Cindy's not talking about the squirrel.

But she has Jameel all wrong.

"He's okay once you get to know him," I say.

"Andy, I'm not going to tell you who you can and can't be friends with."

Something about this makes me really mad. Because she *is* telling me who I can't be friends with. That's exactly what she's telling me.

"Jameel *is* my friend," I say.

"I just don't want anything to happen to you, is all. You should be careful."

"Well, you should mind your own business."

"See, you never used to do this."

"Do what?"

"You never used to snap at me like this. And you skipped Movement on Monday. You know I covered for you? I told Mrs. Ocampo you weren't feeling well. It wasn't until you and Jameel—"

"Me and Jameel. Me and Jameel! What about you and the tall girls!"

"What tall—"

"From Movement! I saw you at the mall!"

Cindy opens her mouth. Her eyes flick to the sliding glass door. "*Andy, shhh*. They'll hear—"

"That. That's exactly what I'm talking about. Bleaching our hair, joining Movement. You decide something and we do it. You never ask me what *I* want."

Cindy's still watching the door, trying to keep her voice down. "If you hate your hair so much, why don't you just cut it? Shave it off for all I care. And I thought you *liked* crew."

"I—That's not the point." She's trying to change the subject from her to me. "You lied," I fire back. "You told me we were too old for trick-or-treating, but then you went to the Halloween store with Viola and them."

"Alexandra's throwing a party, okay? It's not the same—"

"How is that different?"

Cindy folds her arms across her chest. "I don't have to tell you every little thing about my life."

"Neither do I."

She presses her lips into a thin line. She wants to be done with this conversation. But I have more to say.

"I made my first real friend who's not you and you don't want me to hang out with him."

"That's not true," she says. "That's not why."

"It is." I flick one of the pinecones off the railing. Then I remember the time Jameel flicked the Hi-Chew wrapper off our desk. I remember when he made fun of me in the hallways, and blew air at Kevin's—

"Andy, he's a bully."

"He's not . . ."

"He *is*. I mean, he still calls you 'Irish.' You don't see a problem with that?"

"But—it's different now . . ." Even as I say it, my words sound hollow. "Maybe I can help," I tell her. "Maybe he just needs a friend."

"Are you hearing yourself right now?"

I've seen a side of Jameel she hasn't. Even if he still gets in a bad mood sometimes, that doesn't make him a bully, does it?

Cindy throws her hands up. "Look. Do whatever you want. Just don't say I didn't warn you."

"Fine. I will."

"Fine!"

The glass door opens. Hao Bu pokes her head through. *"The old man wanted to come out here,"* she says, helping Ah Dia over the threshold. Cindy slips around them and goes back inside. She even forgets her dinner plate on the patio table.

Hao Bu looks between me and the open door. *"What's going on? Is everything okay?"*

I don't answer. I stare out at the trees and flick another pinecone off the railing.

WEIRD SUPERHEROES

"Still time to change your mind," Jameel says.

He hovers behind me with the hair clippers. In the wide bathroom mirror, I watch him flip the switch on and off. *Bzzzzzzt. Click. Bzzzzzzt.* It'd look like some kind of torture—if we weren't best friends.

I adjust the garbage bag around my neck. The metal folding chair squeaks under my butt. Our eyes meet in the mirror.

"You don't gotta worry," he says. "I've done this a million times. Or at least a dozen."

"I'm ready," I tell him. "Let's go."

Clumps of black and orange start falling from my head and sliding off the garbage bag, landing on the tile floor. The clippers' plastic grooves feel good against my scalp. I close my eyes and picture the waxy orange peel coming off a clementine.

The buzzing stops.

"Yo, what's this bald spot right here?" asks Jameel. He rubs it with his index finger. "You get into an accident or something?"

I shake my head.

Jameel turns his own head to the side and pulls back some of the thick black hair around his ear. He's got a bald spot too, except it's more of a line. I've never noticed that scar before.

"Swimming pool." He shrugs, without going into detail.

"I pull my hair," I tell him. "I don't know why I do it. Sometimes I don't even realize I'm doing it. It's, like, a bad habit, or something."

He's the first one I've told. The only one. It feels like I've been carrying something heavy—and I finally get to let it go.

"Bad habit?" Jameel chews the side of a fingernail, as if to demonstrate. "Got plenty of those." He looks at my hair again. "I'll leave the top half a lil' longer. That way you can't really see it. Cool?"

Something unhooks in my chest. "Okay."

He turns the clippers back on. I close my eyes again. *Bzzzzzzzzzz* . . .

"Fade, right? Sideburns or no? I could cut a lightning bolt if you want . . ." When he's done, Jameel has a huge smile on his face. He's proud of his work. He makes a show of grabbing a mirror so I can see the back. Thankfully, there's no lightning bolt.

"I guess this means I have to stop calling you Irish," he says, talking about the new cut. But maybe he's talking about something else too. I run my hand through my hair. It's short enough that the orange is gone, but long enough to hide the bald spot.

Jameel smirks. "Think I'mma start calling you Yamcha Jr. instead."

"*Dragon Ball Z* Yamcha?"

"Tournament Yamcha. From the original, *duh*."

I laugh. Jameel will be Jameel.

"Hey, I get to give *you* a name then," I shoot back. "It's only fair."

"Go ahead and try. You can't nickname me, bruh!"

"Jameerkat."

"Just sounds like you added *cat* to my name. I'd be a tiger anyway. That's what kind of cat."

"Jameelworm."

"Too long."

"Worm for short."

"Too wiggly."

He's right, he's fidgety but not wiggly. "Gumby!"

"Gumby?"

"Yeah, 'cause you're all lanky and awkward."

He frowns and I instantly regret it. I didn't realize he felt weird about his body. It's wild how fast you can go from joking around to hurting someone's feelings.

I wonder—did he ever feel bad calling *me* names before?

I remember that I did already give him a name. A name I don't say out loud now: *Dementor*.

"How about . . ." I start, a little more carefully. "Lizard boy."

"Lizard boy," he repeats, as if trying it on. "Lizard *man*."

"Captain Lizardpants."

"Yamcha Jr. and Captain Lizardpants," he says, like he's naming a superhero team. "I think we just figured out our Halloween costumes."

We look at ourselves in the mirror. We burst out laughing.

NOVEMBER

SLOTHS & TALKING HATS

"Andy, *wait*," says Baba. *"We'll drive you to school today."*

He takes a sip of coffee and goes back to ironing his work shirt. Mama, in her 88 Mart polo, is packing him a container of leftovers.

"Why? It's not *that* cold," I tell him.

"It's okay, we'll drive," he says. He throws me his keys. *"Go start up the car."*

Outside, I unlock the car doors and stick the key in the ignition. I picture a hibernating beast, waking from slumber. Up and down the street, rows of paper leaf-bags line the curbs of houses, and front lawns are sparkly with ice crystals. Last night, Hao Bu made *nugu migeda*— a thick stew of chunks of sweet kabocha squash and chewy nuggets of dough.

The crunch of gravel. Cindy's parents backing out of the side driveway. Her mom sees me and waves, and I wave back, then look for Cindy. But she's not in the car. I've skipped Movement three weeks in a row now. This'll be the fourth.

Cindy's parents pull away just as mine come out the front door. Once we start driving, there's a weird kind of quiet that reminds me of when my parents first told me we were moving to Hazel Heights. We were in the car then too, turning down streets I didn't recognize. I caught Baba grinning in the mirror, and after a while, I asked him where we were going.

"We moving to new house!" he said, like he couldn't keep it a secret any longer. "Is not own house, but almost like own house. Share with Cindy family. Have backyard and front yard . . . have whole floor for ourself!"

"You're going to a new school too," said Mama. *"Better than your current one."*

"Maybe someday we have own house," said Baba, more to himself.

Before I could even react, we turned up the driveway and Baba announced, "We here!" And then, I think for no other reason than him being excited, he honked the car horn.

This time, though, Baba's not smiling. And once he starts talking, his tone is more serious. I flash to the quiet conversation he and Mama had the other night—the low voices coming from their room while I was brushing my teeth.

"Andy," he says. "Today your mama last day working

88 Mart. She will staying home, help taking care Ah Dia."

Something doesn't feel right. Ah Dia's been doing a lot better lately, moving around more like before his fall. Then I remember his tests.

"Did they find something in his MRI?"

"Doctor say MRI fine." Baba shakes his head. "Think is not physical but in he brain. Is nur . . ."

"Neurological."

"Yes. Doctor want Ah Dia go seeing specialist."

Baba doesn't say it, but I know what that means: It's going to cost even more money. But wouldn't Mama leaving her job mean we have less to pay for it? After the emergency room, Hao Bu tried to shove her envelope of cash into Baba's hands, but he kept refusing. They got into a huge fight over it.

I can't see Mama's face in the mirror like I can Baba's, but she stays quiet as he talks. She started working at 88 Mart a couple years ago. Before that, she was home taking care of me. Maybe I'm imagining it, but her shoulders look a little slumped.

"Did you hear what I said?" asks Baba.

"Isn't Hao Bu already taking care of Ah Dia?"

"Andy. If Ah Dia fall again and we at work, you at school, what Hao Bu do? Better Mama staying home too, okay? Family is most important."

Baba unlocks the doors. We've already stopped in front of my school. I watch other kids stream into the entrance with their big backpacks, like we're all going to work at some factory.

"Is going be okay," says Baba. "I can delivering food again on weekend. No problem." He looks over his shoulder at me. "You have Math Olympia today?"

"I'll walk home after," I say, more of a reflex than anything.

When I get out, Baba tells me to study hard, and Mama waves goodbye with a sad smile.

I sit through homeroom feeling like I swallowed something smooth and hard—like a cherry pit—and now it's growing into a tree in my stomach. Everyone else is making sacrifices for Ah Dia, while I've been pretending to be in Math Olympiad to go to Movement, then skipping Movement to go to Jameel's.

In science, I stare at the back of Cindy's head while Mr. Nagy talks about our new unit on evolution. Cindy's hair has gotten duller and messier. Her dark roots show more.

"There will be no test at the end this unit," says Mr. Nagy.

Cheers and fist pumps.

He shushes everyone. "Instead, a third of your grade this quarter will be based on a project with your lab groups."

Groans.

"You'll present your projects in front of the class before break."

More groans, me included.

Then I realize what it means: Cindy and Kevin, Jameel and me. The four of us working together again— or trying to. I look over to see Jameel's reaction. His book is open in his lap, but it's hiding his phone, playing an episode of *One Piece* with the subtitles on.

Mr. Nagy gives us time to talk about our projects. We're supposed to pick a plant or animal species and research how it evolved its different traits. Kevin and Cindy slowly turn around in their seats. Kevin looks at Jameel, then quickly looks away.

"How about let's do sloths," Cindy says, more of a statement than a question. I notice dark rings around her eyes, like Baba has when he doesn't get enough sleep. "We can each pick a trait to write up," she goes on. "Then everyone can send their part to me and I'll put it all on a poster. Okay?"

Kevin nods repeatedly. Cindy sees Jameel's phone and glares at him. "Jameel, are you listening?"

I nudge him with my elbow. I know he can hear her. I also know that he's seen this episode of *One Piece.*

Cindy rolls her eyes. "Whatever. Andy, you can do the drawings. I'll leave room for them on the poster."

"Fine by me," I tell her. I don't have the energy to fight her orders right now. I'm more annoyed that Jameel isn't even trying. Isn't his mom going to take Vegeta away if he doesn't do better at school?

Kevin gets a laptop from the laptop cart and Cindy starts listing out the different traits of sloths. I nudge Jameel again. He nudges me back, but he keeps ignoring the project.

In social studies, I finish my surprise essay about market economies a few minutes early, and Mx. Adler lets me out for lunch. They haven't acted any differently toward me these last weeks—probably because they haven't even noticed I've been skipping Movement.

In the cafeteria, I barely touch my nuggets and fries. Instead, I just doodle in my sketchbook as I watch the tables around me fill up. There's a group of Black kids at one long table, a bunch of Chaldeans at another, and a half table of Koreans. Other groups are more mixed, but they're definitely their own groups: the athletes, the hardcore gamers, the three kids who sit in the corner and play Magic: The Gathering. My old group is part of a bigger STEM-kids table, but I haven't seen Cindy eat with Thuy and Annie in weeks.

I guess Jameel and I have our section too, with usually just us. Maybe it was like this before, and I didn't notice—how everyone's sorted themselves, no magical hat required.

Here come Cindy and the tall girls. They're all wearing the same purply tie-dye sweatshirt I saw Cindy in this morning—their new uniform for fall, I guess. But instead of taking their usual turn toward the hallways, they head straight for my table, almost as if they want to talk to me. I look over my shoulder: The only thing behind me is a brick wall.

"Andy! Where have you been?" says Viola. Her hair's freshly dyed—a deep turquoise instead of the pink before. "We've missed you at Movement!"

"You have?" I scratch my head and my fingers graze the bald spot. Cindy stands back and stares at her own feet.

"Mrs. Ocampo's been asking about you," says Mai. "I have art with her and I saw the mountain y'all painted. It looks so good!"

"Oh, that's mostly Eva and Lucy," I explain. "I was working on the boar mask. And stuff."

"I'm sure that'll be great too," says Alexandra.

"We can't wait to see it!" says Viola.

The girls float off toward the lunch line, and Cindy along with them—without adding a word. Seeing all the tall girls together, I notice that Cindy's gotten even thinner. Her legs are almost as skinny as Alexandra's now.

"Yo, what was that about?" asks Jameel, setting down his lunch bag. He looks between me and the tall girls, eyes wide. "You *know* those chicks? Through your girlfriend, right?"

The joke's so old that it's not funny anymore. And something else he said bugs me.

"They're not chicks," I tell him.

"Huh?"

"You called them *chicks*. They're not chicks."

"Chicks, girls, whatever."

"No. Not whatever. Girls aren't chicks."

"Bruh, what's your problem today?"

My problem is he basically ignores the science project and now he wants to joke around. I glance over Jameel's shoulder at the table where Cindy used to sit. Where *we* used to sit. Jameel looks too, and when he turns back around, there's a glint in his eye.

"Hey, why you sit with those girls anyway?"

"I'm sitting with you."

"I mean before. When you sat with your girlfriend. Your table was all girls."

"It wasn't."

Jameel looks at me like, *Come on, really?*

"Okay, it was," I admit. "I don't know why." Maybe because Cindy was my best friend, and Thuy and Annie were her other friends. Without her, I probably wouldn't have had anyone to sit with.

But that's not what Jameel's getting at.

"Are you, like, gay or something?" he asks. He says it in a weird way, like he means it half as a joke and half not. I feel like whatever answer I give—it's going to be the wrong one. Even if I said no, he'd just start joking that I was gay. And it's not like I *don't* like girls . . .

"I mean, if you were . . ." Jameel trails off. He stares at my lunch tray. It gets so awkward that I can't sit any longer. I get up to go somewhere else—to the bathroom, to the library . . . anywhere but here.

Jameel calls out after me. "Bruh, you didn't eat your nuggets!"

As I walk out, I realize something that's always bothered me about the sorting hat. I know it's magic and all, but it's ridiculous that a weird talking hat gets to decide your whole future. Because what if you get sorted into the wrong house? Are you just stuck there forever?

UNHATCHING

The boys' bathroom is too smelly. And the library is too quiet.

I roam the halls for a while, with nowhere to go, and stop in front of the glass courtyard. The tree inside's lost half its leaves, its skinny branches sticking out over the rusty ferns and dried grasses. Leaves swirl around the bench and heating ducts, threatening to throw up a mini tornado.

I watch them swirl and swirl, and wonder why I'm so mad at everything lately. Are Jameel's angry parts rubbing off on me? If Cindy hadn't said anything at the Chinese party, would I have even cared or noticed? I rub my bald spot. Then I keep walking.

Before I know it, I'm standing in the doorway of the art studio, as if my legs decided to go there without telling my brain.

To my surprise, Jason and Eva are inside eating their lunches. The tall girls weren't the only ones who'd noticed I was gone. Eva actually asked me about it in the hallways last week, and Lucy came up at the end of honors math and told me to let her know if I need a ride. Even Jason tried to ask in his own way, I think, when he put a set of vampire-themed temporary tattoos on my desk after Halloween. I gave him some candy the next day, from Jameel and my trick-or-treat haul.

Jason sees me iceman staring: "Ahndy! Velcome!"

Eva waves me in: "Come have lunch with us."

"Oh, I already ate. Kinda." But I walk in anyway.

Eva and Jason get up and show me everything they've been working on. The backdrops are finished, painted in big colorful polygons—the jungle in shades of green and the mountain in crystal-y blue and pale purple—as if Picasso made an island. Jason pulls the parachute out from a cabinet—cords and straps and everything—and Eva turns on her fan with the flame strips. The bright cloth flutters like a real fire, and makes the chute billow. There's also a metal costume rack with a bunch of old dress shirts that they're turning into the kids' school uniforms.

It's overwhelming, how much they've done. And pretty awesome too.

"Andy! There you are!"

"Hi, Mrs. Ocampo."

She tosses her keys onto a table and sets down her lunch bag. "We've missed you!"

"Everything looks so good!" I tell her. I glance at the set pieces again, and my eye falls on something big and round and covered with a cloth, sitting on top of one of the wall cabinets. Is that . . . ?

"Don't worry," says Mrs. Ocampo. "It's exactly as you left it."

She pulls the bundle down and lifts the cover. I stare at the wireframe boar mask, still waiting to be paper mache'd—like some video game glitch. It's exactly as I left it, all right: completely unfinished.

Mrs. Ocampo sits down to eat her lunch. Eva and Jason go back to theirs too. It's almost as if they're giving me and the boar some time alone. I think back to working on it after school, here in this room, under these tall ceilings. When Eva gets up to wash her hands at the wide metal sink, I get a whiff of all the art studio smells—paint and pencil shavings, pastel and clay. I remember the other thing Cindy said to me at the Chinese party: "I thought you *liked* crew."

I don't know if she's right about Jameel, but she's right about that. I *do* like crew. And I miss it. I miss being here with Eva, Lucy, and Jason. I miss Mrs. Ocampo's chill music. I even miss Mx. Adler's warm-ups, like the time we ran a slow-motion race and the winner was whoever finished last.

So why am I avoiding something I like, just because of Cindy? Wouldn't that still be letting her decide what I can or can't do, only in a different way?

* * *

If Cindy's surprised to see me in the auditorium after school, she doesn't show it. Neither does Mx. Adler, who tells us that today, for warm-ups, we're doing Egg again. We scatter on the stage and take our spots on the floor. Knees up, arms wrapped around, head down, eyes closed. I'm small, like always. Tiny, unmoving egg.

But after a while, a weird thing happens. I feel how much I'm squeezing, and straining, just to hold myself small.

So I relax my arms. And it sets off a chain reaction in my body. My shoulders drop, my chest gets looser. My belly, which I was sucking in like I was trying to give myself a six-pack, puffs out like a balloon.

I lean back and plant my hands. I'm crab-walking. Then I bounce to my feet, like someone tied a cord to my chest and pulled me up by it. I start shaking my head and arms, letting my hands flop back and forth, like I'm shaking off something, shaking off every time I've felt bad about Cindy and Jameel and kids that pull their eyes into slits and being a good friend and a good grandson and doing something because of someone else or because *I* want to do it, because *I* like doing it, and then I'm crying, but it's not the big crying where you can hardly breathe but a different kind of crying, where tears are just leaking, like snipping the corner off a ziplock bag filled with water.

"Time's up," says Mx. Adler.

I stop moving and open my eyes. I wipe the tears away. We get into our closing circle and bow. And as I'm about to follow the other crew kids off the stage, Mx. Adler says, "Andy."

We look at each other for a second. Then Mx. Adler nods. As if to say *Welcome back*, or *Good work today*. Or maybe, *I understand*. Maybe all of those things.

That afternoon, I finish the first layer of paper mache and set the boar mask over the heating vents to dry. I help the others cut and rip the dress shirts and rub charcoal all over them. We do the same to a bunch of neckties that Jason sewed out of striped fabric. Afterwards, they definitely look like they could've been through a plane crash.

As I work on the second paper mache layer my mind starts to wander. Even if I think really hard, I can't remember when Cindy and I first became best friends. Our families were around each other all the time. It's like we just always *were* best friends.

But the more I hang out with Jameel, the more I realize that Cindy and I don't actually have that much in common. She's not into anime the way Jameel and I are. I'm not into dancing the way she is. If we'd only just met this year, would we still have become best friends?

Not just *best friends*—would we even be friends at all?

Maybe it doesn't matter how it happened. Maybe the fact that you were once best friends is enough of a reason to try to stay that way, even when things are awkward.

Now I'm not sure if I'm thinking of Cindy or Jameel.

I paper over the last part of the boar's tusks. Then I notice Mrs. Ocampo closing some of the cabinets, and turning off the lights in her supply closet office. The music's stopped. Everyone else has already left. The clock says it's almost five p.m.

"They knew not to disturb you." Mrs. Ocampo smiles. I look out the windows. The sky's such a flat gray that I can't tell if it's clear or cloudy. My feet feel cold all of a sudden, even through my thick socks. I start cleaning up the newspapers and flour paste.

"You can leave those," she says. "I'll get 'em in the morning."

"Okay. Thanks." I quickly wash my hands at the sink. I grab my backpack to leave.

Mrs. Ocampo turns off the rest of the lights behind us and locks the door. As we walk down the hallways, I feel like she's going to ask me any second why I haven't been at Movement these few last weeks. And I have no good answer.

Instead, she says: "That was a great idea you had today—adding tusks. How did we forget about those?"

"It kind of just popped into my head," I say.

She nods. "You know, I think that a lot of being an artist is noticing what's in your mind's eye. And trusting it."

I'm not totally sure what she means, but—did she just call me an artist?

"What if you see bad stuff in your mind's eye?" I ask. "Like, stuff going wrong."

We stop in the front entrance. Mrs. Ocampo looks at me for a second. "I think everyone worries about things going wrong at times," she says. "But when something's so vividly in your mind's eye, good or bad, I think that's your intuition telling you to pay attention. What you see might not be exactly real, but the feeling underneath it is. Does that make sense?"

Not really? But I nod like I get it.

Mrs. Ocampo aims her car keys at the front parking lot and presses the unlock button. There's a faint beep, but it's kind of far away. And behind us.

"Oops! Forgot I parked in back!" She laughs. I do too.

"See you next week?" she asks.

I nod. "Definitely."

She smiles, then gets more serious. "Andy, if you ever want to talk about anything that's going on, inside of school or out, just let me know."

I squeeze my backpack straps. "Okay. I will."

Mrs. Ocampo turns around. I step out into the cold air, and reach back and touch my bald spot again. The hair around it's grown in even more since Jameel cut it, but it's not yet long enough to pull.

That's probably a good thing.

SOMETHING, ANYTHING, NEW

There's more frost. It's gray and drab the rest of the week, maybe a sneak preview of the winter ahead. Mama sleeps in late in the mornings. She's still in bed when Baba and I leave. Some afternoons, I hear Ah Dia complaining to her and Hao Bu about his joints being sore.

At school, the eighth graders take their annual trip to Washington, DC, leaving the hallways eerie and quiet. Ms. Daly puts up Christmas decorations early—Thanksgiving isn't for another couple of weeks—and comes to class with extra-large mugs of coffee. Jameel's mostly quiet in science and at lunch, watching *One Piece* again on his phone. He tries to talk about the show, and I try to ask him, but our conversations never go anywhere. I imagine a car engine sputtering, struggling to start.

Is this what Mrs. Ocampo meant by seeing things in my mind's eye? I'm not sure what it has to do with being an artist, but I try to notice it.

Then on Friday, while I'm standing in the lunch line, Jameel gets in line behind me—with Paul and Aiden. At first they all ignore me. They laugh and talk about annoying teachers and girls they think are hot. They make fun of each other too. I grab a lunch tray and stare straight ahead, and try to keep moving with the line.

But just as I get my sloppy joes and fruit cup, there's a tap on my shoulder. I turn around and it's Paul, leaning in with a smirk. He points at Jesse Mays, this popular girl in front of us near the checkout.

"Andy," he says, "I'll give you a dollar if you ask Jesse out."

Aiden snickers. "Go ahead, Andy. Work your—"

Jameel sticks his hand out. He almost touches Aiden's chest.

"Yo, Andy's cool," he says. We make eye contact. Jameel nods.

Aiden backs off. "All right, you do it, then," he tells Jameel. "Go talk to her."

"For a dollar?" Jameel says. "Naw, you gotta pony up more than that."

"Pony up?" Paul laughs. "Who says *pony up*? You some kind of cowboy?"

I turn forward again. I punch in my student number at the register and hurry out before they can follow. I avoid our usual table and head into the hallways. I'm glad Jameel stood up for me back there, but why does he have to hang around them at all?

How I feel about Jameel being around those guys—is that how Cindy feels about me being around Jameel?

I end up in the art studio again. Eva, Jason, and Mrs. Ocampo are all in a chatty mood, but I'm not. I scarf down my sloppy joes and use the rest of my time to paint the boar mask. I borrow Mrs. Ocampo's laptop to find pictures of wild boars, then I mix together globs of tempera paint to match the dark grays and browns of their fur. I paint the gray first, then layer on splotches of brown, which against the darker gray looks kind of orange. It looks almost like my hair did.

I've already lost one best friend in Cindy this year. Am I losing another?

When I finish painting, the mask feels . . . not so menacing. More like the complete opposite.

Still, I feel better just to have done something new to it.

After school, I find Jameel at his locker. He's got his earbuds in, hood over his head, watching another episode of *One Piece*. He's holding the phone with one hand and trying to fill his backpack with the other. His mood feels different than earlier. Quieter and darker. Was it because I ditched him at lunch again?

"Which episode are you on?" I ask.

He takes out one earbud. "What?"

"Which episode?"

"Hundred-something. Nico Robin just joined." Jameel

shuts his locker. He looks at me like he's about to ask me to come over to his place. But then he just pops his earbud back in.

Outside, weird bulgy clouds hang over us, like a sheet of gray Bubble Wrap, and the air's cold enough that I can see our breath. Jameel and I walk, but it doesn't feel like we're walking together—he's a couple steps ahead, still glued to his phone. At one point, I have to stop him at the intersection because he doesn't see a car coming.

As we get near my house, though, he slows down. Maybe he *is* paying attention. Jameel pulls his hood back. He takes out both earbuds.

"You wanna come over?" he asks. "We can watch together."

I hesitate. It feels like too much, too soon. Like the other day when the school's heating system finally came on during honors math. It went from being kinda chilly to the ceiling vent blowing right in my face.

"I don't think I can," I tell him.

"Oh."

I watch him fiddle with his earbuds.

"But I feel like walking a little," I say. "I'll go to the bridge with you."

Jameel looks at me for a second. He puts his earbuds back in their case and pockets his phone. He keeps his hood off. We don't say much, but we go past my house toward the freeway, slower than before, like we're both trying to make the short walk last as long as we can.

At the edge of the bridge, Jameel stops.

"You sure you can't come over?" he asks.

I think about Ah Dia at home, Baba working overtime, and Mama leaving her job. I flash to the cafeteria again—when Jameel asked if I was gay. My backpack feels heavy from all the books. I wish there wasn't so much happening all the time.

I shake my head. Jameel's face hardens. That hallway between us feels dark, doors closed on both sides. I have to say something—anything.

"Is your brother coming back for Christmas?" I ask.

His mouth tightens. "Couldn't get time off."

"Oh. Sorry."

Jameel puts his hood back on. He turns forward, holds up a peace sign, then starts walking to the other side. Down on the freeway, the blocked-off lanes have been demolished, leaving just rough, grooved dirt. Cranes and excavators sit along the side of the road, next to mounds of gravel and big concrete pipes. If they don't hurry, they won't finish before winter. Then it'll be too cold to do anything.

I remember something.

I look up. Jameel's halfway across the bridge.

I call out, "Wait!"

He stops. Looks over his shoulder. I run up to meet him.

"You wanna go to the cider mill this weekend?"

CIDER & DOU-NAS

The clouds don't break—but we go anyway.

Jameel comes over Saturday and squeezes into the car with my entire family. We drive northwest, to where the roads are more winding and hilly, not flat like where we live, until finally we spot a barn-red building with a water wheel: Jameel's favorite cider mill.

Inside, the air smells sweet with apples and burnt sugar. Framed newspaper and magazine clippings line the walls, and a sign brags that they've been open since 1874. Nothing else I know around here is that old, but I guess people probably wanted cider and donuts back then too.

"*Ba, look,*" Baba says to Ah Dia. He points to the massive gears and axles that run across the ceiling and connect to the water wheel. "Before no electricity," he tells us. "Energy from water is use for machines. Like dam."

Jameel and I look at each other. We start cracking up.

"Why laughing?" asks Baba.

"No reason," I try to say with a straight face.

Baba hands me some cash and tells me and Jameel to order, while they go find a seat outside. We scan the menu board and wait our turn. The employees behind the counter are filling cups with piping-hot cider, and handing people sacks of warm donuts, the frying oils already seeping through the sides. The donuts are just a little smaller than normal—Cindy would love these. But she's not here.

Jameel and I decide on a dozen each of plain and cinnamon sugar. Ciders for everyone, and a couple caramel apples to share. While we wait, he eyes the tip jar by the registers, and I catch myself expecting him to do something bad. What if he's just thinking about how much of a tip to leave?

It's our turn. I tell the cashier lady our order, and she repeats it to another worker who starts pulling it all together. The cashier adds up the cost of each item on a handheld calculator. I do a quick count in my head and get out the bills and coins.

"That comes out to forty-six seventy-five," says the cashier. "Oh—look at that, you already have the exact change!" She winks and sorts the money into the register slots. "Us Americans aren't so great at math."

Spider-sense. Then something in me snaps: "I'm American too," I tell her. I take the donuts and go. I don't leave a tip.

Outside, I'm shaking a little. I can't remember what else I was thinking about.

Jameel comes out with our drink tray. "Yo, you shoulda seen the look on her—" He stops. "Bruh. You all right?"

I take a deep breath. "Why does that stuff always happen when you're least expecting it?" I wonder out loud. "It's like, you go for days or weeks and . . . nothing. Like, you're just a regular person—"

"But then they remind you you're *this* kind or *that* kind." Jameel nods. "Yeah."

The worst part is, I get what that lady was trying to say: That I'm not American the way she is—white American. But I'm not fully Chinese, either. And I *am* good at math, even though I know it's a stereotype. So am I just supposed to hide it?

Jameel touches my shoulder. And leaves his hand there. I wonder, then, if he has any parts of him that *he* hides.

"Bruh, I'mma leave a one-star review for them," he says, face hardening. "I'mma tell everyone to never come here again."

His words calm me a little. "Thanks," I tell him.

"Andy! Jamee!" Mama's waving from a picnic table. "Over here!"

Jameel takes his hand off my shoulder. But I can almost still feel it there. We put on smiles and join my family. If it were earlier in the year, and a little warmer out, it'd probably be packed here. But I'm glad it's not.

We pass the donuts and cider around, and I watch everyone peel back the flaps of their plastic lids, steam wafting out. I take a sip from my own cup. The hot, sweet cider warms my throat and belly.

Baba, Hao Bu, and Ah Dia all really like the cinnamon sugar donuts. Jameel eats only those. I have one plain, then two cinnamon sugar, which Mama says are *too* sugary. I watch her dip a plain donut into the cider, take a bite, and close her eyes. The sleepiness is gone from her face, like maybe instead of jet lag she had a kind of work lag, that she's just getting over.

"Comwing to cider mwill vwery gwood widea, Andwy!" says Baba, mouth full.

"It was Jameel's idea," I tell him.

"Then very good idea, Jamee!" says Baba. He raises his caramel apple in a toast. We all toast with our half-eaten donuts. I'm not sure if it's just the chilly air, but I think Jameel's cheeks are red.

Baba takes a bite of the apple, then furiously licks his teeth to get the stuck caramel off. Mama sees that we've eaten almost all the donuts and goes to get another dozen to take home. When she comes back out, Jameel tells us that there's a hiking trail near here. Bellies warm with cider, sugar on the corners of our lips, no one complains—not even Ah Dia.

The trail takes us into the woods along the creek. The water's not quite as fast as a rapid, but it moves quick, and ripples in a soothing way. Mama and Hao Bu walk in front, elbows linked, talking and laughing. My dad and grandpa follow closely behind, Baba trying to encourage Ah Dia.

"Old man, it's nice to be out of the house, isn't it? Better than being cooped up inside," he says. *"Maybe we can do some traveling over Christmas and New Year's. Drive to Washington, DC, or Niagara Falls. Go visit New York City!"*

"Aiya, it's going to be too cold then," says Mama, overhearing. *"The falls are going to be frozen. And you want your ba to sit in the car for that long?"*

Baba goes up to avalanche-talk with Mama. I explain to Jameel what they're arguing about. He nods, then looks out at the creek, his mind somewhere else. I wonder if mentioning Christmas reminded him of Yousif, or of their dad.

In front, Ah Dia stops by a wooden staircase—six steps down to a small platform sticking out over the water. It looks big enough for a handful of people.

"Ah Dia, do you want to go?" I ask.

Ah Dia nods. He looks kind of funny with his poofy jacket and all his extra layers. This morning, Baba and Hao Bu wrapped him up like a baby. He has two sweaters on.

I call for Baba, and everyone comes back to the staircase. Baba looks it over for ice, then tells us to be careful. Jameel and I go down first, followed by my dad and Ah Dia, who take it step by step at Ah Dia's pace. When the four of us are on the platform, Mama has us turn around and smile. She snaps a picture.

Mama and Hao Bu tell us they're going to go check out more of the trail. The rest of us spread out along the wooden guard fence. The platform hovers over the creek's edge, so we're not in the water, but we're not exactly on the shore, either.

From here, I watch a group of ducks floating in a calm part of the riverbank, quacking and flapping their wings. One of them dives its head below the surface, sticking its butt and webbed feet up in the air. Another duck stands on a flat rock apart from the others, cleaning its feathers, while water flows past on either side.

I notice Ah Dia watching the ducks too.

"Ah Dia, did you like the donuts or the cider better?" I ask. Then I repeat the question in English so Jameel doesn't feel left out.

"Dou-na," says Ah Dia. I think that means he liked the donuts. He stares at the ducks again and goes on. *"Andy, did you know? When I was your age. In Shanghai. Sometimes I'd skip class. Go to the river."*

"Was it a river like this?"

"Huangpu River," says Ah Dia in English.

"Is main river," Baba explains. "Much bigger than this! Is divide Shanghai in half—Puxi and Pudong."

"One day, the water level was real low," Ah Dia says. *"There were places you could walk. Out on the sand. A good ways into the middle. When I went out there, I saw a purple color."*

I try to translate for Jameel. He perks up, listening too.

"When I walked farther out," says Ah Dia, "the purple color started moving. Parting. Like a wave. I thought, this can't be water . . ."

"What was the color from?" Jameel asks.

"Crabs. River crabs. Tens of thousands of them. They were so tiny. Smaller than my fist."

"That's wild," Jameel says.

"That must've been beautiful," I tell Ah Dia.

"Wild." Ah Dia nods. "Beautiful."

We all smile. Then it gets quiet again. I listen to the trickling babbling water. A pale leaf falls from a tree, and lands on the surface, then drifts past us, back toward the mill. Ah Dia starts coughing hard, like maybe he talked so much, his throat got dry. Baba, with a worried look on his face, pats Ah Dia's back, asking if he's okay.

I look at Jameel. He blinks a couple times.

"Andy, come," says Baba. "Let's go. It's cold standing here."

Baba helps Ah Dia back up the staircase. It takes them longer than when we came down. At the top, he adjusts Ah Dia's scarf and zips his poofy jacket up a little tighter. Jameel and I run ahead to find Mama and Hao Bu. We finally meet up with them at a spot where the trail forks into two. But we don't explore any further. We all turn around and head back home.

A CLOSE CALL

Ah Dia's cough won't go away. Baba wants him to stop walking outside. Mama volunteers to take my grand-parents to the Chinese Community Center during the week—there's space there for them to walk indoors. So Monday morning, as I head to school, everyone else leaves in the car, with Mama driving.

At school, the eighth graders are back from their DC trip. The hallways feel alive again, and I almost can't believe that even a few months ago, we had no locker combinations or class schedules. No bells that ring every fifty minutes. No Movement.

In homeroom, during morning announcements, I flip through my planner: Ten weeks have already passed. More than a quarter of the school year is over.

In science, Jameel's late—again. He rolls in just as

we're finishing our quiz on Charles Darwin and natural selection. Mr. Nagy has him make up the quiz at the table in front, and gives the rest of us time to work on our group projects while he grades.

Cindy and Kevin spin around. "Okay guys, how's it coming?" Cindy asks. "I basically just have to type this up." She shows us a couple website printouts from her folder. She's already highlighted the important facts.

"I found out about their claws," says Kevin. "Did you know they're actually bone? And not, like, fingernails?"

"Cool," says Cindy. "But are they convergent or divergent?"

"Compared to what?" Kevin asks.

While they talk it over, I see Jameel get up and hand his quiz to Mr. Nagy. Is he done already? He hurries over to us and thwaps his notebook on the table as he sits down. He flips to a blank page, clicking a clicky pen. "What'd I miss?"

Cindy glares at him. "We were going over our research for the project," she says. "How's your part coming?"

Jameel leans back and puts a hand on his chin. "Yo, what if we did a lizard?" He looks at me. "Like, a bearded dragon."

Cindy huffs, almost a laugh. She's incredulous. "We already decided on sloths," she says.

"Who's 'we'?" asks Jameel. "I didn't decide on no sloths."

"Andy, Kevin, and me," says Cindy. "If you'd been pay-ing attention, you would've heard—"

"Sloths are boooring," says Jameel. "Right, Andy?"

Does he remember that there was a sloth on the birth-day card I gave him? I nudge his knee under the table. "Jameel, it's due next—"

"Sloths are *not* boring," says Cindy. "They spend eigh-teen hours a day—"

Jameel pretends to snore. Cindy folds her arms across her chest. Then he leans in and says, looking at Kevin, "Maybe Kevin should decide."

He says it in that half-mean way again. The same way he asked if I was gay: *Choose wisely . . . or else.* I don't get why he has to pick on Kevin, though. Because he has red hair? That first day of class Kevin happened to turn around when Jameel called me "Irish." He got caught in the crossfire, and now he's stuck. It's like that sorting hat business all over again.

I try to focus. Kevin's looking back and forth between Jameel and Cindy, like there's no right answer. But maybe there's a compromise.

"Cindy, I know we've already done a lot of sloth research," I say carefully, an idea bubbling up. "But it doesn't matter what we pick, right? As long as we get a good grade."

She gives me a death stare.

"That's right." Jameel nods. He clicks his pen.

I nudge him under the table again.

"Jameel has a bearded dragon for a pet," I go on. "So he knows a lot about them already. We won't have to look up as much."

"And I could even bring Vegeta in for the presentation!" says Jameel. "If old man Nagy over there lets me."

Just then Mr. Nagy comes around to our table. He gives Jameel a look, and hands back our quizzes. Jameel grumbles when he gets his. The score's low enough that there's a slip his mom'll have to sign.

"Vegeta's his bearded dragon's name," I explain for Cindy and Kevin. "Maybe Mr. Nagy will give us extra points for it?"

Cindy's arms are still folded. But it looks like she's thinking about what I said. I watch Jameel again to make sure he's not doing anything else mean to Kevin. I feel like I'm juggling a bunch of balls in the air, trying to keep them all from falling.

"Kevin, what do you think?" Cindy finally asks.

Kevin looks between her and Jameel again.

"Um, the bearded dragon . . . I think?"

Jameel smirks. "Looks like it's three to one! Team Vegeta!"

Cindy takes a deep breath, like she's trying not to bop Jameel on the head with her science book.

"Fine," she says. "We're wasting our time fighting about it. Just write up your traits and send—"

"Hold up," Jameel says. "This is supposed to be a *group* project. We should meet after school *as a group* and work on it together."

Cindy gives him a look like *Are you kidding me?* "No way," she says. "*Some of us* have after-school activities—that aren't detention."

"Should we ask Mr. Nagy how group projects are supposed to work?" Jameel starts raising his hand.

I pull it down. "Look. Maybe we can each can work on a different part on our own," I offer. "And then just meet in person to do the poster and practice what we'll say."

"Sounds good to me," Jameel says, clicking his pen.

Cindy rolls her eyes. "Fine."

"Is that okay with you, Kevin?" I ask.

Kevin nods. But I can tell he doesn't really have a choice.

We settle on Friday, after school. At my and Cindy's house. When the bell rings, it seems like the only one who walks out of class happy about it is Jameel.

At lunch, when he's cracking jokes about how he can't believe he only just found out that Cindy and I live together, I catch myself tuning him out, thinking about the boar mask instead, wishing I were in the art studio working on it.

On my way to the auditorium after school, I wonder if painting more individual hairs onto the mask, enough so you could see the bristles in the fur, would make it look less bad. More realistic. But right as I'm about to go through the open doors, I spot Jameel coming down the hallway.

I veer away just in time and walk up to him instead.

"Yo, you going to Math Olympiad?" he asks.

"Yeah—I mean no." I catch myself. If he tries to come with me, he'll find out it's not real. "I gotta go home for, uh, family stuff," I tell him. I glance at the auditorium. Inside, Cindy and the tall girls are goofing around on stage, recording a dance challenge together.

When I look back, I see Jameel looking toward the auditorium too.

I start walking. Down the hallway.

Jameel follows me, thankfully. On the way to the front entrance, I keep looking left and right in case someone from Movement sees me and tries to talk to me. When we turn the corner around the glass courtyard, I notice that the door to the art studio is open—and we're going to walk right past it! What if Mrs. Ocampo's inside?

I stop and turn around. I go back the way we came.

"Yo, where—" Jameel starts, quickly catching up. "Hey, I thought you were going home."

"I feel like taking the side entrance."

"Why you walking so fast?"

"I'm not." I slow down a little. I try not to look at him in case my face gives me away. Why don't I just tell him? That Math Olympiad started as a lie to our parents and it got out of hand. That I'm in crew, working on sets and costumes. He'd understand, wouldn't he?

I push through the side entrance. But then I notice, after a few steps, that Jameel's not with me anymore. When I turn around, he's standing back in the doorway.

"You're not walking home?" I ask.

"Uh, no. I gotta stay after. I told you at lunch." Jameel's forehead crinkles a little. His eyes narrow. "Why you acting so weird?"

"I'm not." I totally am. I take a breath, then think of something. "Hey, can you, like, not be mean to Cindy and Kevin?"

Jameel raises an eyebrow. I changed the subject on him. It's a very Cindy move.

"Just—try to be cool when we work on our project," I tell him.

"Your girlfriend put you up to this?" he asks.

"I'm serious. Do it for me."

He takes a long second to think about it.

"*Please.*"

"Okay, chill. Don't get your panties in a bunch, bruh."

"Promise."

"What, you want me to pinkie swear?"

"Just promise."

"I'll be on my best behavior. Cross my heart." He crosses his heart. "Scout's honor. Signed, sealed, delivered."

I sigh. I guess that's the best I'll get out of him.

He looks down at the coat in my hands. The coat I

haven't put on yet, even though it's almost freezing out. He looks back up.

I turn so we don't make eye contact. "Okay, gotta run," I say, trying to walk and get my coat on at the same time, all without stopping or letting go of my backpack. I end up just putting the coat *over* my backpack, which probably looks even more ridiculous.

I can feel Jameel's eyes on me as I hurry away. I can't go back to the school. Not while he's there. So I walk all the way home, wondering again why I didn't tell him just now. Because he'd probably make fun of me for being in a dance club.

But it's not just that—I can take a joke. It's more like if I told him now, he'll think I didn't trust him enough to be honest with him.

And he'd be right. And maybe the fact that I didn't confess it all means I still don't trust him.

But aren't you supposed to be able to tell your best friend everything?

I'm home, stopped on the sidewalk in front of the porch. Our car's parked in front and the living room curtains are drawn. I can hear a few muffled sounds from inside.

I run my hand through my hair and touch my bald spot. Only it's not completely bald anymore. I feel a short, soft fuzz that tickles my fingertips. It's not as thick and full as the hair around it, but it's growing.

I go up the porch steps. Just as I reach for the knob,

the door opens from the inside and a couple stumbles out carrying an old coffee table and an air fryer. The guy's Asian and he has a man-bun. He does a weird face when we make eye contact. My first thought is: Are we being robbed?! But then I notice Mama standing in the entryway, counting twenty-dollar bills.

"Eh? You're home early," she says, seeing me.

"Yeah," I say, so I don't lie again.

It's not until I get inside and see all the stuff laid out on the floors and counters that I realize what Mama's doing. She's organizing all the junk in our basement. And selling it.

She shows me the app on her phone that she's been using to list everything.

"Your mama's been busy!" laughs Hao Bu, on the sofa watching TV with Ah Dia.

There's a pile that Mama has to take to the post office, and another that people are coming to get in person. Down in the basement, she's even cleared a path to the shelves along the wall. She smiles at me, and reaches for the pull-string light.

"Don't tell Baba yet," she says.

IT'S ALL IMPORTANT

The doorbell rings. It's Friday afternoon, and Cindy and Kevin are here to work on our project.

As soon as I open the door, though, Cindy brushes past me and heads upstairs. I ask Kevin to take off his shoes, then help him hang up his coat. By the time I show him our living room, Cindy's back with her poster and science folder.

"Where'd your grandparents go?" she asks, looking around like she's seeing if anything's changed. I can't remember the last time she was even here. Was it when we bleached our hair?

"My mom took them to the Chinese Community Center," I tell her.

"Oh right. She's staying home now." Of course Cindy already knows. All of ChinaNet knows, probably.

Cindy spreads her stuff on the dining table, next to

the scissors, markers, and glue sticks I already set out.

"Is Jameel not coming?" Kevin asks, looking out the window.

"He'll be here any minute," I tell him and Cindy. "He had to grab something from home. Shouldn't we wait for him?"

"My mom's, um, picking me up at four thirty," says Kevin.

"We can start on the poster at least," says Cindy. "We still have to practice the presentation together. Jameel already sent me his part."

"He did?" I ask.

Cindy nods. Maybe this is going to go smoother than I thought.

Kevin asks to use the bathroom, so I go show him where it is. When I come back, Cindy's cutting out the blurbs from her printouts, and I notice she's already marked the places on the poster where the different sections are going. I turn on the TV and find a YouTube channel with chill music.

Cindy gives me a look.

"What? I'm used to drawing with music now."

She shrugs.

I sit down across from her and lean over the poster board. I start penciling in a bearded dragon along the right side, where she's left me a space. I've drawn Vegeta enough times that I pretty much know him by heart. I sketch his spiky head and tiny hands, the slight curve of his tail. As I draw, it reminds me of being in the art studio with Eva, Lucy, and Jason. A couple weeks ago, Mrs. Ocampo called our skills *complementary*. Meaning we're each good at different things, and those things go well together.

I watch Cindy, quietly cutting, a wisp of hair dangling in front of her face. I'm close enough that I can smell her perfume, faint flowery orange.

"How're rehearsals going?" I ask.

"They're okay." Cindy yawns. "Excuse me."

"Mrs. Ocampo said we're going to watch you guys run through the entire show on Monday."

"Cool."

"We were working on the costumes last week—the kids' school uniforms. I think you'll like them."

"I'm sure they're great," she says. I don't know at first if she's being sarcastic, but then she looks up at me and smiles a little.

I smile too.

The toilet flushes. Kevin comes back and Cindy hands him a glue stick. I check the wall clock in our kitchen, then look out the window. Where the heck is Jameel?

A half hour later, after the three of us have basically finished the poster, there's a loud knock at the door. Before I can even get up, Jameel barges in, bringing with him a rush of cold air. He kicks off his shoes and unzips his coat, revealing a small duffel bag. I go close the door behind him.

"What took you so long?" I ask.

"They blocked off the bridge," he says, breathing hard, his nose and ears red. "Construction. I had to go all the way to the next one. But look who I brought!"

Jameel goes over to the coffee table and sets down the duffel, which I notice has black mesh along the sides. He unzips the front and takes out Vegeta, holding him up in the air for everyone to see—like the beginning of *The Lion King*.

Cindy leaps out of her chair. "Ugh, get that thing away from me!"

"His *name* is Vegeta," Jameel says, scowling at Cindy. I catch Kevin staring, wide-eyed. I can't tell if he's interested in Vegeta or afraid of Jameel. Maybe both.

"Can I see him?" I ask. Jameel lets me put Vegeta over my shoulder. I give him a few light scratches under his chin, then I bend down near Kevin and ask if he wants to try petting too. Kevin nods and lightly pats Vegeta's back. Vegeta sticks an arm up and waves.

We all laugh—except for Cindy.

Jameel leans over the dining table and points along Vegeta's back and sides.

"You see how he's darker than before?" he asks me.

"Oh," Kevin says. "That means he's shedding soon, right?"

Jameel beams. "That's right!"

I notice Cindy standing back with her arms crossed. I don't want her to feel left out. "Are you sure you don't want to see him?" I ask. "He won't bite or anything."

She shakes her head.

"Don't forget to wash your hands after," Jameel tells Kevin. "Or you'll get salmonella."

Kevin snatches his hand away. Jameel laughs.

"You guys. Quit messing around," Cindy says. "We've gotta practice our presentation."

"She's right," I tell Jameel. "Let's finish our project, *then* we can play with Vegeta."

"All right, all right." He puts Vegeta back on his shoulder. Cindy takes the poster to the living room and stands it up against the TV. The rest of us sit down on the sofa.

"So, I'll do the introduction and talk about reptiles being cold-blooded," she says. "Then we can just go in order. Kevin, you'll talk about their diet—"

"Wait a minute," says Jameel. He walks up to the poster and points.

"Oh. We got started without you," I explain. "Because Kevin has to go at four thirty."

Jameel looks at Cindy. "This ain't what I sent you."

"It is," she says.

"I wrote more than this. Where's the rest?"

"I had to shorten it," Cindy says. "We agreed on three lines per trait, remember? Any more and it won't fit on the poster. I kept all the important stuff."

"It's *all* important!"

I jump to my feet. "Maybe we can—"

"We can't have one trait with four paragraphs and

the rest with one," says Cindy, rolling her eyes. "It's fine, we'll get a better grade this way."

"No, not fine," Jameel says. "You changed my words. You didn't ask or nothin'!"

"Ugh, why do you have to be such a baby!"

Jameel's whole face is red. He's about to explode. I step between him and Cindy. "You guys, let's just—"

Jameel freezes. He pats his shoulder, then twists his head around.

"Where's Vegeta?" he asks.

He spins in a circle, checking the back of his shirt. Vegeta's not there. I search the carrying case but it's empty. Jameel looks frantically under the sofa and coffee table. Kevin gets up and starts looking too, in the gaps around the TV stand.

Jameel's pulling pillows off the sofa now. He's almost in tears. "Where is he!"

Then Cindy shrieks.

"Kevin," she says. "Don't. Move."

We all look. Vegeta's slowly crawling up Kevin's back, toward his neck. I almost laugh, but then Cindy grabs her binder and starts swiping at Kevin like she's swinging a baseball bat. Kevin freaks out, trying to shake Vegeta off. Jameel spreads both hands. "Stop! Stop!"

Kevin yelps.

The next thing I know, there's a bearded dragon

flying through the air, almost in slow motion, limbs and tail flailing until . . . he lands on all fours on the sofa.

Jameel rushes over and scoops him up, hugs him close to his chest. He gets right in Kevin's face and shouts: "Are you trying to *kill* him!?"

Everything goes quiet for a second. Then Kevin starts crying.

Cindy steps between him and Jameel. She jabs her finger at Jameel's chest. "It's *your* fault," she says. "You shouldn't have let him run loose!"

Jameel's still comforting Vegeta, completely ignoring Cindy. Completely unaware that he just made Kevin cry.

Cindy pulls Kevin away. She grabs the poster too. "We're leaving," she says. "Come on, Kevin. We can wait for your mom upstairs."

"Get outta here, then!" Jameel reels around, his mouth twisted up. "Lizard murderers!"

Cindy takes Kevin away. The kitchen door slams behind them, leaving just me and Jameel, who's pacing back and forth in the living room with Vegeta still hugged to his chest. It's only now that I unfreeze.

"I can't believe you just did that," I tell him. "It wasn't Kevin's fault. He wasn't trying to hurt him!"

Jameel clicks his tongue. "You too? I thought you had my back."

I'm silent. Fire flows up my chest.

"What, I'm supposed to stand here and let 'em kill

Vegeta?" he says. "No. Uh-uh. Besides, she changed what I wrote—"

"So you go and yell in *Kevin's* face? And isn't your mom going to take Vegeta away if you don't do better in school? If you don't stop getting in trouble? If you really cared about him, you wouldn't be so nasty to everyone!"

Jameel presses his lips into a line. Then he says, almost under his breath: "Why you care so much about this anyway?"

"Because you're my best friend!"

Jameel blinks at me. I point toward the front door.

"You should go," I tell him.

He puts Vegeta back in the duffel, zips it up, and leaves without another word. I close the door behind him, fighting back tears. In the main room, markers, glue sticks, and cut scraps of paper are scattered in one big mess all over the table and floor.

We should've done sloths.

ALMOST LIKE BEFORE

I wish it was Thanksgiving already. Because once it's Thanksgiving, it'll almost be Christmas. And once it's Christmas, New Year's isn't far away. Maybe everything will be calmer, and easier, in the new year.

Too bad I can't skip ahead. Monday, when I walk into science, Jameel's already in his seat—talking to Kevin.

I hurry over. By the time I get there, he's holding out his fist to Kevin for a fist bump, like maybe he just apologized. I can't really tell. Kevin returns the fist bump carefully, but what else can he do?

I slide into my seat. Jameel looks at me, then looks away. Just as the bell rings, Cindy comes in with our finished poster board. When Mr. Nagy asks for groups to present, she volunteers us to go first. Probably to get it over with.

Cindy gives her intro, then she and Kevin each read

their different parts off the poster. Jameel does his without complaining, but also without any real energy in his voice.

I was so focused on what Jameel did wrong that I ignored what Cindy did. I get why she had to make his part shorter. But she should've asked him if it was okay—or asked him to do it himself.

Maybe none of this would've happened if I'd defended him then. Maybe we'd be here as a real group, a real team, with Vegeta too.

"Andy," Cindy says. "It's your turn."

Iceman stare. Everyone's waiting for me to talk. My chest feels heavy as I read my lines about why bearded dragons have spiky beards. It's to protect them from bigger lizards and dingoes. When they're afraid, they'll puff up their throats to make themselves look more dangerous.

We sit back down. After all the other groups have gone, Mr. Nagy hands out the grading sheets for everyone's projects. We get an A. Jameel flashes the paper in my direction. "Wait till my ma sees this," he says with a sad smile.

I try to smile back. But I wonder if the grade was worth it.

I have lunch in the art studio again. I need some time away from Cindy and Jameel. Away from everything. Lucy's here today too, but I don't really talk to her or anyone else. I mostly just eat quietly and paint a bunch of thinner hairs on the boar mask, which turns out not to help much. Something's still missing.

In Movement that afternoon, the stage curtain is drawn. When we walk in, Mx. Adler tells everyone to find a seat in the front rows.

"Our show might seem like a ways away," they say once we're all here. "But with Thanksgiving in a few days and winter break soon after, February will be here in no time."

I almost expect a *bah humbug*.

Mx. Adler goes on: "Our work is cut out for us. We'll all have to do what we can to be ready—Mrs. Ocampo and myself included."

The curtains behind Mx. Adler start opening. There are gasps and excited murmurs all around. Jason says, "Oh vow . . . ," then I see it too, lit up by the stage lights: our set. The one *we* built. Lucy's mountain stands tall and sharp in front of the other backdrops, and Eva's fake fire is center stage, fan on and flames waving. Jason's parachute hangs from the rafters, and someone brought in a couple fake palm trees. Even my boar mask is there, stuck on the end of a mop handle—a Lord of the Flies . . . sort of.

Mx. Adler clears their throat. "Today, we'll be running through the entire show from the top. Dancers—you've been rehearsing with tape markers. From now on, it'll be the real deal."

Mrs. Ocampo comes out from backstage. Mx. Adler nods to her. "Let's hand it to our production crew," says Mrs. Ocampo, "for all their hard work!"

Everyone claps and cheers. Eva, Lucy, Jason, and I look at each other. We're all beaming.

Mx. Adler waves everyone up. "Don't just sit there, people. Come familiarize yourselves with the set. Then we'll start our warm-up."

We all rush onto the stage. Everything looks even more amazing under the colorful lights—except maybe the boar. The dancers check out the backdrops and set pieces up close, admiring all the detail. They touch our shoulders and tell us we did a great job.

Including Cindy.

She gives me a big hug, almost out of nowhere. I feel my face go hot, but then I hug her back. I get a weird knot of feelings: It's like before, like the old times—like nothing's changed. But so much feels different too.

"I knew it'd be great," she says. "You're so talented. All of you."

I'm still blushing, but I don't care.

"I'm sorry about Jameel," I whisper, wanting to say more.

She shrugs. "It's okay," she says. Even though she could've said *I told you so.*

Mx. Adler claps twice. "All right, people. Circle up. Then we'll do Egg."

We get into our warm-up circle and link our arms.

Everyone's still wearing big smiles, and I can see Alexandra and a few others bouncing in place. We all take a big bow. And as we come up, I hear a click in the distance.

I look toward the auditorium entrance. That's when I see him, in the doorway, standing completely still: Jameel.

Jameel.

But before I can read his face, he's gone.

LIFTING

At dinner, Hao Bu is the first one who notices.

"Andy, what's wrong? Did you catch the flu? You're barely eating."

Baba puts his palm over my forehead. *"A little warm,"* he says.

I sat through the rehearsal numb. I stayed in Egg the whole time during our warm-up. At first I wondered if I should've gone after Jameel. Then I *knew* I should have. But I couldn't. Why couldn't I?

Mama gets a bottle of American cold medicine from the cupboard. Hao Bu goes into her bedroom and comes back with a finger-sized vial of that Chinese medicine that tastes like gross licorice. I try to wave them both away. "I'm not sick," I tell them. At least not in that way.

I flop into the sofa bed. Bury my face in the pillows.

Mama comes over and covers me with a blanket, and

puts both medicines and a glass of water on the side table. She sticks a thermometer in my mouth. Maybe I could stay home sick tomorrow. And the rest of the week. The rest of sixth grade.

Nope: The thermometer says 98 degrees. The next morning too. My parents make me go to school.

As I walk there, unraked leaves crunching under my sneakers, garbage and recycling trucks roaring and squealing down the streets, I replay everything that's happened between me and Jameel, from him making fun of me to Hi-Chews at 88 Mart. Meeting Vegeta after school and his brother at his birthday party. Wontons with Hao Bu, the cider mill, the group project. Then in the cafeteria . . .

I think back to that vision I had, of a dark hallway between us. There's not just one door in the hallway, there's two. Has mine been closed this whole time?

I know he's going to be mad. I know he's going to feel hurt.

He's probably already both mad and hurt.

But I also know that if I just pretend like nothing's happened at all, everything will only get worse.

So I'll start from the beginning. I'll explain it one step at a time. And if he doesn't want to be friends anymore after that, then I won't bother him ever again.

* * *

I find Jameel in the hallways before the start bell. He's by the courtyard, hanging around Paul and Aiden again. The three of them are laughing at something on his phone. I ignore my spider-sense. I walk up anyway.

Aiden spots me first. "Yo, there he is," he says.

Paul laughs. Jameel turns around. There's a sharp look in his eyes.

"Can we talk?" I ask him. I try to keep my voice down. "Just us?"

His answer comes extra loud: "You wanna talk? Looks more to me like you wanna dance!"

It's then that I see what's on his phone: a video of Cindy and me with plastic bags over our hair. The two of us dancing in my living room.

My face gets hot. How did he even—

"Hey, why don't you show us your moves?" Paul laughs.

"Yeah, let's see whatchu got!" Aiden snickers.

Jameel laughs with them. I try to hold it together. But I barely have time to process what he does next.

"Here, ballerina," he says. "Lemme give you some help." He whips behind me and grabs me around the waist. He lifts me up toward the ceiling and starts spinning around. The other kids in the hallway turn and stare. Paul and Aiden laugh. Everything's so loud and fast.

Then he throws me a little, down the hall. I land one foot on top of another. I trip and crash to the floor.

Everyone's smiles disappear.

It all comes out: a flood. The kind of crying where I'm taking big heaving breaths, the kind of crying that I can't stop. Everything around me muffles and blurs. I'm underwater.

"What's going on here?" says a familiar voice.

It's Mrs. Ocampo.

She helps me up and asks if I'm okay. Paul, Aiden, and most of the other kids scatter. But Jameel's still standing there, staring. He's making a face I've never seen him make before.

Mrs. Ocampo looks back and forth between us.

"My office. Let's go."

I don't even know how I end up there, but I do. We both do. We sit in Mrs. Ocampo's closet office in the back of the art studio while she talks on the phone to the principal, and tells him what happened—what she saw herself and what she found out from the other kids.

Jameel's quiet. And I'm quiet, except for my snuffling. The one time I glance over, he's staring at his feet.

Mrs. Ocampo takes him to the main office first. Then she comes back for me.

As I follow her out, I notice the boar mask on top of the cabinets, glaring down at me.

They call Mama at home. She brings Baba with her, from work. I sit with them in the principal's office while Mrs. Ocampo tries to explain to my parents what happened.

They're both confused, and I can't translate for them. Not just because of language.

After going back and forth a while, the principal calls in Mrs. Hu, the eighth-grade language arts teacher, to help.

With Mrs. Hu translating to Mandarin, Mama and Baba start to understand. Their questions to me and the principal get more specific.

"Jamee? But Jamee is friend," says Baba. "Andy go to he birthday party!"

"Andy, he doing this before?" asks Mama.

"Why he say Andy dancing ballet?"

"He doing art for dancing club? But Andy no in dancing club. He in Math Olympia! With Cindy together!"

At this last statement, everyone stares at me.

At home, Hao Bu and Ah Dia are watching TV when we walk in.

"Eh? How come you're back so early?" asks Hao Bu.

Baba tells me to go to my old room so they can talk and decide what to do. I shut the door behind me and sit down on the bed.

I've been sleeping out in the living room for so long, my room feels smaller than it used to. It smells different too— like my grandparents, but also like China, even though I have no idea how I remember what China smells like.

Once I confessed everything about Movement, Mrs. Ocampo tried to tell my parents that I was doing really well in crew. But then she said, looking at me as she said it, that she had to leave it up to them to decide the consequences for lying about it.

Not that I care what happens to me anymore. In the car I begged Mama and Baba not to tell Cindy's parents. Even though the lying was her idea in the first place. She warned me about Jameel, and I didn't listen. I didn't want to believe.

I don't know what to believe.

My eyes fall on the knickknacks on the dresser. A bowl of uncooked rice, holding burnt sticks of incense. In Hao Bu and Ah Dia's pictures, there's one of Baba's side of the family, all four generations, taken right before my parents and I left China. There I am, just three years old.

I remember the look on Jameel's face in the hallway, the look that stayed on his face in Mrs. Ocampo's office. I just know that *he knows* what he did was wrong. I know he regrets it. But it doesn't make it any less horrible. In fact, it only makes it worse. It's worse than anything a faceless Dementor could have done. Because Jameel's my friend.

My *best* friend. Is. Was.

I feel a sharp pain on the back of my head. I look down.

In my left hand, pinched between my fingers, are five short hairs.

After a while, there's a knock at the door. Mama tells me to come back out. My dad and grandparents are at the dining table, looking worried—or maybe just sad.

Mama sits down too, and I drop into the empty chair between her and Ah Dia. Whatever punishment they have for me, it can't be worse than what's already happened.

"Mama and I talked it over with Hao Bu and Ah Dia," says Baba. *"We decided that you can keep going to your after-school activity."* He switches to English. "Keep make art for dancing club."

I look over at Ah Dia, and he blinks at me through his glasses. His hands are trembling a little in his lap. I just know he had something to do with this.

Baba goes on: "But we have tell Cindy mama and baba."

"No. Baba, please don't."

He shakes his head. "Is not my choice. You are me and Mama son. Cindy is Cindy mama and baba daughter."

Tears fall into my lap.

"What about . . . Jameel?" I ask.

Baba stares at me, a little confused. Then he looks to Hao Bu. We all know that she especially liked Jameel.

Hao Bu puts her hand over mine. *"That's for you and Jamee to figure out,"* she says.

Baba gets out his phone to call Cindy's dad. I walk quickly back to the bedroom and shut the door. I hear Hao Bu tell Mama, *"Let him be."* I hear Ah Dia coughing.

That night, I know the exact moment Cindy's parents tell her she can't go to Movement anymore—that she can't be a part of the winter show. Because I can hear her dad through the ceiling, yelling.

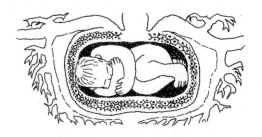

GORGON LIFE

Jameel's suspended the rest of the week—I won't see him until after break.

By the next morning, word of what happened has gotten around. I catch kids avoiding eye contact in the hallways—even Paul and Aiden—as if I'm one of those creatures in Greek mythology that can turn them into stone or salt. Gorgons, I think.

Mr. Nagy doesn't wait for Jameel to get back to switch Aubrey Martinelli into his seat. But I'm still right behind Cindy, who's ignoring me for a very different reason. Later in the lunch line, I notice her sitting with Thuy and Annie again. Not only did her parents take her out of Movement, she probably got kicked out of the tall girl group too. All because of me.

Still . . . at lunch in the art studio, Eva gives me her

bag of beet chips, and Lucy shares the *loukoumades* she helped her grandma make. Even Jason slides over his tray of tater tots.

"Have as many as you want," he says.

My jaw drops. Lucy and Eva stare at him. Lucy points.

"What?"

"You didn't say that in a Dracula voice," I say.

He shrugs.

And I think: Maybe I'm not invisible to everyone.

I've been so focused on Jameel and Cindy, I didn't realize . . . I didn't see I'd made other friends too. Not just Crew Friends or Lunch Friends. *Friend* Friends.

Thanksgiving. Finally. I spend the day helping Mama and Hao Bu get dinner ready, while Baba and Ah Dia watch the parade on TV ("Andy, *we should show your grandparents around downtown more!*"), followed by the annual Detroit Lions football game ("Let's go! Home run!").

Baba's set, as usual, on an authentic American-style holiday for my grandparents. But Mama and Hao Bu have other ideas. Hao Bu takes one look at the jar gravy and boxed mashed potatoes and stuffing he got for this meal, and shoves it all back in the cupboard.

Instead of bread stuffing, Hao Bu fills the bird with a mix of sticky rice, chestnuts, and boiled peanuts. Mama uses real potatoes for the mash, and Hao Bu has the idea of putting taro in there also. We're going to make our own gravy too, by adding flour to the drippings.

I help where I can, peeling potatoes, peeling taro, basting the turkey and checking to see if the little red button's popped up. I open the can of cranberry sauce, flip it over a bowl, and give it a couple shakes. The three of us watch the glossy maroon cylinder squoosh out.

And stay a perfect cylinder.

"This is cranberry?" asks Hao Bu, poking it with a chopstick. The cylinder jiggles for a little too long. She tastes it and makes a weird face. *"It's too sweet,"* she says.

"It has to be," says Mama. *"The meat's very bland and dry."*

How good is Thanksgiving dinner? It's the best. It almost makes me forget about school.

The sticky rice stuffing, soaked in the juices from the turkey, is probably my favorite. Baba loves the turkey, but only after drowning the dry meat in gravy. Hao Bu has to cut Ah Dia's into extra-small pieces so he doesn't have trouble swallowing with his cough, but he likes it too. We all eat so much that we're still full the next morning.

When Mama goes shopping with Cindy's mom and some of their other friends, Baba suggests showing Hao Bu and Ah Dia around Detroit. We went once already, to a barbecue restaurant on Michigan Avenue. But it was rainy that night and we couldn't really walk around. This time, Baba's ready with all kinds of ideas: *We could see the big Christmas tree downtown, or go to the riverfront. There's also the* DIA, Motown Museum . . ."

"*What's the* DIA?" asks Hao Bu.

"*It's an art museum*," says Baba. "Detroit Institute of Arts."

"DIA," says Ah Dia. "Okay."

The best part of the museum is the murals in Rivera Court, which is named after the artist Diego Rivera.

"*Ah! I saw this in a book once!*" Hao Bu says when we step into the echoey room.

The murals cover almost every inch of wall, and are divided into panels like a comic book. The large bottom ones show workers in a car factory, but the panels toward the ceiling skylight are much weirder: lungs that look like tree roots; black, brown, and yellow fists clutching gems and minerals; a baby in a womb, curled up, eyes closed, like in Egg. They don't seem like they have anything to do with the car factory, but they also feel like they have everything to do with it. Diego Rivera didn't just notice what was in his mind's eye—he painted it for us all to see.

Afterwards, we go down Woodward Avenue, past streetlamps hung with garlands and red bows, and drive around until we finally find a parking spot. We walk past the Fox Theatre and Comerica Park, with its huge stone tigers clutching baseball bats in front, that make me wonder what aliens might think if they came to this planet and saw our stadium. Would they think we worshipped tigers? Or had duels like in Roman gladiator times? Would they think our whole species was tigers instead of humans?

Further downtown, near the big Christmas tree, they've set up a holiday market, with stores in tiny huts shaped like gingerbread houses, selling candles and scarves and dog toys. We get hot chocolate from one, then go over to the ice rink and watch the skaters. Little kids cling to the walls, while the hockey-player-looking ones weave in and out of the crowd. Then everyone comes off the ice for the Zamboni.

I've never seen a Zamboni up close before, the way it uses steam like a clothes iron to smooth out all the skate marks, leaving behind a shiny, clean sheet of ice—as if the marks were never there in the first place. As if no one ever struggled or fell.

When nobody's looking, I reach under my hat and rub my bald spot.

Finally, we get coney dogs from a coney restaurant shaped like a tall slice of cake with windows on the cut sides. While we're waiting for our food, Baba asks: "Andy, *have you thought about what you want to do for your birthday this year? Where do you want to go with your friends?*"

I shake my head. "I don't want to do anything."

Normally my mid-December birthday means this time of year feels like one long holiday, but the last thing I want right now is a party.

"We can have a quiet one at home," says Hao Bu.

"We'll get a cake from 88 Mart," says Baba.

I look at Ah Dia and realize that I've been so wrapped up in my own problems that I forgot about his tests and doctor's visits.

"Baba, did you or Mama take Ah Dia to see the specialist?"

My dad shakes his head. "Specialist is all book. No appointment until next year."

I remember something else. "Are we going to Niagara Falls?" I ask. "For Christmas?"

He shakes his head again. "Is too far for Ah Dia. Better staying home." His voice softens. "Maybe next time."

The waiter brings our coney dogs and fries, everything piled high with chili and chopped onions. Cheese on the fries too. I pop a couple in my mouth, the cheese stringy and gooey and warm.

Hao Bu points at the tray. *"Eh, how come you don't need this stuff separated?"* she asks me. *"Isn't the chili and cheese touching the fries?"*

"It's a topping," Ah Dia says. We make eye contact.

"Ba's right." Baba pokes a fork into the fries, then twirls it a couple times like he's eating spaghetti. *"It's not its own food. So Xiaolei's okay with it."*

I watch Hao Bu pick up one of the coneys and carefully turn it around in her hand, then take a big bite, chili dripping down her sleeves. I can't help but laugh. I hand her a stack of napkins.

"*Wits gwelicious!*" she says, her mouth full.

I cut one into smaller pieces for Ah Dia. He loves the coneys too.

On the way home, we drive through whole neighborhoods of big old houses. Whole parts of Detroit I've never seen or heard my parents talk about. We have to exit early because our usual one is closed for construction. We follow the detour and along the service drive, closer and closer toward Jameel's apartment.

When we pass the building, though, something feels off. I glance out Hao Bu's window, and that's when I see what's changed: the pedestrian bridge is gone. Demolished.

All that's left are the twisty ends of rusted metal bars, sticking out where it used to be.

DECEMBER

FOG JUICE

The weather changes. No snow yet, but definitely below freezing. It's cold enough that my parents want me to stop walking in the mornings. The Monday after Thanksgiving, when I pile in the car with the rest of my family, everything's sleepy and nobody talks. I stare out the window the whole way to school.

As soon as Jameel shows up in science, though, my body wakes up. I try to ignore him but it's almost impossible—his new seat is right near the front. In the hallways, turning random corners, I flash back to that day. Not even the art studio feels fully safe. Walking in at lunch, I remember the two of us sitting in the back office. The look on his face.

It's only when the others stroll in that I start to relax a little. Lucy and Jason seem especially chatty, and Eva brings in a black metal box that looks like a mini cannon, along with a jug labeled FOG JUICE. She plugs the box in and turns it on. A minute later, the art studio is shrouded in mist.

Mrs. Ocampo rushes in, her eyes wide.

"Eva, you almost gave me a heart attack!" she says, realizing it's not smoke. She waves her hand to clear the fog. "This'll be great for the show, though."

Mrs. Ocampo shares some Filipino desserts she made over break—these yummy fried banana rolls called *turon*. Everyone eats and talks about their Thanksgivings, and new ideas they've had since we saw the dancers rehearse—since the day Jameel saw me. Lucy wants to cut bushes from our plywood scraps and put wheels on them to roll around. Jason, back to doing his Dracula voice, wants to make a parachutist to attach to the parachute—"Like a scarecwoah, ah!"

The whole time, my boar mask sits on top of its cabinet, glaring down at me. I wish I liked it more than I do.

Without Cindy, Movement feels different. The tall girl group feels incomplete. After we circle up and stretch, Mx. Adler has us widen our circle even more. They tell us that we're doing a new warm-up today, that not even the eighth graders have done before. It's called "The Machine."

It sounds kind of menacing.

"Who'd like to start us off?" asks Mx. Adler.

We all look at each other. Nobody wants to be the first. Then Jason raises his hand.

Mx. Adler has Jason stand in the middle and imagine that he's part of a bigger, complicated machine. "Now perform a repetitive motion with your body," they tell him. "Everyone else, pay close attention. One by one, you will be adding to the machine."

Jason thinks for a second and starts flapping his arms up and down. Lucy and I giggle. After a while, Viola jumps to one side of him and acts like she's pulling his arm. It looks like she's working an old water pump.

I'm not the only one who thinks that. Eva goes in front of Jason and pretends his mouth is the spout, and she's catching the water with a bucket. She catches it and dumps it out. Catches and dumps.

One by one, we all add to the machine, laughing as it gets bigger, weirder. Some of the movements are specific, like Arj Patel doing the backstroke on the floor. Others are more general, like Mai stomping her feet, or Lucy twisting left and right with her arms in front of her. Soon, everyone's found their part in the machine except me.

But then I see an opening: I put myself in the space between Lucy and Jason. I pretend she's moving a heavy weight, and I grab it and hang it on Jason's other, free arm. I close the loop.

We all move together. I'm amazed that we're so in sync. Then Mx. Adler adds a twist. They tell Jason to slowly speed up. And because he speeds up, the rest of us do too.

We go faster and faster. But right before we go too fast—so fast that the machine's about to break—Mx. Adler says, "Slow down."

We start slowing down.

As we do, a weird thought pops into my head: This machine wouldn't work if even one person was out of sync. If even one person refused to do their part.

"Slow all the way to a stop."

We grind to a frozen halt.

"Well done," says Mx. Adler. "Now circle back up."

We all look at each other, like we can't believe it's over. My heart's pounding, not just from the movement. We unfreeze and step back into our closing circle, smiling and laughing. I feel like something inside me scrambled—in a good way.

As usual, Mx. Adler doesn't explain what this exercise is supposed to teach us. They leave us to figure it out for ourselves.

NOT SO BOARING

It's like that for the rest of the week.

At lunch I help everyone with their new ideas—help Eva paint and Lucy cut plywood, help Jason sew patches onto an old green jumpsuit. If I keep my hands busy, it keeps my brain busy. As long as my brain's busy, it doesn't go where I don't want it to go.

I catch Jameel looking at me a couple times in science. On Thursday, he stays after to talk to Mr. Nagy, and he glances at me then too. I try my best to ignore him, and doodle in my sketchbook. But I just swirl my pen in circles and don't draw anything real. My mind's eye is completely blank.

Then: Saturday morning. I wake up to Baba's phone voice. Footsteps and the jingle of car keys. The sound of a zipper—Mama zipping up Ah Dia's poofy winter coat. And in the background, violin. Cindy's parents making her practice upstairs.

"Andy, *you're awake?*" asks Hao Bu.

I rub my eyes. "I'm awake," I tell her.

She sits down on the edge of the sofa bed and hands me a plate with a pair of steamed buns. One pork, the other a green onion roll. When I smell them, I'm suddenly starving, like I haven't eaten in days. I take a big bite of the pork bun, then unfurl a ribbon from the roll. It's salty and pillowy and good.

"Yes. Yes. We understand," my dad's saying. At first I think it's about Ah Dia again, but when Baba looks at me, I get the feeling that maybe it's Jameel's mom, calling to apologize. Like one of those conversations that parents have with each other, then don't really talk to us kids about.

"Andy, *your baba's off work today,*" says Mama. *"We're taking Hao Bu and Ah Dia to the CCC first, then we're going to* Costco." She grabs my coat from the closet and holds it up. *"Do you want to come with us?"*

Hao Bu pats my knee, then takes the empty plate from me. *"Come with Hao Bu and Ah Dia,"* she says. *"We'll go together.* Okay?"

The violin screeches on a broken note. It starts over again. I roll out of bed and put on my clothes.

The community center used to be an old elementary school. Being here on Saturday takes me back to when Cindy and I would come for Chinese school. We only stopped because she convinced our parents that we weren't learning much vocab—that we could learn more by watching Chinese dramas with the subtitles on. I definitely don't miss the vocab.

But walking down the halls today, passing rows of wooden cubbies overflowing with backpacks and coats, and seeing kids in classrooms practicing watercolors and calligraphy, and hearing basketball dribbles and squeaky shoes echoing from the gym . . . there's something I do miss. Maybe it's all this traditional Chinese stuff—even though basketball isn't exactly traditional.

Or maybe it's just seeing so many kids who look like me. Enough to fill a whole school.

Baba takes it all in, like it's been a while since he's been here too. We go to the cafeteria, where a bunch of older people are sitting at square tables, drinking tea and playing mahjong. Others are walking laps along the edges of the room, as if it's a race track.

Inside, Hao Bu helps Ah Dia take off all his winter layers, and my parents spot some people they know and go say hi. I notice a faint drumming in the distance, different than the basketball dribbles coming from the gym. This beat is faster and less random. I think I hear cymbals too. While no one's looking, I slip away.

I follow the sound. Down one hallway, there are pictures on the walls with little plaques like at a museum. I see news articles about Detroit's original Chinatown, and black-and-white photos of parades and protests, and a girl wearing a big button that says

I AM AN AMERICAN CHINESE. Another photo shows a memorial for someone named Vincent Chin.

It's not stuff we ever learned in school—my regular school—and it's not stuff that Mama and Baba ever told me. On the next wall is a row of maps of Michigan and other Midwest states, showing the Chinese population of each county over time. The 1920 map says there were eight Chinese people living in ours—just eight! Then in 1970, there were 763, and by 2000, there were 10,874.

I wonder what the number will be in the next map. Whatever it is, three of those people will be Mama, Baba, and me.

The drumming's louder, the beat faster. I'm getting close. I follow the sound to a room near the gym.

There, my eyes immediately go to the pair of giant colorful animal heads bopping around. They have big round eyes and shocks of yellow fur, and red nose pompoms and flaming green skin. They're lions! For a Chinese lion dance!

The drumming stops. The lions stop. They disassemble into two pairs of teenagers—like a reverse-Voltron. Each mask also has a long cape connected to it, with its own ripply yellow fur, that covers the dancer who's the butt. The guy in charge tells the dancers and other kids watching to take a water break, and pulls out his phone. Wait—is that Lang Uncle?

"Xiaolei, there you are!" Mama says, coming in from the hallway with Baba.

The guy turns and waves at us. It *is* Lang Uncle. Baba spots him too. "Kingston? *Perfect! I've been meaning to talk to you.*"

When they start talking about visas and green cards, I look at the masks again, the closer one sitting next to me on the floor. I can't take my eyes off it. I remember seeing lion dances here as a kid, but I never paid that much attention to them. Now I try to soak up all the details: the wide flappy mouth, full of big white teeth. The round dome mirror in the middle of the forehead. The fuzzy gold horn curling up the back!

The mask feels so alive, even when no one's wearing it. It's colorful and fun . . . but also *menacing*.

"*They're not issuing green cards like they used to,*" Lang Uncle's telling Baba. "Not with the current political situation. But I'll get you the website for—" He catches me staring at the mask. "Andy, do you want to try it on?"

I nod.

He hands me the lion mask. I grab it by the collar and twirl the cape behind me. I lower the mask down over my head, careful not to drop it. It's both lighter and heavier than I expect—something about the way it balances. Inside, the frame's made of strips of wood instead of wire, and there's a pair of plastic handles behind the mouth opening. The ceiling lights filter through, a kaleidoscope of colors. I shake the head a little and the mouth flaps up and down. I almost want to start dancing right then and there—I'm a lion! *Roar!*

When I take the mask off, everyone's smiling at me.

"So what do you think?" asks Lang Uncle. "Do you want to join our lion dancing team?"

I shake my head. "I'm busy with school," I tell him.

He laughs and says to my parents, "Our kids' schedules are more packed than ours!"

"Andy is in dancing club at he American school!" Baba says, proud.

"Is that so?"

I nod. "I do crew—mostly costumes and stuff." When I hand back the mask, I think of a question. "Lang Uncle, did you . . . make it?"

"What, this thing?" He laughs again. "We ordered it online!"

"Oh."

The kids on the lion dance team come back in, talking and laughing. Most of them are teenagers, but a couple look like they're my age. Baba and Lang Uncle finish talking and wave goodbye, and Mama pulls me toward her and puts her hand on my shoulder.

As we leave, I can't help sneaking one last look at the masks. They're so much better than my boar mask. My boar looks dull and wimpy by comparison.

But . . . maybe I can do something about that.

FIRST FLAKE

I draw more boars. Boars with fuzzy beards and eyebrows, with big teeth and tusks, and flames all over. I draw them in neon highlighter colors, bright pinks and yellows and greens. I fill page after page in my sketchbook.

Monday at lunch, the first thing I do is pull the mask down from on top of its cabinet. I grab a pair of scissors and cut a slit along the bottom. I start peeling off the gray-brown skin.

"Vhat are you *dooing*!?" Jason says, his hands over his head like the Jackie Chan meme.

"I'm fixing it," I tell him. The others gather around me. Eva nods a few times, like she approves of the destruction in general. Lucy looks a little more worried. I hand her my sketchbook.

I peel off every last shred of skin. All that's left is

the wire frame. Mrs. Ocampo comes in, and I show her the sketchbook too, along with videos I found over the weekend—one of lion dancers parading up and down Mott Street in New York City's Chinatown, a couple others on how they traditionally make the masks.

By the end, everyone's as excited as I am. Eva says she has a bunch of fake fur that she can bring in from when she dressed her dog up as the Grinch. Jason says he can help me sew the cape. Lucy offers to weld on metal handles, which . . . I think involves some kind of blowtorch? And Mrs. Ocampo's interested not only in my designs, but also that there are *two* dancers for the lion instead of just one.

"I think Mx. Adler should see this right now," she says, and goes off to get them. It feels like an avalanche of a different kind.

I'm too excited to eat. I grab the spool of craft wire from the cabinets, and Jason says he'll help me cut some newspaper strips for the paper mache, forgetting to do his Dracula voice again. When I sit back down, there's a knock at the door—that was fast!

But it's not Mrs. Ocampo and Mx. Adler.

It's Jameel.

Jameel.

Alarm bells. Sirens. Lightning striking a tree. Eva cuts Jameel off at the doorway. Jason comes over next to me. Lucy pops up too, suddenly holding a power drill. I clutch my sketchbook like it's some kind of shield.

"You can't be here," Eva tells him.

"Can I talk to Andy?" Jameel asks.

Eva glances at me. I'm too frozen to nod or shake my head.

"He doesn't want to talk to you," she says.

"I wanna apologize."

"I think you should go."

Lucy's drill whirs a couple of times—I don't think by accident. Then Mrs. Ocampo and Mx. Adler show up.

At first, I think Jameel's just going to run off. But he turns his attention to the two of them instead. They go out into the hallway and talk in voices too low to hear. Everyone else relaxes a little.

Jason asks me if I'm okay. I nod but go sit by the window. I notice that I'm breathing hard, like I just ran a mile. For Jameel to show up to the art studio—How did he even know I was here? Just seeing him at the door made it all come flooding back. The auditorium. The hallway. The principal's office. Cindy's dad yelling upstairs. A long line of dominos tipping over.

I feel that itchy feeling, not just on my head but all over. I sit on my hands so I don't pull any hairs. I think about Cindy again: Why haven't I tried to tell her I'm sorry, the way Jameel's trying?

Maybe because it doesn't feel like any of it's my fault. I never wanted to bleach my hair. I never wanted to lie about Movement. I never even wanted to *do* Movement.

Or maybe it's that *everything*'s my fault. For not speaking up. For keeping the lie going. For not believing her about Jameel. For trusting him too much.

Or not trusting him enough.

The door clicks. My shoulders tense. Mrs. Ocampo and Mx. Adler come back inside—without Jameel. Mrs. Ocampo pulls a chair up next to me, and asks if I'm okay. I don't know.

She sighs, and says softly, "Jameel asked me to pass along a message, if that's all right with you."

I look into Mrs. Ocampo's face. She looks sad. I nod.

"He said he wants to come see our show. But only if you want him there."

I feel a lump in my throat.

"He also said that Mr. Nagy is going to adopt Vegeta. He said you'd know what he meant."

The lump gets bigger. I know how hard it must've been for him to ask Mr. Nagy that. But I'm not sure if it's too late. I'm not sure if I've already closed my door in that dark hallway for good. Locked it and threw away the key.

Mrs. Ocampo glances over her shoulder at Mx. Adler, who's looking over my wireframe boar mask, and at all the ripped scraps of paper mache.

"Andy, do you want to show Mx. Adler your idea?" she asks gently. "Or would you prefer that I do it?"

I flip open my sketchbook and hand it to her.

We all gather around while Mrs. Ocampo talks Mx.

Adler through my drawings. She plays the videos too.

"That's really interesting—having a pair of dancers for the boar." Mx. Adler points.

"Exactly what I was thinking," says Mrs. Ocampo. "Can we spare any bodies?"

Mx. Adler thinks for a moment. "We're already one short with Cindy gone. But maybe Arj could be the second. I'd also want someone with lion dancing experience involved. We have to be responsible and respectful if we're to work in a Chinese cultural element."

My mind jumps to Lang Uncle. But I can't find any words.

"I'll ask around," says Mrs. Ocampo.

"Might be too short notice anyway," says Mx. Adler. "We only have a handful of rehearsals left."

Mrs. Ocampo looks at me. "Even if we don't change the choreography, do you agree that it'd make sense to go forward with Andy's new designs? I just think they're wonderful."

"Looks like we're already committed." Mx. Adler nods at the pile of scraps. Then they add: "Great idea, Andy."

Eva slaps my hand, and Lucy touches my shoulder. Jason looks at me like, *Did Grumpy Teacher just say something nice?* Then the end-lunch bell sounds. Mrs. Ocampo hands me back my sketchbook.

"Andy, if you'd rather, you can stay here next period while I teach my class at the elementary school," she says. "I'll write you a pass."

I shake my head. I want to work on the boar, but I also don't want to be here alone. So I take off with the others.

On my way to class, I stop at the courtyard. Inside, the tree's leaves are mostly gone, and the few that are left are shriveled up and brown. Steam billows out from the heating ducts, almost covering the bench and dried plants.

For some reason, I think of Baba's face at the community center—when we were walking down the halls. We used to go there for events around Mid-Autumn Festival and Lunar New Year too, I remember. But that was more when we first moved and didn't know a lot of people here yet. Once my parents found their group of Shanghainese friends, we pretty much stopped going.

This whole time, Baba's been trying to show Hao Bu and Ah Dia what life is like in America. I think maybe he forgot that Chinese stuff is a part of it too.

I watch the steam in the courtyard float up and up, blending into the gray sky. It's then that I see, drifting down from above, a single snowflake.

I let out a small breath. I hurry back to the art studio. I catch Mrs. Ocampo just as she's leaving.

"I know someone," I tell her. "Someone who can show us the lion dance."

Outside, the snow keeps falling, flakes big and soft— though it's not quite cold enough for them to really stick.

That night at dinner, while Hao Bu ladles turkey soup

with hunks of winter melon into our bowls, and Mama's on her phone secretly selling more stuff from our basement, Baba and Ah Dia stand in front of the living room window, watching the snow. When Baba helps Ah Dia back into his chair, he gets his best idea yet—or at least what he *thinks* is his best idea.

"This year, for holiday, we go to camping!"

I can't help laughing. Camping's a perfect combination of the American life stuff Baba's been trying to show my grandparents. He even counts it out on his fingers:

"Have fishing . . . have hiking . . . have BBQ grill . . ."

It'd make total sense, if it wasn't freezing out.

Mama says it first: "Aiya, is too cold for fishing. Too cold for camping!"

"Ice fishing! Lake Michigan! We can build camping fire, sleep next to camping fire. Make hot chocolate!"

"And s'mores," I suggest.

"*What about your ba? We might as well just rent a cabin!*"

"Log cabin! Like on bottle!"

"What bottle?"

Baba goes into the cupboards while Mama explains to Hao Bu and Ah Dia what we're talking about. He brings back a plastic bottle of pancake syrup. Right there on the label is what he's picturing: a little log cabin, glowing warm windows, smoke from the chimney, all blanketed in snow.

Mama sighs. She knows she can't talk him out of this now. *"At least let's find one that has central heat."*

Baba gets the tablet from the living room and hands it to me.

"Andy, you find for us. Let's staying for Christmas and New Year!"

"Make sure have nice kitchen too," adds Mama.

I wake the tablet and open the browser. There's a search results page up from before, for "How much cost America nursing school."

I look at my parents. My mom's making sure we all have napkins, then checking her phone for new sales. My dad takes a big bite of winter melon and immediately spits it back into the bowl. He starts fanning his mouth.

"Still too hot," he says.

Mama laughs, then goes back to her phone. I feel my insides twist. Maybe she's not checking for new sales at all.

"Andy, *did you find anything?"* Baba asks, blowing on a spoonful of soup.

I open a new tab and search for cabins on Lake Michigan. I find a site that lists a bunch—some of them up north, but others a little closer, in West Michigan, halfway between here and Chicago. A lot of the cabins are nestled in the woods, and the descriptions say they're within walking distance of the lake. A couple of them remind me of the Langs' house.

I ask before I forget: "Baba, can Lang Uncle come show my dance club the Chinese lion dance?"

"What? Your dancing club want doing lion dancing?"

"Well, it's a boar, not a lion, because the show's based on this story about—" I stop. It'd take forever to explain. "Just . . . can you ask him if he can come to my school sometime?"

"Okay, I ask." Baba shrugs. "You find log cabin?"

I hand him the tablet and he scrolls through the listings. *"Wah, the nice ones are kind of expensive,"* he says.

"How much?" asks my mom. Baba shows her the screen. She stares at it for a while, looks at my grandparents and me, then goes to the bedroom and comes back with a wad of cash.

Baba's eyes get wide. *"Where did that come from?"* he asks, soup dribbling from his mouth.

"I want to show you something," Mama says.

She leads him down into the basement. I follow along. When Mama pulls the string for the ceiling light, Baba shouts, *"We've been robbed!"*

Mama sighs. *"We haven't been robbed."*

"It's really strange," says Baba, looking around. *"They only took stuff from our side of the—oh."*

I giggle. Mama actually rolls her eyes.

When we go back upstairs, my dad starts scrolling though the cabin listings again. *"Maybe we can get one with a hot tub,"* he says.

After dinner, I help clear the table while Mama loads dishes into the dishwasher.

"Is okay," she says. "You leaving for Mama wash."

But I stay and help anyway. We form a little line, her scraping the gunk off a plate or bowl and me putting it in the dishwasher racks. Baba's the outgoing one, the one who leaps before he looks. But Mama's always been there to clean up after him, sometimes literally. I think about that day in the car when he said she'd be leaving her job at 88 Mart. How he said, "Family is most important." I know he was talking about Ah Dia then, but what about Mama? She's obviously part of our family too. What about what *she* wants?

"*Okay, enough,*" says Mama. She wrings out a cloth to wipe down the table. "*Go watch TV with Hao Bu and Ah Dia.*"

I do what she says.

Outside, the snow's letting up, barely powdering the sidewalk. And my dad's in the other room, talking loudly on the phone with Lang Uncle.

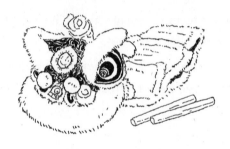

A DEMONSTRATION

Over lunch the next week, I completely redo the boar's eye sockets. I widen the opening for the mouth and make bigger tusks that curve up like horns. Lucy adds a pair of thick wooden dowels for handles, and after I paper mache, Eva paints black and gold flames on the skin. Jason sews a cape, frilled with fake green fur, and together we glue more of it around the eyes and mouth. We even find a tiny round makeup mirror for the middle of the forehead.

When I look over the finished mask, I see, in the mirror, my own reflection.

At the next Movement, Mx. Adler tells us all to have a seat in the front rows again—then sits down with us. It's Mrs. Ocampo who takes the stage.

"You've all worked so hard in the past few months," she says. "Mx. Adler and I thought it'd be nice to take our last meeting of the year off. And have a little party to celebrate how far we've come."

Cheers and hoots. Mx. Adler twists around in their seat. "Now, now, we'll be back at it in the new year. Remember, we only have four more rehearsals leading up to our—"

"And rest is important too." Mrs. Ocampo shoots a look at Mx. Adler, who turns back around and folds their arms. "We have some snacks and drinks set up backstage. But before that, we have a different treat, thanks to our very own Andy Zhou."

Mrs. Ocampo smiles at me. I get a few claps and cheers. Jason pats my back.

"Let's give it up for the Metro Detroit Lion Dancers!"

Everyone claps and murmurs. Mrs. Ocampo exits stage left, and Lang Uncle and a teenager wheel in a barrel drum stage right. Four more dancers come out, each pair carrying a lion mask. They're all wearing pants fringed with fur too, which they weren't wearing when I first saw them at the community center. They set the masks down in front of them.

The drummer lifts up two drumsticks, and Lang Uncle opens a pair of hand cymbals. Everyone goes quiet.

Lang Uncle crashes the cymbals together. The drummer goes into a drumroll. The dancers bow, then hurry under the masks and capes. The two lions lie still for a second, as if they're both sleeping. Then they wake up.

They shake their heads left and right, slowly at first, then faster and faster. Lang Uncle crashes the cymbals again and the beat changes. The lions leap up, bow three times, and start dancing around the stage.

Everything swirls inside me. The drums feel like my heart thumping. The cymbals sound like crashing thunder. Other kids clap and hoot, and I suddenly wish Cindy were here to see this. We cheer when the lions kick and duck and dodge and knock each other out. We cheer again when they come back alive. We leap to our feet as they prance down the side steps and run the row between the seats and stage. We stay standing for the big finale, when both lions rear up toward the sky. I see the dancers in the back, lifting the front ones by the waist.

It's too big, almost, every sound and feeling at once. I don't know whether to laugh or cry. I clap and cheer, at the top of my lungs, with everyone else.

And maybe it's watching them live in person like this, or knowing that I made it happen—I helped bring them in. But it's the best lion dance ever. Better than any of the videos I found, and for sure better than anything I could have imagined. It isn't until the lions go back to sleep at the end, and the drumming stops, and the dancers take off the masks and capes, that I remember again there are kids under there—because the lions just feel so alive.

Lang Uncle and the dancers bow. We give them a standing ovation.

* * *

Afterwards, my whole body tingles—in a good way. Kids swarm the stage to talk to the dancers as if they're celebrities. Mx. Adler and Mrs. Ocampo go up to chat with Lang Uncle. While they talk, I run and fetch the boar mask from the art studio to show him.

"Andy, you made this?" he says, putting it over his head and looking around. "It's great! How did you learn to do this?"

I explain how everyone in crew helped, and also I found some YouTube tutorials.

He takes off the mask and laughs. "You can learn anything on YouTube. You really can."

While everyone else is digging into the snacks and juice boxes backstage, Mx. Adler calls Alexandra over and has her do her part of the boar hunt number for Lang Uncle. He watches carefully, nodding a lot.

"Now, is it ever traditionally done with just one dancer?" Mx. Adler asks afterwards. "Or is it always a pair?"

Lang Uncle thinks for a second. "Ideally you'd have two, but I think you could make it work with just one. You wouldn't do any jumps or dips, but those are more advanced moves anyway."

I glance at the Chinese teenagers, all still wearing their frilly lion-leg pants, and I remember how much fun Cindy and I had recording dance challenges in my living room, before everything blew up. If she were here, she'd be the first one to volunteer to be the extra dancer. I picture a ghost version of Cindy, haunting the stage.

I shake the vision away. Cindy's not here. It's just me.

"I can do it. I can be the butt," I say. Out loud.

Mx. Adler and Lang Uncle look at me.

"I mean, if that's okay."

Lang Uncle laughs. "We call it the tail. You might be the first kid I've met who didn't want to be the head."

Mx. Adler puts their hand on their chin. They look between Alexandra and me, thinking, maybe, *It just might work.*

I thought that being the tail would mostly mean rocking my hips back and forth. But it's hard work, staying in sync with Alexandra. Lang Uncle suggests a few moves to make the boar dance more like a lion dance, and he coaches us through them while Mrs. Ocampo records it for us to watch later. We're not doing any lifts, thankfully.

At home, I practice by myself after dinner. I don't want my whole family seeing—at least not until the actual show. So I do it instead in our newly cleaned basement. I practice the stance Lang Uncle showed us called horse stance, where you crouch a little with your feet planted shoulder-width apart. I wonder what Jameel might think knowing that I'm also a dancer now, that I'm not just in crew.

And what would Cindy?

It doesn't matter. I'm doing this for me.

Soon, it's Friday. The last half-day before winter break. Outside it's unusually warm—warm enough that I'm walking home. On my way out, as I say goodbye to Jason and Lucy, the hallways are alive with smiles and laughter. I picture a flock of sparrows, all in the same tree, tweeting up a storm, then flying away.

Before I leave, though, I stop by the art studio to see Mrs. Ocampo—she said she wanted to give me something before break. When she goes into her back office to get it, I pick up the boar mask and admire it one more time.

Is it weird to admire something you made yourself? Maybe it's not so weird—because I'm proud of it. Proud of the work that my friends and I did. I put the mask on and get into horse stance. I hold the mouth flap closed and bow, like Lang Uncle showed Alexandra, then shake from side to side. I know I'm supposed to be the tail, but still.

"Ah, a man of many talents!"

I take off the mask, blushing a little. Mrs. Ocampo smiles.

"I heard it was your birthday recently," she says. She hands me a wrapped present, flat and rectangular, almost the size of a portable game console. "Go ahead, open it!"

I rip off the wrapping paper. It's a watercolor set! One of those nice ones where each color is in its own little tray.

"Thanks so much!" I tell her, staring at all the colors.

"Happy birthday, Andy," she says. "Happy holidays too."

I tuck the gift carefully into my backpack, where it won't get jostled around. I wish Mrs. Ocampo a happy holidays back.

"See you after break," she says. "Keep practicing."

"I will." I smile.

On my way out, I walk toward the glass courtyard, and slow to a stop in front of it. The whole courtyard is glowing from the sun, lit up like a jewel. Every last leaf has fallen off the tree, leaving just the thin, bony branches. It almost reminds me of a person, old and frail.

"*Cornus kousa,*" says a voice. It's Mx. Adler, wearing a wool coat and fingerless gloves, and a gray knit hat that looks two sizes too big.

"Huh?"

They nod toward the courtyard. "That tree, it's a *cornus kousa*—kousa dogwood. Interesting story: They originally planted a different dogwood species there—*cornus florida*—but it died from a fungal disease. So they replaced it with a kousa, which isn't native, but does much better against the fungus."

"Is it a . . ." I try to remember the term. "Invasive species?"

Mx. Adler looks at me. They open their mouth but

take a moment to answer, like they know I might be asking about something more, something else.

"They're not native to this area, no," they finally say. "But neither are apple trees. Or the honeybee. And those big catalpas outside the school? They were brought up from the Mississippi valley."

Mx. Adler looks back at the dogwood.

"Not everything non-native is necessarily invasive. It's only invasive if it takes over, makes everything the same. And I'd rather there be a tree there than not, wouldn't you?"

I stare again at the barren tree. I try to imagine what the courtyard would look like without it. It'd feel emptier—the old bench more lonely. There'd be no branches for cardinals to land on, no shade for the grasses and plants underneath. Now, instead of seeming thin and frail, the dogwood feels almost proud, like it's holding up the sky.

Mx. Adler clears their throat. Their face changes, as if they just remembered they're supposed to be the grumpy teacher. They sling their bag over their shoulder and leave.

"Happy holidays," I tell them.

They wave without turning around.

THE WAY IT WAS

"Andy, *go get your hao bu and ah dia*," says Baba. He takes my backpack from me and stuffs it in the trunk next to the fishing gear. *"We're almost ready to go."*

"Do you want to bring your pillow too?" asks Mama, lugging over a pair of suitcases. *"Just grab it."*

I pop back inside. *"Hao Bu, Ah Dia, we're leaving soon,"* I tell them. Hao Bu's putting on a scarf, and Ah Dia's already dressed, watching TV from the sofa. I grab my pillow from beside him. He turns off the TV and sets down the remote. Then he tips forward to get up, like I've seen him do hundreds of times.

Except this time, he freezes halfway. As if he's a robot that suddenly ran out of batteries. He's stuck.

I rush over to help. Hao Bu comes too.

"What's the matter, old man?" she asks. *"Come on, just a little more."*

"I can't," says Ah Dia, still frozen. His face is red. A string of saliva falls from his mouth.

"What do you mean you can't? Just sit and try again!" Hao Bu holds his arm and puts one hand on his back to help him sit. He still won't budge.

"What's the matter with you?"

"I can't!"

My parents barge in the front door. They must've heard us from outside. I stand back to give them room. Baba tries to help Ah Dia but the same thing happens. He eventually has to pick up Ah Dia's entire body and lay him flat on the sofa, before Ah Dia can relax.

"Old man, we don't have to go," Baba says, his voice shaky. *"We can just stay here for Christmas."*

"Nonsense," says Ah Dia, eyes closed. He takes slow, shallow breaths. *"I just need to. Lie down. For a second."*

Hao Bu sits on the edge of the sofa and holds Ah Dia's hand. Baba stands and stares, his face full of worry. Mama comes up behind me and runs her hand through my hair. Everyone's so still that I picture a Christmas manger, or a scene from an old oil painting.

Mama's hand grazes my bald spot. She leans in for a closer look, and pulls back some of the hair around it. *"Eh, what happened here?"* she asks.

I keep looking at Ah Dia. He blinks a couple times, the corners of his eyes wet. His breathing starts to calm.

"I pull it sometimes," I tell Mama in Chinese. *"When I feel uncomfortable, I pull it."*

She smooths my hair over the spot. Then kisses the top of my head. Something in me feels lighter.

"Why don't you go put your pillow in the car," Mama says softly.

Outside, there's an icy wind that I'm pretty sure wasn't there before. I start to put my pillow in the trunk, but then I move it to the front, in case Ah Dia needs extra cushioning. When I shut the door, I hear the crunch of footsteps on gravel. I turn and see Cindy carrying a bag of trash to the bins along the side of the house.

"Cindy!" I call out. I walk quickly over.

She lifts the garbage bin lid and puts the bag in. She looks at me. Something in her face says *What do you want?*

I want to talk. About everything that's happened this year. I want to tell her about lion dances and boar dances, and going to Chinese school again and missing it. About how Ah Dia just froze like a robot running out of batteries. Most of all, I want to tell her I'm sorry, and ask her if she'll ever stop being mad at me. If we'll ever be friends again. Not even *best* friends—just regular friends would be okay.

"So, um . . . how's it going?" I ask.

"It's fine," she says. She folds her arms across her chest. She curls her toes a little in her slippers. But she doesn't leave.

"Lang Uncle came to Movement last week." It's the

only other thing I can think to say. "His lion dance team did a demonstration for everyone. We're going to make it part of the boar hunt number. And I'm gonna be the tail. It's not called the butt, it's called the tail. I just thought you should know. So thanks, I guess."

That didn't come out the way I wanted. Why did it sound like a mix of me bragging and being mad at her?

"That's great," she says, her voice flat. "I'm happy for you." She turns to go.

"Wait."

Cindy looks at me. Her hair's almost half black now. Even through her sweatshirt and layers of clothes underneath, I can see the shape of her collarbones.

"I'm sorry," I tell her. "About Movement."

She sighs. "It's okay, really. I'm not mad about Movement."

"You're not?"

She shakes her head. "Just . . . forget it, okay? I forgive you."

I watch her walk up the side driveway. I thought that once you apologized to someone and they forgave you, everything's supposed to go back to how it was before.

The front door opens with a loud squeak. "Andy, *where are you?*" Baba calls. "*Time to go!*" His voice softens. "*Come on, old man . . .*"

I turn around and notice that the lid to the garbage bin is still open. When I go to close it, the top of the bag Cindy put in untwists. Inside is a Faygo Red Pop, a bag of airline pretzels, a taxidermy baby squirrel—her entire collection of mini things.

I look up the driveway again. Cindy's already gone.

I reach into the bin and fish out Eliza the squirrel. And when I do, what's under it makes me almost knock the lid shut:

Ziplock bags. Filled with food—cooked food, all touching and mushed together. Almost entire meals, barely eaten.

Chinese people hate wasting food.

So what—

How . . .

IT JUST KEEPS GOING

Is everyone just carrying around big secrets all the time?

That's what I think about as we drive away from the house. I remember one of the moms at the Langs' party saying how much thinner Cindy was. I think about how tired and cranky she's seemed. Is it—is she not eating? Why would she not eat? Could it have something to do with me . . . being friends with Jameel?

Then I watch Mama next to me, looking out the car window, and wonder if she was saving that money she made selling stuff to go to nursing school. Or if she's even told Baba about it. I remember the questions Baba had for Lang Uncle about green cards and visas. I know those things have to do with my grandparents staying here longer, so Ah Dia can get treatment. But I don't know if my parents have even talked it over with them.

When we merge onto the freeway, I look at the cars around us, and picture the people inside with their own secrets, all following them around. Like shadows only they can see.

The maps app says the cabin's two and a half hours away. But it takes longer because Baba pulls over every thirty minutes and makes Ah Dia get out and stretch.

Driving west on the freeway, we leave behind the houses and stores, and the four lanes each way shrink down to two. Baba finds radio stations that play Christmas music and sings along—even when he doesn't know the words—while Mama hums to the ones she knows. There are long stretches with walls of pine trees on either side of the road. When I look closer, I realize there are other, leafless trees mixed in too. *Deciduous*, I remember from science. It must've been nice to do this drive earlier in the fall, right when the colors changed.

It's midafternoon when we finally reach the cabin. The town it's in is tiny—there's a convenience store, a post office, and an antiques shop. That's pretty much it. My parents say we'll have to check out the antiques shop later, probably because it looks like a permanent garage sale.

We follow the directions onto a gravel road, and the reception goes from one bar to NO SERVICE. But luckily we're close. We pass cabin after cabin, some of them painted bright white, others dark greens and blues and browns—almost camouflaged in the pine trees. I imagine a pond with tall reeds, a mix of swans, ducks, and geese.

"*Why are there so many for-sale signs?*" asks Mama. She's right—every other house seems to be up for sale.

"Is near beach." Baba shrugs. "Probably no one want staying in winter."

"But why all selling now? Still can staying in summer. *Are you sure this isn't a scam?*"

"*It had good reviews!*" says Baba. "Anyway, is good for us. Cheaper for rent!" He points. "*That's the one!*"

Then he honks the horn. We're here—a cabin made of painted brown logs. A real log cabin! It looks suspiciously like the one on the syrup label.

Baba hands me his phone with the instructions on how to get the key out of the lockbox. I grab my backpack from the trunk and go open the front door. Inside, it's the most cabin-y cabin I've ever seen. The walls and ceiling are all knotty wood paneling. There are plaid couches, wooden ducks, ceramic fish lamps, and, like Mama wanted, a big kitchen with shiny new appliances. And bedrooms for everyone.

I find the one that's clearly a kid's room. I fall into the bed face-first. I stay like this for a while: on my belly, still wearing my backpack. Soft light comes through the pull-down window shade to my left. Next to that, above the night table, is a poster of different bird species.

I almost forgot what this feels like—to have my own

room. If Hao Bu and Ah Dia stay with us for good, am I just going to keep sleeping in our living room? Or would we move to a new house . . . Would I go to a new school?

Doors opening. Luggage wheels and avalanche-talking. I go back out to help. Mama turns up the thermostat and opens the fridge to see what's inside, while Hao Bu unties Ah Dia's shoelaces and swaps his walking shoes for slippers. Baba brings in loads of stuff from the car, including a box with old wooden tennis rackets Mama wasn't able to sell—which Baba said we could use as snowshoes if there's a blizzard.

Along with syrup bottles, I think maybe my dad's whole idea of winter comes from old Looney Tunes cartoons.

"We need to get a few things from the store," says Mama.

"Old man, come take a look at our room!" says Hao Bu.

"I'll see if the hot tub is ready," says Baba. *"They said they turned it on for us!"*

I follow Baba onto the back deck to see the hot tub, which was definitely not on the syrup bottle. Baba lifts the top cover and the water underneath is gently rippling. He swishes his hand around inside, then frowns and shuts the cover.

"Hopefully it'll warm up by tonight," he says.

Mama and Hao Bu end up going to the store while my dad, grandpa, and I go out for a walk—"Only us boy!" says Baba. I think I'd be fine staying in bed and never leaving the cabin at all, but Baba wants to take Ah Dia to see Lake Michigan. It's supposed to be a short walk away.

The houses along the water are bigger and nicer, and there are even more for-sale signs than before—and very few cars. It's like we're in a ghost town. Down the road, there's a sign that says PUBLIC BEACH ACCESS, and we follow the bend until we see a narrow wooden staircase tucked between some trees. It goes all the way down to the lake, and it's *tall*—there have to be more than a hundred steps.

Ah Dia starts toward the steps, but Baba pulls him back.

"Not these stairs, Ba. Look—part of it's collapsed."

I look too. Where the bottom steps should be, there are logs and boulders scattered across the beach. I remember the freeway overpass near our house. The metal rods and piles of rubble.

"Come on, let's find another staircase," Baba says. "Andy, *you too.*"

Ah Dia looks down the steps one more time, before Baba pulls him along.

We find a different way down. This one's a sloping car road that ends in a boat launch. I go ahead to make sure it's not too slippery.

The beach here is narrow, not much wider than the beach at the Metropark. The tide crashes and roars, and the ground is littered with smooth flat rocks the size of my fist. The water close to the shore is clouded with sand, but farther out it's a clearer cobalt blue. It doesn't exactly look like the kind of beach where tons of people swim, even when it's warm.

Still, Lake Michigan is so . . . *big*. It just keeps going.

"Wah, it's like an ocean," says Baba, coming up next to me with Ah Dia. *"You can't even see the other side."*

Ah Dia stares at the churning waves, then squints out at the horizon, like maybe he spots something in the distance. I squint too, but I don't see a single boat.

When I look at Ah Dia again, his glasses are fogged over. I tell Baba, who wipes them clean, then adjusts Ah Dia's coat hood to better cover his face.

"Let's keep walking," says Baba. *"We'll get cold if we don't keep moving."*

We walk along the shore, with Lake Michigan to our left and grassy dunes and bluffs to our right. We pass a bunch of tall wooden staircases with PRIVATE PROPERTY signs on them, but all of those are collapsed toward the bottom too, just like the public one.

A word floats up in my brain: *erosion*.

At almost the same time, Baba says, *"Oh. No wonder everything's for sale."*

He points up at one of the houses, standing on stilts over the bluffs, almost like the backs of our set pieces for the dance show. One day, maybe soon, those stilts aren't going to be enough to keep the house up. I think about all the work someone did—probably more than one someone—to build that house. It makes me sad in a way I can't describe.

We keep moving. I walk ahead, looking once in a while out at the water. Everything else—school, Movement, Jameel, Cindy . . . it all feels so far away, and not entirely real. I imagine Cindy taking dinners to her room and secretly dumping them into ziplock bags. I picture Jameel's mom making him give up Vegeta, the two of them getting into a huge fight about his dad. I see Jameel breaking open my birthday gift to him, ripping up the drawing.

Or maybe none of this happened. Maybe it's just easy to make up stories about what a person does, or who they are, when you're not in the same place as them. Easier than actually talking.

I see someone down the shore. A teenager in a University of Michigan hoodie, along with a black-and-white sheepdog. The kid's Asian, maybe Vietnamese. They're skipping rocks on the water, while the dog's rolling around in the sand.

I pick up a couple rocks too. I try to flick my wrist in the right way to skip them, but I can only get two hops at most. Then the dog perks up and comes over, tail wagging. I let it sniff the back of my hand. It turns and leans its butt into my leg, like it wants me to rub. So I rub the top part, right above the tail.

The teenager laughs. "Oh, Penny likes that."

I keep rubbing. The dog licks her lips.

The kid nods down the shore, toward Baba and Ah Dia.

"You all visiting?"

"Yeah."

"Where are you from?"

"We're from Hazel Heights. It's around Detroit."

We make eye contact. Then they nod, as if they understand something about my answer.

"Cool," they say. "I'm from Chicago."

"Are you going to U of M?"

"How did you know?!"

I point at their hoodie.

"Oh. Yeah." They laugh.

I look up and down the shore. "Are all the stairs like this?"

"Yeah. The water level's been really high the last couple of years. It's wild—all this used to be beach. See that stone pillar? That used to be eight feet above the water."

I spot the nub of a pillar, barely sticking out from the surface.

"Is everything just getting worse all the time?"

"Whoa. Kinda grim, dude."

"Sorry."

"But yeah. I get it." They look out at the water. "It'll get better. I have to believe that. 'Cause if I don't, I've already given up, right?"

Penny's ears perk up. Baba and Ah Dia are coming

toward us. Penny goes over to lean her butt on them too, but Ah Dia looks like he might be a little scared of her.

"Penny!" The teenager whistles. "Get back here."

The dog comes prancing back, then lies down on the sand.

"Good girl. *Stay*."

The teenager wraps their arm around Penny. Clips her leash back on and holds her still. They nod farther down the shore. "There's a working staircase that way. Probably five, ten minutes."

I tell them thanks and "Go Blue."

"Go Blue!"

We keep walking, and after a while we reach the staircase. Baba points out that this one collapsed too, but someone rebuilt it. Unlike the weathered gray wood at the top, the bottom is made of a fresher, greenish color, with a metal frame reinforcing it.

I start up the steps, thinking about what the kid said. But when I look back halfway, Baba and Ah Dia are still near the very bottom.

"Do you know the way back?" Baba shouts.

"Right, then left!" I shout back.

"You go ahead! We'll meet you there!" Baba turns his attention to Ah Dia again.

I can't hear them over the roar of the water, but I just know Baba's saying, *"Come on, old man. One step at a time."*

* * *

For dinner, Hao Bu makes another one of her pork shank soups. Only she makes it with a different squash instead of winter melon because that's what they had at the store. There's stir-fried veggies and rice also—we brought our rice cooker.

"What's the point of staying in a cabin if we're just going to eat Chinese food?" says Baba. At the same time, he's slurping empty his soup bowl.

Mama says they got bacon, eggs, and pancake mix. We'll have an American-style breakfast. They got bundles of firewood too, and after dinner my dad starts a fire in the wood-burning stove by crumpling up paper grocery bags to use for kindling. To everyone's surprise, he gets it on the first try. Baba was also hoping the hot tub would be ready, but the water was still lukewarm.

That night, the five of us sit on the sofas around the wood stove, my parents and grandparents telling memories about life in Shanghai. I get my sketchbook out to doodle, and realize that I only have a couple of blank pages left. I run my hand over the tattered leather cover, its cracked spine and stickers, and nicks from being in my backpack. Then, starting with the first page, I flip through all my drawings from the last four months:

Hi-Chews and trays of roast duck.

Crickets and lopsided lizards.

Costco sneakers and twisted-up glasses.

Ah Dia's hands, like knobby tree trunks, from the back seat of a car.

And boars. Lots and lots of boars. Even more than bearded dragons.

When I get to the end, a few things fall out of the back pocket: vampire tattoos and a scrap of orange cloth, a fishing hook and short line, a leaf from the sidewalk.

But also: a business card from the cider mill, a ticket stub for Reptomania.

And nothing from Cindy.

Mama sets a mug of hot chocolate on the table next to me. While my dad and grandparents talk, I watch her bring mugs of hot chocolate to everyone, rinse the pot, wipe down the counters, check the thermostat, lock the doors, and turn off the light that'd been left on in the other room. When she sits back down, my insides feel full and heavy.

So much has happened these last four months. And so much is happening, all the time. I feel myself melt into the thick sofa cushions. In my mind's eye, I turn into a puddle of water. I slowly evaporate and disappear into the warm, dry air.

ROOTS

I wake up to the smell of bacon. When I go out into the main room, my mom and grandma are cooking up a storm. Mama's making pancakes, and Hao Bu's frying eggs the Chinese way—with lots of oil and hot enough so the edges get crispy. There's already a big mound of bacon and breakfast sausage on a plate lined with paper towels. The rice cooker's going, but instead of *zhuo*, there's oatmeal inside.

"Finally awake?" Mama smiles, seeing me. I nod and pop a slice of bacon into my mouth. It's crunchy and chewy at the same time. She grabs a stack of plates and opens the drawer for the silverware. *"Come, help Mama set the table."*

As I do, I see Baba outside on the rear deck, getting out of the hot tub. He hurries back in, teeth chattering, and darts for the shower, leaving a trail of water behind him. I finish setting the table and wipe the water up with a towel. Then Mama tells me to go wake Ah Dia. It's almost time to eat.

I knock softly on the door to my grandparents' room. Then I open it all the way. The blankets are crumpled up into a ball—it looks like Ah Dia already got out of bed. But I check both bathrooms, and only Baba's in the one, taking a hot shower. I check the other bedrooms too— nothing. I get a chill through my body.

I hurry back out to the main room.

"I can't find Ah Dia," I tell Mama and Hao Bu.

"What do you mean you can't find Ah Dia?" asks Hao Bu. *"He's not in our room?"*

I shake my head. *"He's not in the bathroom either."*

"That's impossible," says Mama. *"He was asleep a minute ago."*

"See for yourself."

Mama and Hao Bu go look in the bedrooms. They check in the basement, everywhere. I hear doors opening and closing.

"Ba, where are you?"

"Old man, come out, it's time to eat!"

It's then that I notice the front door cracked open a little. Ah Dia's poofy coat is gone from the coat rack on the wall. His shoes are missing too.

"He's outside!" I shout. I throw on my own coat and shoes and burst out the door, into the road. I look left and right, but I don't see him. I run to the end of the

road, where it bends by the water. He's not down that way either. I turn around and wave at my family, who are just coming out of the house—Baba too, hair wet, wearing only a towel.

Then I get a weird feeling. Something makes me check the public beach staircase—the broken one. And when I look down, I see Ah Dia, standing at the edge of the water.

How the heck did he even get there? Did he teleport? The broken staircase has a drop from the last step down to the sand. He couldn't have used that, could he? I call out to him, but he doesn't hear. The waves are too loud.

I don't wait for my parents. I book it down, as fast as I can, watching where I step so I don't slip. What was Ah Dia thinking? Does he want to jump in? Go swimming? He'll freeze!

Near the bottom, the drop is even steeper than I thought. Then I notice, to my right against the bluff, the exposed roots of a tree, running almost all the way down to the beach.

I grab a couple of the thicker roots. They're cold but strong and secure. I pull myself against the bluff and climb down.

I take it slow. And it's funny—wherever I reach, there's another root there to meet my hands and feet. It takes my total concentration. But little by little, step by step, I make it all the way down.

When I look again, Ah Dia's still standing at the shore.

The wind's blown his hood off his head. Out past him, waves crash against the sand. I imagine them rising higher, the surf becoming a big gaping mouth, taking bites out of the shoreline, closer and closer to Ah Dia's feet, until . . .

I finally get it. I finally see the reason Baba's been so adamant about Ah Dia getting his tests, seeing doctors here, trying to figure out insurance and visas and green cards. Even showing him a good American time. The reason my parents have both been making sacrifices.

It's because this trip might be the last time we get to see Ah Dia in person. The last time he gets to see us.

Maybe Mama and Baba never said it out loud because they didn't want to make me sad. Or maybe they only knew it deep down and didn't want to admit it, even to themselves. Because then it might come true:

Ah Dia is dying. Not today, not tomorrow. Probably not even in a year. But there'll be a day, maybe soon, when he's not here anymore.

I look down and see a footprint in the sand. I step in it. Then I see another, in front of the first. I step there too. I notice other footprints, all around, and see that even though the staircase was broken, the bottom washed away, it hasn't stopped people from finding other ways down. Maybe the same way I found.

I come up next to Ah Dia. I grab his bare hand and give it a squeeze. We look at each other, and in that second, his eyes are crystal clear.

Ah Dia knows it too. He knows what's coming. Not today, not tomorrow, but maybe soon.

"Ah Dia, do you like America?" I ask him. *"Do you and Hao Bu want to stay here? Do you want to come live with us?"*

He stares out at the lake again, at the water that goes so far, it's hard to believe there's another side. I remember the story he told by the creek, about walking into the Huangpu River at low tide, the tiny river crabs parting in front of him in a shimmery purple wave.

"America is very beautiful," he answers in English. "But is your home, not my."

I squeeze his hand again.

"Ba! Andy!" my dad shouts. Our car's at the boat launch. My whole family's running toward us. Baba gets here first, wearing his winter coat over a bath towel, his hair frozen solid. When Mama and Hao Bu reach us too, everyone bursts into an avalanche of worry and scolding. But Ah Dia keeps looking out at the water, like he doesn't hear them.

Or maybe instead of the shouting, he hears the feelings underneath.

A shiver runs through me. It's not my spider-sense, but a different kind of sense, one that makes me look over my shoulder. I follow the roots of the tree by the staircase, from the sand up, thickening and merging at the short, gray trunk, then splitting apart again into thin, bony branches.

It's a dogwood.

JANUARY

A NEW YEAR

We come home to a city covered in snow.

It keeps snowing through the weekend, though it's not enough for school to close. The first Monday back, everything seems quiet and cozy, wrapped in a thick white blanket. Mr. Nagy has us read from our textbooks, silently to ourselves. Mx. Adler gets called away in the middle of class, but before they go, they actually put on the movie version of *Hamilton*.

At lunch in the art studio, we all tell each other what we did over break. I talk about how my whole family, Ah Dia too, crammed into an outdoor hot tub on Christmas Eve. How we explored the little towns in the area, went to antiques stores and fudge shops and ate delicious food—both homemade and at restaurants, Chinese and American. And how sad Baba was that it wasn't until New Year's Day—the day we left the cabin—that it finally started to snow.

Then I leave early. For the second half of lunch, I sit with Cindy at our old table in the cafeteria. We don't really talk that much, but I notice again how little she's eating. I want to ask her about it—but not here, not in front of other people.

When I walk by the courtyard, I remember being with my family on the shores of Lake Michigan, and I feel that cyclone of feelings again. Happy, sad—everything.

I remember too what happened in the car, on the drive back. Mama, saying suddenly, to all of us: *I want to get my American nursing degree.*

After school, there's a frantic energy in the auditorium. A bunch of kids are huddled around someone on stage. And it's not until I go up there that I see who: Alexandra, holding a pair of crutches, with a cast on her leg.

I spot Eva and Lucy off to the side.

"What happened? What's going on?" I ask them.

"She broke her leg snowboarding." Eva shrugs.

"I think Mx. Adler's freaking out a little," says Lucy.

I see Mx. Adler and Mrs. Ocampo talking backstage. I hurry over to them.

"We can have Arj fill in as Piggy," Mx. Adler's saying. "It'll be a lot, but I think Arj can handle it. Then we'll move Christina to—"

"Andy! There you are," says Mrs. Ocampo. "How would you feel about stepping in for Alexandra as the boar? Aside from her, you're the one who best knows the routine."

I look back and forth between the teachers. Me—the boar?

"But if I'm the head, who's going to be the tail?" I ask.

"It'll be just you," says Mx. Adler. "We can't spare anyone else, unfortunately."

Mrs. Ocampo leans in a little. "I know it isn't what you signed up for. And you can say no if you don't feel comfortable doing it."

I look over at Alexandra, chatting away with the other dancers. Kids are taking turns signing her cast. I picture the stage empty, me coming out as the boar—just me, alone—under the bright lights, to a full audience. I remember my and Cindy's audition, the way I froze and forgot my moves . . .

And I get an idea. A *great* idea.

"Okay," I say.

"Okay?" asks Mrs. Ocampo. "You'll do it?"

I nod.

"Oh, you're a lifesaver!"

Mx. Adler lets out a breath. "Andy, thank you." They check their watch and call out to all the kids on stage. "Arj! Christina! A quick word. Everyone else—warm-up circle."

I want to ask something before I line up.

"Mrs. Ocampo?"

"What is it?"

"Can I take the boar costume home with me?"

* * *

"You wanna do *what*?" Cindy says at the door.

But then she lets me in anyway. Maybe a part of her wants to hear me out.

I follow her into her room, like I've done a million times back when we still hung out a lot. Inside, the shelf that used to hold her mini things now has some books and a small cactus. That's not the only thing that's different: She's moved her K-pop posters around, and white twinkly lights are wrapped around her curtain rod. Maybe they're left over from Christmas, but I like that they're still up.

There's a pile of unfolded laundry on Cindy's bed. She sits down and starts folding her tie-dye sweatshirt. I lean my backpack against the wall and try convincing her again.

"Think about it, it could totally work," I tell her. "If your parents saw how good of a dancer you are, they'd have to let you rejoin!"

"Have you *met* my parents? There's no way."

"Can't you say that we're, like, representing our culture?"

She shakes her head. "Andy, it's too late." She lays the sweatshirt flat on the bed and folds one edge over. "Besides, I'm just gonna do what they want from now on," she says, almost talking more to the sweatshirt than to me. "I'm only making it harder for myself when I push back. If I lay low and do all my work, then—I don't know, maybe I can skip a grade. I'll get through high school quicker and go to college somewhere far away, like New York or California or London. Then they can't ruin my life anymore."

I picture a flower, petals wilting and falling off. "You can't do that," I say.

"Watch me."

"I mean, you're going to die inside if you try to do that."

She sets the folded sweatshirt aside and fishes out a pair of black yoga pants from the pile. I watch her pull at a loose thread near the waist. My heart grows a size.

"I never really wanted to bleach my hair," I say. "Or join Movement."

She rolls her eyes. "Are you really going to keep bringing this up every—"

"But I'm glad you made me do it."

She looks at me. "You are?"

"Because I had to try it to figure out what was me and not me."

"So did you?"

"Did I what?"

"Figure out what was you."

I think about making sets and costumes in the art studio. I think about garage sales and cider mills. Chinese school and lion dancing with Lang Uncle. Standing on the shores of Lake Michigan with my whole family. The other day I did my first watercolor in years, of the dogwood in the courtyard the way I remembered it in the fall—full and bright and peachy-pink.

"Not yet," I tell her. "Not all the way. But I think it involves being an artist."

Cindy stares at the yoga pants. She runs her hand over the legs, but doesn't fold or do anything with them. She snuffles a little, then looks at me.

"Even if we *did* go ahead with this," she says. "My parents have been watching me like hawks. They'd shut us down before we could even start. When would we do it?"

"Next Saturday, when everyone's here for the Lunar New Year party," I tell her. "We'll come up with a distraction—that's what they always do in movies."

"Andy, we're not trying to rob a casino."

"Let me worry about that. You just focus on dancing." I unzip my backpack and hand her a pair of boar pants. She runs her fingers along the frills of green fur, then quickly hides the pants behind some boxes under her bed. She does it so naturally, I wonder if that's where she hides the—

"You said you have a video of the choreography?" she says, straightening up.

I try not to look flustered. "I'll send it to you," I tell her. "We might not have time to practice together." I turn to leave.

"Andy—"

"What?"

"What happened to you?"

"I saw some tree roots." I smile.

Her eyebrows go up. "You've gotten way weirder," she says. But then she smiles too.

Walking out, I take one last look before I head downstairs. Through the open doorway, Cindy's still sitting on her bed, staring at her laundry, looking like she's not entirely convinced. Like she's still figuring it out.

I guess we have that in common.

THE GROWING, GLOWING HEART

At school the next morning, Cindy tells me she's on
board with the idea. I'm so relieved I could float away.
But I don't. Because now I need to figure out the perfect
distraction for the party.

The last time her family and mine hosted a Chinese
party at our duplex, it was warmer, and people could go
back and forth between our bottom floor and the backyard. This time though, everyone will be inside. We'll
have to find a place to put on the costume, then somewhere with enough room to dance. We'll have to make
sure her parents are—

I almost run into a big muscle-y guy coming out of the
science room.

He gives me a weird look. Speaking of distractions, I
need to pay more attention to where I'm walking. I glance

at the VISITOR sticker on his chest. There's something familiar about him . . .

"Thanks for your help—" Jameel stops in the doorway. He goes quiet.

Oh. That's why the guy looks familiar.

"Andy, uh, you remember Uncle Leo?" says Jameel.

I look back and forth between the two of them. Does Uncle Leo know what happened?

"Good to see you, Andy!" he says. "If you ever want to try pacha again, come down to my restaurant for Easter! Bring your whole family!"

I nod. He turns back to Jameel. "I'll pick you up later."

"I'll be out front," Jameel says. "Thanks for this."

Uncle Leo fist-bumps Jameel, then fist-bumps me too. He walks down the hallway, twirling his keys around his finger.

Jameel and I look at each other again. Neither of us says a word. We head inside the classroom.

I find out why Uncle Leo came into school today—to help bring Vegeta's terrarium to the science room. By the time class starts, all the other kids have noticed the new addition, and it seems like everyone's divided into two groups: those who want to hold and pet Vegeta, and those who want nothing to do with him.

Mr. Nagy has Jameel do a show-and-tell at the front of the room. Jameel mumbles a few things about temperature and brumation, then tries to answer questions, getting quieter and more mumbly. I picture a Jenga tower, about to topple over. When Jameel sits back down, he tugs the hood of his hoodie over his head. As soon as class ends, he books it.

And I go after him.

Once I'm close enough, I call out: "Jameel!"

He whirls around. And the instant he does, I stop in my tracks. My whole body locks up. I see a Dementor—the Jameel from September.

He takes off his hood. Underneath, his eyes are puffy and red. I realize, then, that we'll never go back to being friends the same way as before.

I think I also understand what Jameel was really asking on his apartment balcony. I'm still not sure if the world's fair. It might not be. But that doesn't matter, because I feel—I *know*, deep in my bones—that Jameel's not a bad person. That he's a *good* person. That you can be good and still make mistakes. Maybe unforgivable mistakes.

It's not one or the other. It's both.

I let out a breath. I take a couple steps closer. "I know you care about Vegeta," I tell him. "I know you care a lot."

"I can still take him home over break," he says. "I won't see him all the time, but . . . it's better this way." He looks away for a second. I'm not convinced he believes the last part.

Cindy walks past us on her way to next period. She glares at me. I try to tell her, with my eyes, *I know what I'm doing.* And I'm not sure if she gets my message, but she stops. She waits for me by the lockers.

"I'm really sorry about"—Jameel wipes his eyes—"you know."

A random laugh in the hallway. I picture Dementors again, swarming, sweeping me up. Then I picture my heart growing, glowing. I remember what Mrs. Ocampo said, about not just the image but the feeling underneath. The feeling's real.

And I say out loud, "I don't know if I can ever forgive what you did to me."

Jameel stares at his feet. "Oh."

"But that doesn't mean we have to stop talking."

He looks at me again. "If there's anything I can do . . ."

In the distance, light glints off the courtyard glass. I notice Cindy's face soften. I look between her and Jameel, my two best friends—or they used to be. Now I'm not sure what we all are.

"Actually, there is something," I say.

"Anything. Whatever you need."

"What are you doing next Saturday, around dinnertime?"

LUNAR NEW YEAR

The snow melts and turns to slush. The floors in the school entrance are caked with mud, and the skies go gray and stay that way.

But there's a bright spot—one I hear more than see. Some afternoons, there are new sounds coming through the ceiling at home. Not violin music, but the thumps and smacks of Cindy's feet, practicing the boar dance.

The next Monday after school, we have our first full dress rehearsal for the winter show. It's kind of a mess. During the first number, the music keeps starting and stopping because of the auditorium Wi-Fi. Jason forgets to lock the wheels under one of Lucy's shrubs and it rolls right into Arj and Mai. Eva's mixture for the fog machine is too strong, and the custodian has to come clear the stage with heavy-duty fans.

Viola drops the conch.

And I don't do much better with the boar dance. I remember most of my steps, but my timing is completely off, and I almost crash into one of the Hunters. Afterwards, I try to keep my plan in mind. Because if it works, it won't be just me under the boar—it'll be me and Cindy both.

The music for the last number ends. We all stand around on stage, like a field of deflated soccer balls. Mx. Adler claps twice. "All right, bring it in."

We stumble into a loose circle.

"This is why we have rehearsals," they say. "To get this all out of our system before the show. Now, I want you to stop thinking about your steps and routines. You already know them. So trust that you know them. And just dance. Can you do that?"

There's a half-hearted *yes*.

"What was that?"

"Yes!" we shout.

"Good. Everyone, spread out. You can leave your costumes on. We're doing Egg."

We scatter for Egg—maybe the last before the show. I remember the first one, how I held myself small. And the next, when I let myself go. This time, I end up somewhere in between.

I start flat on the floor and float my arms up. Then I roll over, onto my hands and knees. I crawl a while, and slowly rise, first my left foot, then my right.

I plant my feet.

Take a deep breath in.

I raise my hands, and slowly wiggle my fingers, and let my arms sway.

Back and forth, like the limbs of a tree in the wind.

By Saturday morning, the slush is gone. The streets are dry again. Cindy's family and mine spend the whole day cooking, cleaning, and getting ready for all their Shanghainese friends. Afternoon comes, and cars and SUVs start pulling up, and people start rolling in, bringing food and wine—and red envelopes for us kids—to celebrate Lunar New Year.

The party's spread on both floors, the dads and grandparents downstairs with all the platters of food, while the moms and kids hang out mostly upstairs. When the adults have had enough wine to be in deep avalanche, I find Cindy in her room, brushing her hair in the desk mirror. She's gotten it cut again, and there's only a little blond left at the tips. It looks nice.

I close the door behind us, muffling the party sounds.

"I got you something," I tell her. "Late Christmas present. Or early New Year's."

She sets the brush down and swivels around in her chair. When I hand her the gift, she frowns a little. "I didn't get you anything."

"It's okay."

Cindy unwraps the gift. She gasps. *"Eliza."* Her baby

taxidermy squirrel. She gives me a big hug. "How did you—"

She pulls away, an unsure look on her face. She knows that if I saved Eliza from the garbage, I must've seen what else was in there.

Or maybe she doesn't. Maybe we can't read each other's minds the way I thought. If we could, I would've known sooner something was wrong. I would know why she stopped eating, and if there was anything I could do to help. So I tell her:

"I saw ziplock bags full of food in the garbage. Then I noticed you weren't really eating at lunch, and I—"

"Andy, it's no big deal," Cindy says, looking away. "I'm just on a diet, that's all."

"Oh. I'm—" I trip over my words. Has she just been on a diet? Did I get it completely wrong? But—the food bags. What about—

Our eyes meet, and all my thoughts and questions melt away. Even if I'm not sure what's really going on with Cindy, I know how *I* feel. I know what's true for me.

"I'm worried about you," I tell her.

Cindy stares down at Eliza. Turns her around in her hands.

"I know." She snuffles. "Thanks. For being worried."

Cindy wipes the corners of her eyes. Then she laughs a little, as if there's something ridiculous about the two of us talking like this when we're about to secretly dress up as a boar and dance in front of our families and all their friends.

I chuckle too. It *is* ridiculous.

"So, when's Jameel getting here?" Cindy asks, sitting up straighter. "Is he going to be on time? Because if he's late—"

I take the phone out of my pocket. "He's going to text me."

"Your parents got you a phone?"

"It's not mine," I tell her. "Jameel let me borrow his." She gives me a look.

"Trust me," I say. "I know what I'm doing."

She stares at me for a second, and finally nods. "Okay."

Then she gets up and walks over to the wall shelf, puts Eliza back in her old spot. The tiny squirrel looks good, tucked between her books and the new cactus. It looks like it belongs.

Just as the sun's about to set, Jameel texts me from his uncle's phone. They're on their way.

I go down into the basement and put on my costume pants and grab the boar mask. Then I slip out the back and wait from the side driveway. After a while, a red SUV pulls up and lets Jameel out. He spots me and gives me a thumbs-up. I watch him unzip his backpack and take out my Halloween Jake mask, a metal cooking pot, and a wooden spatula. I text Cindy: *Get ready.*

Jameel puts on the Jake mask and pats the side of the

SUV. Music starts playing, then the volume gets louder. He starts banging away on the metal pot. And after a while, the sounds inside the house change. I hear the avalanche voices move toward the front to see what's happening in the street.

What's happening is: Jameel . . . *dancing.*

He's doing the weirdest dance I've ever seen—and I've seen a lot of weird dances. First he wiggles like a worm. Next he flaps his elbows and pecks like a farm chicken. Then he crouches and leaps like a frog. I have to cover my mouth so I don't laugh too loud.

The back door snaps open. Cindy shuts it quietly behind her, hurries to put on her boar pants. I hand her the mask and get into position, bending over and holding her waist while she covers me with the cape. It takes us a few steps to get in sync, but we quickly do, even though we haven't practiced the dance together.

Because it's Cindy and me. We're the boar!

We strut down the driveway, gravel crunching under our feet. The gravel turns into pavement, then grass. Cindy crouches low, and I crouch with her. A second later, I hear the song change. Jameel bangs faster on the metal pot.

Cindy and I bounce up into horse stance. We swing our hips. We shake and skip across the lawn. We groove to the music. I can't see what's going on, but I picture everyone looking through the windows, standing on the front porch, pointing and smiling and laughing. I picture

Jameel next to us, still in the Jake mask. It must be a weird sight: a fuzzy dancing boar and a yellow cartoon dog banging on a metal cooking pot. Weird and fun and funny. We lose ourselves to the music. We dance.

The song only lasts for one minute, but—what a minute! At the end, Cindy leaps up, even though it's not part of the routine. I do my best to lift her. It's not quite a lion rearing on its legs. But it's close.

We throw off our costume, breathing hard. My eyes adjust to the light. The sun's just set and the skies are orange-pink—it's golden hour. My parents and their friends are clapping and cheering. Even some of our neighbors across the street are clapping from their windows. I spot Lang Uncle on our porch. He whistles and gives us two big thumbs-up. Right next to him are Hao Bu and Ah Dia, and Cindy's parents. And even *they're* clapping.

"Now's our chance!" I tell Cindy. I start for the porch, but she pulls me back.

"What are you doing?" I say. "Let's go ask. They *have* to let you rejoin after that!"

"Andy, I don't wanna go back to Movement."

"But I thought—It's your dream . . ."

She shakes her head. "I don't think it's the best thing for me right now," she says.

I flash to her and the tall girls. How she acted around them—like, not entirely herself. Could that be why— And I missed— My chest swells. "I'm sorry I wasn't there," I blurt out. "I mean, if you wanted me to be there. I just—wasn't—" My words jumble together. "I'm—"

"It's okay," she says. "Really." She pulls me in for a hug. A great big hug. We're both crying. I open my eyes and see Ah Dia smiling from the porch. My bald spot tingles.

"What . . . do *you* want?" I say in Cindy's ear. "Can I—Is there someone you want to, like, talk to—like, an adult?"

Cindy snuffles, pulling away. "I don't know, maybe." She swipes at her nose. "But—thank you for this. You don't know how much this— It was really great, Andy."

She reaches down for the boar mask and puts it in my hands. "You're gonna be amazing," she says. "I can't wait to see you on stage."

Cindy walks up the porch steps. She goes back inside with her parents. Hao Bu comes down with Ah Dia and sweeps me up in praise—"*My grandson! Not just an artist, but a dancer too! Your ah dia loved it!*"

Ah Dia nods. "Very good," he says in English. I smile at him and squeeze his hand.

Then Hao Bu points over my shoulder and asks me: "*Does Jamee want to come in for dinner?*"

I look at Jameel, still holding the Jake mask and kitchen utensils, waiting patiently. He glances at the red SUV, its parking lights on, steam coming out of its tailpipe. Through the back window, I see his uncle's silhouette.

"Do you and Uncle Leo want to come in for dinner?" I ask.

Jameel's face brightens. Then he hesitates. "I mean, I don't wanna crash your party. And we didn't bring nothing . . ."

But then Hao Bu grabs his arm and almost pulls him in. *"Nonsense! Come, come,"* she says, as if she knew exactly what he'd said.

I laugh. And I run to invite Uncle Leo too.

MORE THAN I THOUGHT

After dinner, Jameel and I sit out on the front steps—
just the two of us. The sun's gone down completely, and
the only lights left are from windows and front porches,
and a sliver of moon—a thin, pointy fingernail.

Jameel pats his belly. "Bruh. That was so good."

I look at him. "My mouth wants more—"

"But my stomach's full."

We laugh. And as we both stare back out at the street,
it gets quiet—that sad kind of quiet. As if we forgot
everything that's happened this year, and suddenly
remembered again.

Jameel's the one who breaks the silence. "I can't be
at your show," he says. "Yousif's deployment, it's end-
ing. He's coming home. But it's only a few days, then he's
gotta leave for another— And we gotta—"

"It's okay," I tell him. "I get it."

Jameel snuffles. He rubs his eyes.

"You know," he says softly, staring out at the street. "I wish you woulda told me sooner. About the dance thing. I woulda liked to know about that."

I look at his hands, fingers laced together. I feel my chest rise and fall.

"Me too," I say. "Wish I would've told you. But I couldn't."

He opens his mouth to say something, then closes it.

I shut my eyes and tilt my head back a little. I listen to the party, still going inside. There's a faint, repeating chirp, from under the porch.

"Andy, hey," Jameel says. "That time in the cafeteria. When I asked you if you were gay . . ."

We look at each other.

"I want you to know that if you were, I'd have your back. And if you're not, I got your back too."

I look into his eyes and imagine that hallway between us, and see walls and doors flipping down, the floor and ceiling falling away.

I nod. "Same," I say.

I look out again at the barren winter trees, branches holding up the sky. I feel my heart in my chest, warm and glowing.

"I don't know what I am yet," I tell him. "Or if I've found a name for it."

All I know is that it's more than one thing. And I have room for it to be that.

More room than I'd thought.

FEBRUARY

THE WINTER SHOW

I peek through a gap in the curtain.

My family's sitting in the second row, near the aisle. Baba's recording a video on his phone, and Mama's smiling, gently guiding his arms down so he doesn't block the view of people behind them. Next to them are my grandparents, light bouncing off of Ah Dia's thick glasses, Hao Bu, face rosy with makeup, almost glowing. And somewhere, out beyond the glare of the stage lights, Cindy and her family too.

The music stops. A big round of applause. Arj and Mai whoosh in past me and the Hunters, all bouncing in place with excitement. The lights dim and Jason and Lucy dash out stage left, dressed in all black, and start moving the trees and shrubs into place. I glance at Eva and Mrs. Ocampo, sitting at the control table, ready to change the lights and music.

I run my hand through my hair. I rub my bald spot. The hair's still shorter than what's around it, but it's not entirely bald, either. I still touch it from time to time, but I don't pull as often. In a weird way, knowing why I do it makes it easier not to. Sometimes, at least.

Jason and Lucy exit. Mx. Adler taps my shoulder. I hurry out in the almost-darkness, to center stage, with the boar mask. I put it over my head and squat low to the floor, like I'm holding myself in Egg.

It's then that I see, in my mind's eye, a flash of images, one after another:

Me and my friends on a sunny day, walking into the school's courtyard, and sitting on the bench and grass. Eating our lunches under the white spring flowers of a kousa dogwood, roots strong in the earth.

Mrs. Ocampo, working on a fabric collage in the art studio, hearing a knock on the door. Looking up to see, in the doorway, Cindy.

A freeway overpass. Going up in the place of the one they took down. Not a secret passage, just a regular bridge. A new way across.

And an airport departures area, at the end of February.

"Is there anything else?" asks Baba. My grandparents' luggage is checked. Hao Bu has her purse and roller bag, her poofy garage sale coat draped over the handle. Ah Dia's in a red wheelchair, cane across his lap, an airport worker behind him holding the handlebars.

"Andy, *when are you going to come visit us in China?"* asks Hao Bu.

I look at my parents.

"*Maybe next year,*" says Baba, snuffling, his eyes red.

"*Maybe next summer,*" says Mama, running her hand through my hair. "*When I have a break from nursing school. We'll all go together.*"

"*Next summer,*" I tell Hao Bu.

I turn to Ah Dia, and put my hand on his. He grips it back, and gives it a squeeze.

"*Ah Dia, I'm going to miss you,*" I say in Shanghainese.

"I miss you too," he says in English.

Chinese people don't really hug. But *I* do. I smush into him for a big bear hug. And to my surprise, everyone else comes in too, for one long family group hug.

Eventually, we pull away. We wipe our tears and watch Hao Bu and Ah Dia go through the security checkpoint. Then we wave goodbye to my grandparents one last time, before they turn out of view, toward the gate for their flight back to China. Back home.

Maybe all these things will happen. Maybe some of them need my help to happen. Or maybe they're what I see in my mind's eye—not because they're real, but because the feelings underneath them are.

Now the music's playing.

The stage lights brighten and filter through the mask—a kaleidoscope of colors.

I squeeze the wooden handles, bounce a little on my heels.

The melody changes.

The drumbeat starts.

I'm on.

AUTHOR'S NOTE

Dear Reader,

Even though the story you've just read is fictional, many events in it are inspired by real experiences from my life.

Andy's family, like mine, moved from Shanghai, China, to Detroit. At home, I grew up speaking a mix of English and the Shanghainese dialect, which, unlike Mandarin Chinese, has no single standard written form. So throughout this book, I've used Mandarin spellings where it made sense, but in some cases, I've changed them to better convey Shanghainese pronunciations and word choices.

I had a lot of fun reliving, through Andy's eyes, my family's trips to Asian groceries, weekend garage sale crawls, and occasional potlucks with other Chinese families—experiences that were part of ordinary life. What was much tougher was also reliving some of the more difficult memories from those same years.

Every instance of racism that Andy faces in the book I've had directed at me, some even while I was working on this novel.

My mom and five-year-old me at Hongqiao Airport in Shanghai, seeing my dad off on his flight to America. We'd join him in Detroit three months later.

Many are microaggressions—the everyday and sometimes-unintentional forms of prejudice that make the person they're aimed at feel like they don't belong. For Asian Americans, even "positive" stereotypes, like being hardworking or good at math, can hurt those of us who don't fit the stereotypes. This myth of the "model minority" also pits us against other diverse groups by suggesting it's their fault that they're not getting ahead like the "good Asians." Obviously no group of people is any better or worse than any other.

A favorite book of mine on this topic is Ronald Takaki's *A Different Mirror for Young People*. It's the kind of untaught history I was thinking of when Andy sees the posters at the Chinese Community Center. For those curious about Vincent Chin and how his death galvanized the Asian American movement, I also recommend Paula Yoo's young adult nonfiction book, *From a Whisper to a Rallying Cry*.

There are other ways Andy and I are similar. Like him, I too pulled at my hair growing up, particularly when I was anxious. I only discovered years later that maybe as many as ten million people here in the U.S. do this same thing. Hair pulling, also called trichotillomania, is known as a body-focused repetitive behavior (BFRB). The good news is that BFRBs are treatable. If you feel like it's a problem for you, a smart first step is to speak to a parent, guardian, or trusted grown-up. More information can also be found at bfrb.org.

While I've not personally struggled with an eating disorder, I have loved ones who have. They're also proof that recovery is possible. If you suspect that you or someone you know might have an eating disorder, ANAD (National Association of Anorexia Nervosa and Associated Disorders) provides free peer support services regardless of age, race, gender identity, sexual orientation, or background. Find them at anad.org or call their toll-free hotline at (888) 375-7767.

Finally, I wanted to share one more small story. At an event for my last book, *See You in the Cosmos*, a student asked me why I put serious topics—like death and mental health—into my books for kids. My answer: Because they're real things that real kids deal with. And often these serious topics are connected to other serious topics. Bullying happens over race, gender identity, sexual orientation, body image, and so many other things. Mental health struggles can come out of—or be made worse by—bullying. One organization that's working along multiple fronts is STOMP Out Bullying, and they have a free online HelpChat for young people ages thirteen to twenty-four at stompoutbullying.org. Again, talking to a parent, guardian, or trusted adult is a good first step.

Every single one of us deals with our own unique combination of challenges. But knowing that there are people out there who might share our same struggles can help us feel less alone in our journeys. Knowing also that, like Andy, we can laugh and cry and dance and make art along those same journeys, helps even more, I think.

That's why I wrote Andy's story. And why I'm now sharing, with you, my connection to it.

It might be fiction, but it's also real.

With love,
Jack Cheng

ACKNOWLEDGMENTS

Every book takes a village; this one is no exception. Deepest thanks:

To Jessica Craig for being there from the beginning.

To Jessica Dandino Garrison for guiding this novel through its many iterations and false starts to the deeply personal story it is today. To Squish Pruitt, Regina Castillo, Jessica Jenkins, Jason Henry, Nancy Mercado, Lauri Hornik, Jen Klonsky, Jenn Ridgway, and the (many) people and teams at Dial Books for Young Readers and Penguin Young Readers. Yuta Onoda for the phenomenal cover art. And Jarod Lew for the shiny new author photo.

To the Association of Chinese Americans in Madison Heights, MI. Stacey He, T.Y., and the Michigan Lion Dance team. And to Deborah Al-Najjar, Weam Namou, and the Chaldean Cultural Center in West Bloomfield, MI.

To the beta readers from Mr. Blatt's ELA classes at Ferndale Middle School, AKA the Hi-Chew Crew. (Let's do that again!)

To friends, too many to name, who have supported me in various ways throughout this project, including being patient enough to answer my repeated questions about the smallest details: Leo Tominna, Alise Alousi, Sam Conklin, Christiana Laine, Jeff Raudebaugh, Rae Baker, Nari Kim, Eli Borton, Brian Silverstein, Shawn Liu, Danny Wen, Alex Taylor, Jen Kron, and Kelly Yang.

To Show and Tell buddies for twice-monthly inspiration and Zoom camaraderie, and to my *BookSmitten* podcast co-hosts, Kelly J. Baptist, Patrick Flores-Scott, and Heather Shumaker— the closest thing I've had to a regular writing group.

To Kresge Arts in Detroit for helping grow and sustain my practice, and the practices of so many other artists in Metro Detroit. And to my website patrons—my fellow winterers—for keeping me going. The Movement warm-ups are based on a combination of Twyla Tharp's *The Creative Habit* and exercises from Theatre of the Oppressed, which I was first introduced to at an Allied Media Conference session led by Pink Flowers.

To Mom, Dad, and Charlie. Love you.

To Matisse for being the silliest, sweetest shy pup in the world. (Wanna go for a pack walk?)

To Julia, for being my first reader, Halloween costume completer, solitude protector, roadtrip copilot, and sometimes therapist. Love you most. (Don't tell Matisse.)